PRAISE FOR
AFTERMATH OF AN INDUSTRIAL ACCIDENT

"From heartbreaking character studies to exercises in Grand Guignol excess, from scalpel-sharp poetry to sledgehammers of blood-soaked prose, Mike Allen displays not only his own considerable range, but the range of the horror genre as well. *Aftermath of an Industrial Accident* will surprise and delight you at every turn."
—**Nathan Ballingrud, Shirley Jackson Award-winning author of *Wounds***

"Allen overflows the tank with nightmare fuel in this collection of 23 stories and poems that showcase his ability to find the monstrous in almost any setting . . . Readers will be impressed by the variety, intensity, and skilled craftsmanship Allen brings to this collection. These horror shorts are sure to linger in the dark corners of readers' minds."
—***Publishers Weekly*, starred review**

"*Aftermath of an Industrial Accident* puts the weird in Weird Fiction. The stories range from clever twists on the Lovecraft mythos, to the downright madcap (spider demons nesting in suburban souls!). Allen weds the brute visceral punch of early Clive Barker with the demented whimsy of darker Neil Gaiman."
—**Craig Laurance Gidney, Lambda Award-nominated author of *A Spectral Hue***

"From a university library's forbidden collection, to a manse occupied by cursed souls, to seemingly ordinary suburban homes haunted by memories and otherworldly beings, *Aftermath* takes readers on a journey, and Allen deftly imbues each world visited with its own own special kind of dread."
—**A. C. Wise, Nebula Award-nominated author of *Catfish Lullaby***

"Mike Allen habitually upends Lovecraftian tropes with his own brand of cosmic horror."
—**Laird Barron, Bram Stoker and Shirley Jackson award-winning author of *Swift to Chase***

"From World Fantasy Award-nominated author and editor Mike Allen comes a mesmerizingly beautiful, classic horror collection of short stories and poems. Each tale in *Aftermath of an Industrial Accident* packs a punch that will keep you willingly pinned to the wall. A master of the hook and a perfect ending, Allen's fast-paced, fluid prose engages you from the very beginning and does not let you go until it is done with its story; and the stories will keep resonating in your mind like a wonderful, terrible memory that haunts and thrills you. 'Six Waking Nightmares' scared and intrigued me, 'A Deaf Policeman Heard the Noise' had me turning the pages for more, 'The Cruelest Team Will Win' is an arachnophilic thing of beauty, and the title story is an apt reminder of the horrific monsters our god complex creates. Allen writes with a mystical precognition of knowing the deepest terrors in your gut. If you don't want to ever sleep again, read *Aftermath of an Industrial Accident* just before bedtime. It'll be worth it."
—Christina Sng, Bram Stoker Award-winning author of *A Collection of Nightmares*

"As a huge fan of Mike Allen's first novel, *The Black Fire Concerto*, I was excited beyond belief to have the opportunity to devour his new collection, *Aftermath of an Industrial Accident*.

"In this collection, Allen demonstrates again and again his masterful ability to infuse cosmic, existential terror into the most intimate and mundane aspects of our lives, while never failing to point out the self-made horror already there: from his introductory piece that credits Poe as a conjurer of inescapable, psychic horror and a muse-sinister for Allen, to the title story that force-marches the reader through rising terror, like a tea kettle screaming, for which there is no escape, no sanctuary, even within your own mind.

"With every one of Allen's works I get my hands on, I am more and more impressed with his dream-like prose, his knack for seeping cold, inescapable dread into the 'normal' foundations of his tales. Allen is a craftsman and this collection represents him at the height of his game. These stories will stick with you long after you have finished them. I highly recommend *Aftermath of an Industrial Accident* for fans of Allen's work, and for those who will have the envious pleasure of discovering him for the first time."
—R. S. Belcher, Locus Award-nominated author of *The Brotherhood of the Wheel*

AFTERMATH
OF AN INDUSTRIAL
ACCIDENT

Also by Mike Allen

Novel
THE BLACK FIRE CONCERTO

Story Collections
UNSEAMING
THE SPIDER TAPESTRIES

Poetry Collections
HUNGRY CONSTELLATIONS
THE JOURNEY TO KAILASH
STRANGE WISDOMS OF THE DEAD
DISTURBING MUSES
PETTING THE TIME SHARK
DEFACING THE MOON

As Editor
CLOCKWORK PHOENIX 5

MYTHIC DELIRIUM: VOLUME TWO (with Anita Allen)

MYTHIC DELIRIUM (with Anita Allen)

CLOCKWORK PHOENIX 4

CLOCKWORK PHOENIX 3:
New Tales of Beauty and Strangeness

CLOCKWORK PHOENIX 2:
More Tales of Beauty and Strangeness

CLOCKWORK PHOENIX:
Tales of Beauty and Strangeness

MYTHIC 2

MYTHIC

THE ALCHEMY OF STARS:
Rhysling Award Winners Showcase (with Roger Dutcher)

NEW DOMINIONS:
Fantasy Stories by Virginia Writers

AFTERMATH

OF AN INDUSTRIAL

ACCIDENT

STORIES

MIKE ALLEN

INTRODUCTION BY JEFFREY THOMAS

Mythic Delirium
BOOKS
mythicdelirium.com

Aftermath of an Industrial Accident: Stories

Copyright © 2020 by Mike Allen

Cover photograph © 2020 by Danielle Tunstall.

Cover design and interior illustrations © 2020 by Mike Allen and Brett Massé, brettmasseworks.com.

ISBN-10: 1-7326440-2-0
ISBN-13: 978-1-7326440-2-1

Library of Congress Control Number: 2020937119

FIRST EDITION
July 7, 2020

Published by Mythic Delirium Books
Roanoke, Virginia
mythicdelirium.com

Further copyright information begins on page 236.

Our gratitude goes out to the following who because of their generosity are from now on designated as supporters of Mythic Delirium Books: Saira Ali, Cora Anderson, Anonymous, Patricia M. Cryan, Steve Dempsey, Oz Drummond, Patrick Dugan, Matthew Farrer, C. R. Fowler, Mary J. Lewis, Paul T. Muse, Jr., Shyam Nunley, Finny Pendragon, Kenneth Schneyer, and Delia Sherman.

For my brother Ed

TABLE OF CONTENTS

AFTERMATH OF AN EXPLOSIVE IMAGINATION

INTRODUCTION BY JEFFREY THOMAS

I remember seeing Mike Allen's horror collection *Unseaming* all over my Facebook feed in 2014. In my "customers also bought" suggestions on Amazon. It was receiving praise, had nabbed a starred review in *Publishers Weekly*; hell, a copy of it was spotted in a photograph of director Guillermo del Toro's living room. Like any lover of books, though, I'm in constant threat of being crushed by my precarious to-be-read pile, and didn't catch up with *Unseaming*, as tantalized as I was.

Enter Scott Nicolay, a new writer whose work I had caught up with, and admired. Having read Mike Allen's follow-up collection, *The Spider Tapestries*, Scott recommended to Mike that he request a blurb from me. Familiar with my work, Scott thought I'd appreciate the book—and did I ever. This is how I described it in my blurb: "We think of science fiction, fantasy, and horror as genres of the imagination, but someone like Mike Allen shows us how lacking in daring and vision so many of their works can be, by resisting the labels altogether. *The Spider Tapestries* is kaleidoscopically, gloriously imaginative—feverish and fantastical—while never threatening to spin away into the nonsensical. Beyond the gorgeous and poetic mind pictures, he creates real, powerful emotions in the most alien of settings and circumstances. Allen achieves what I find most exciting in any artistic medium: a synthesis of beauty and the grotesque."

I was so impressed, in fact, that Mike was one of only three writers I personally requested editor Brian M. Sammons invite to the anthology *Transmissions from Punktown*, set in my dark future milieu of the title. I had to see what Mike would create, playing in my sandbox, and he didn't disappoint. That invitation resulted in the story that gives this collection its name.

So what does Mike bring to this particular collection? Well, I'm thinking he brought pretty much everything he's got . . . and that's a lot, to put it mildly. What I've said above, and what I'll be going on to say below, illustrate perfectly how extremely versatile Mike Allen is, and that's a quality I highly prize; a quality I am ever striving toward, myself. Many writers endeavor to establish a certain style or voice or tone, to clear a small but distinct plot of ground they can build within, so as to create a kind of brand that inspires recognition in a reader. Maybe this is just their natural inclination, or maybe it's a calculation. Perhaps they do this partly out of fear that if they extend themselves toward too many horizons on the compass, readers won't be able to get a grip on their work overall. And there's nothing wrong with such an approach! But those writers who do as Mike does have a special place in my heart.

And what Mike does, as I say, is just about everything. In these pages you will encounter straight up horror. Experimental horror. High fantasy. Science fiction. Poetry. The consistency, here, is simply excellence.

Just to give you some brief teases and impressions of the offerings herein . . .

The collection's opening poem, *Six Waking Nightmares Poe Gave Me in Third Grade*, seems to establish for us Mike's early obsession with horror. We then move on to *The Sun Saw*, a gruesome Lovecraftian nightmare that mixes themes of racism and war. The unsettling little poem *The Paper Boy* is followed by *A Deaf Policeman Heard the Noise*, which haunts us with the image of ghosts racing across rooftops to keep pace with our cyclist protagonist. *The Cruelest Team Will Win* reminds me of *The Spider Tapestries* with its epic cosmic battle, like something from a classical mythical text that never existed. *Tick Flick* is a surreal, grotesquely humorous affair, while *The Nightmare Avatar's Nightmare* is a poem coauthored with Bram Stoker Award winner Christina Sng. *Tardigrade* impresses greatly with its chilling mysteriousness. *Burn the Kool Kidz at the Stake*, like others in this collection, cleverly utilizes ambiguity to question what is real. *Puppet Show* is a ghastly fusion of Grand Guignol and rock 'n' roll. (Rock 'n' Guignol?) The poem *The Bone Bird* is creepy, mournful, ghostly. *Longsleeves* highlights Mike's impressive range with a fantasy story that confronts mankind's curious habit of mythologizing—while simultaneously oppressing—women. *Toujours Il Coûte Trop Cher* is a poetic dialogue between Gilles de Rais and Joan of Arc. *Binding* is an excellent, spooky and tricky tale of erotic obsession . . . *Nolens Volens* a harrowing and compelling supernatural thriller. The very disturbing poem *Sad Wisps of Empty Smoke* is followed by *Blue Evolution*, one of my top favorites of the stories in this collection; with its awe-inspiring imagery, it's Allen's extraordinary imagination at its finest. *The Ivy-Smothered Palisade*, another work of high fantasy, set in the same world as *Longsleeves*—a thoroughly gripping combination of fairy tale and horror. *With Shining Gifts That Took All Eyes* is a disorienting, nightmarish tale about an enigmatic plant. *Follow the Wounded One* involves the weird intersection of reality with an overlapping dream-like realm, and its open-ended coda suggests that the conflicts that weave these two planes together will go on. *Drift from the Windrows* combines the eco-horror of a Monsanto-like corporation with an ominous alien presence. The book's title story, *Aftermath of an Industrial Accident*, is a suspenseful, phantasmagorical onslaught of body horror, with a clever trick regarding who is truly the story's antagonist. The book ends with *The Night Watchman Dreams His Rounds at the REM Sleep Factory* . . . a poem rife with vivid, horrific imagery.

As you can now tell, you are holding in your hands an overflowing cornucopia of monstrous goodness. Don't spill too much of it onto yourself.

So yeah, Mike Allen. Let his far-ranging gifts transport you to a seemingly infinite number of dark but fascinating worlds. Let his imaginings inspire you.

I know they inspire me.

SIX WAKING NIGHTMARES POE GAVE ME IN THIRD GRADE

1) At night, the light fixture above my bed stretched into a pale blue vulture eye, and the emaciated ghost of the man it belonged to swirled out, craggy face contorted in silent accusation as he reached for me, but

2) I didn't dare turn my head, for fear of the man with the toothsome smile who would emerge from my closet and disassemble himself like a thing made of paper tabs and glue, and what he would look like as he kept crawling towards me. Yet

3) If I shut my eyes, the old man would never leave me alone, the pounding I heard not the pulse of blood in my ears but the beat of his heart, thumping, thumping, thumping, as he lay dismembered beneath my bed, and

4) If I kept my eyes shut, I would feel the deadly rush of air as that long curved blade swung from above, swept lower and lower as I lay wrapped and trapped in my blankets. I could never, ever sleep, and

5) If I did, I would wake up buried, faceless men dumping dirt on me from above as I screamed in my coffin, smothered and alone with the gold bugs that bit and the deathwatch beetles and hideous throngs of conqueror worms. But

6) None of it mattered, no matter how many nights I stayed awake and afraid, because soon the great raven that hid in every shadow would pluck out my pale and fluttering soul, and I knew then I would nevermore see happiness or Heaven.

THE SUN SAW

A gainst his better judgment, John Hairston did these things:
Parked his Plymouth across from Pollard's book shop, in the shadow of an ash tree, the same tree where a mob strung up another black man just seven months ago, set him on fire as he begged for mercy.

Stepped out of the car into the shade of the tree, the murdered man's howls still breathing in its leaves.

Popped the trunk, as a red-haired boy on a shiny blue bike rounded the corner and stopped to stare.

Picked up the cloth-wrapped parcel inside the trunk, big as two cinderblocks bound together, tucked it under his arm, ignoring the gawking boy.

Crossed the street to the shop's front door, keeping his cool, acting as if he weren't a brown-skinned man out alone in a town full of racist whites who would savor putting him in his place, whooping and hooting at every cry of pain.

Pollard, Lord be praised, wasn't like that. He was white as a painted picket fence, but Hairston was alive to make this nerve-wracking drive to Grandy Springs because Pollard had killed for him as their squads fled Kunu-ri, felled a Chinese sniper with a bead on Hairston's back. Not three days later, Hairston saved Pollard from a lonely death in a wind-swept rice paddy.

This was no matter of trading favors. Their debts to each other could never be repaid and didn't need to be.

Only because Hairston knew Pollard's goodness in his bones did he dare bring his uncle's book to Grandy Springs.

Pollard's last letter had been dire: "I never wish to witness such an awful thing again . . . Come in the morning, before ten.

I'll assess your uncle's treasure and have you out by noon. Again, I apologize that I can't instead come to you."

This bowel-knotting fear discombobulated Hairston worse than that awful quiet before the Chinese bullets came slicing over the dam in Kunu-ri. It shouldn't be this way, he shouldn't have to live every moment on the blessed ground of his home country like a sniper might sight between his shoulder blades, like that boy on his fucking bike was an enemy scout. He so admired the bravery of the boycotters in Montgomery, that woman in Oklahoma leading the lunch counter sit-ins.

Their bravery could not save him if a mob came.

Not gonna take me alive, he thought, and knocked.

"Come in," Pollard called, his voice sounding oddly close, as if no door stood between them. Hairston stepped into his friend's bookshop, the "appointments only" sign clacking as he swung the door closed. Hardbound books in muted golds, reds and browns filled tight shelves in a room too small to house a proper business. The pleasing must of aged paper summoned thoughts of how easily it all might combust if the townsfolk chose to teach Pollard a lesson over his choice of friends.

Get the business done, get back to Baltimore. "Bill, where you hiding, brother?" Hairston called, advancing between the tall, narrow shelves. Pollard had to have spoken from just inside the entrance, but the shop was empty. Hairston paused, listened, pictured how many moves it would take to drop the book, pull the switchblade from his inside jacket pocket, spring it open. Its weight where he normally kept his cigarettes reminded him that he wasn't helpless.

Uncle Mansfeld was convinced a fortune could be had, that this hide-bound, illuminated tome recovered from the Franklin property didn't belong in the estate auction, instead should be offered to people who'd recognize its real worth. Convenient that his nephew made a white friend in the war who happened to be an antiquarian book expert, because maybe, just maybe, the Big Apple fat cats would give credence to a white man's appraisal.

"I'm in the back," Pollard said. Sheer reflex kept Hairston from smashing into a bookcase, because it sounded like his friend spoke right in his ear. At the same time he thought he heard a pained shout, the kind made by a man bleeding out in an empty rice field.

Maybe the high shelves were distorting the acoustics. He stepped into Pollard's back office, its desk crowded close by more books in stacks upon stacks. Something huge and white wrapped an arm around his neck and pressed a cloth to his face. A searing stench of fruit-sweet gasoline.

P ollard shook his shoulder, rousted him to the icy wind, the rocks like molars pressing into his back.

"It's really me this time, John," Pollard hissed. "My owner's fed good tonight, so he's sleeping. But he's gonna send the overseer for you when he wakes up. You gotta wake up first, you gotta. You can free us both."

Hairston had slept with his helmet on, though it failed to mute Pollard's jabbering. "What are you talking about?" When he opened his eyes, the sun saw them both across the Korean hills and chose the moment to meet his gaze and blind him. "Damn." When his focus returned Pollard was leaning down to whisper in his ear. Blood sheeted his face.

"What got you?" Hairston started up, Pollard shoved him back down.

From the other side of the hill, thunder, and the eerie whistle of a mortar round.

Deep corrugated slits regular as ladder steps marred both sides of Pollard's face from temple to jawline. "You gotta wake up for real, John. NOW!"

Flames licked out from his wounds.

Wake up, John!

Cold soil under his back became cold concrete against his cheek. He lay face down with arms and legs twisted at painful angles. His head throbbed with hangover agony. The coarse mesh of a blindfold blotted his vision.

His new accommodations stank of singed meat and sawdust. He coughed involuntarily, almost split his chin on the concrete, tried to move again, deduced he was hog-tied, tight cords pinning his wrists and ankles behind his back.

That cough could have given him away. He listened, heard nothing but his own breath. The wise bellow of his non-com in his head, *Let your guard down, you're dead.*

He relaxed, took inventory. His hands were not touching his feet; there had to be a length of cord between them. He was still dressed. The lumps of his wallet, keys and matchbook still weighted his trouser pockets. The switchblade pressed against his ribs.

John Hairston did these things next:

Rolled awkwardly onto his side.

Bent his arms as far left as he could, gathered the fabric of his coat in swollen fingers, shook it to drop the knife out.

Suppressed a gasp of relief as it clattered loose.

Carefully rolled over so his back was to the knife, wincing at the strain on his shoulders.

No one watched him. A guard would have acted by now. Who had taken him? Couldn't be the Klan. They'd have beaten him awake, made sure he was alert for every minute of his drawn-out death.

His fingers found the handle's smooth wood, circled it with a solid grip. Despite his caution, he nicked his forearm when he opened the blade.

Didn't scream at Kunu-ri when the sniper notched his ear with a bullet. Wasn't going to now.

Were someone observing him, sadistically biding their time, their moment to intervene had arrived. No one did.

The cords, butcher's twine it seemed, wrapped his wrists in layers: still, he praised the Lord that he didn't have to cut rope or wire. Careful as he was, severing strand after strand with each stroke, he cut his wrists over and over, the blade slicked with his own blood.

He heard a moan and stopped. He counted to ten, holding his breath. Quiet.

He resumed worrying at the twine.

Abruptly the cords went slack. He stretched his arms apart, sat up and pulled off his blindfold.

His first sight, a wall hung with saws, drills, miters, hammers, pristine as a catalog spread. A thick, fresh-planed board supported by four sawhorses dominated the chamber like the posh mahogany table in Uncle Mansfeld's meeting room, where he sat down with grieving families and their lawyers to talk business. A single lighted bulb hung from a chain above the workbench, and past it squatted a gas-powered generator the size of an icebox, with an equally cumbersome device hooked up to it by steel belts, some kind of bandsaw.

The wall behind him held two exits, one at each end of the long chamber, a single plaque mounted equidistant between them. If someone stood at the workbench with their back to the tools, they'd be looking up to that plaque as they worked, just like a chapel cross.

Hairston had never seen letters like those on the plaque. Not Arabic, Russian, Greek, Hebrew or Chinese.

Both doors were open. Whoever had intended to hold him here lacked military discipline. Maybe it was the Klan, out celebrating their big catch, too stupid to properly secure him.

After five years spent grateful that his rifle no longer burdened his shoulder, he sorely missed it now.

"You have to kill us all," Pollard whispered.

Right in his ear again. Ingrained survival instinct kept him from screaming.

Hairston finished freeing his ankles. When the pins and needles sufficiently subsided, he stood. He picked a toothy backsaw from the shrines on the wall. It had a symbol scratched on its gleaming blade, like one etched on the plaque, vaguely recalling a seven-pointed sun.

Another moan.

Weapon in each hand, Hairston stole to the door closest to the source of the noise, peered into a dim cinderblock hallway. One end opened into light. At the other end, behind a shut door, a man bleated in pain.

No one in sight. The man moaned again. At the same time Pollard's voice whispered, "John, get the gasoline."

Hairston whispered back, "You a ghost?"

"You'll see soon enough. Please buddy. You gotta hurry." He had never heard Pollard's voice so high-pitched with fright. "When my owner wakes I won't be free to talk. I'll say what he makes me say."

"What do you mean, owner?" No answer.

Pollard's repeated use of slavery terms amplified the nightmarish disconnect that threatened to make Hairston's head swim. Though he damn well knew he was wide awake.

Two big metal gas cans stood sentry by the generator. He stuffed knife and saw into his outer coat pockets, picked up both cans. Hall still clear, he hurried to the shut door, pressed his ear to the wood. This time, when the man moaned, he detected other sounds, a dog-like whimper, someone else softly blubbering. He set the cans down, re-armed, eased the door open. He did not at first comprehend what awaited in the shadows.

Seven figures crouched naked, sealed in a circular pillory, their filthy bodies down on all fours outside the wooden cylinder, their heads and hands trapped inside, facing one another, their faces practically mashed together. Except that couldn't be, because their shoulders weren't touching. Their heads were inflated somehow, misshapen.

He groped, found a light switch, flipped it.

The gray, fly-swarmed corpses of Korea lay five years behind him, but sometimes, at night, as he fought for sleep, their maggoty skins stirred. Those memories fortified him against the overwhelming urge to scream.

Whatever demons did this had burned and sliced these captives beyond recognition, their faces scabbed together in one raw, continuous wound. Hairston spotted stitches in the crusted flesh, regular as zipper teeth, binding each face to its neighbor, but that didn't explain how the skin stretched and fused. No chemical agent Hairston knew about could do that.

"John, help me." Pollard in his ear.

"Where are you?" Hairston whispered.

"Find my eyes. Find the book."

The poor saps trapped in the pillory moaned with one voice. He paced around their shaking, atrophied bodies—men or women, he couldn't tell, it was as if their very bones had twisted, their bellies bloated red, pale spines jutting like fins. He spotted Pollard's eyes staring straight at him from a ruined face within the circle.

"Shit," he said, no longer whispering. "I'm gonna get you out of there."

"There's only one way to help me."

"Yeah, spring you loose, my brother." He crouched beside Pollard's rib-jutting, skin-sagging, excrement-reeking form. The hollow cylinder of the pillory seemed to be carved from a single tree trunk. He found no seam, no way to pry it open. "How the hell they got you in there?"

"Kill us, John. Before it wakes up."

Worse than finding no seam, he found no separation between the oddly-smooth wood and Pollard's neck.

Panicked, he groped the other bodies. They too were melded in seamless. All shuddered and flinched at his touch but one, whose skin was like ice-packed meat.

"That one . . . the overseer means to replace him with you," Pollard said. "You have to get the book out of there, and end us."

Hairston blinked at his friend's mangled face. "The book?"

"The *Necronomicon* your uncle acquired. My owner recognized it from the description in your letters." Pollard's gaze flicked down.

His uncle's book lay open on the floor inside the cylinder, beneath the circle of heads. It rested on a complex pattern of runnels, its leathery cover soaking up the blood that filled them. It was open in the exact center, an inhuman eye with a star-shaped pupil staring up, a drawing that spanned both leaves, surrounded by indecipherable symbols. Hairston could not stop a second's heart-skip of dismay at the damage done to his uncle's hoped-for fortune.

"Tell me how to get you out!"

"You can't. My owner's awake now. End this, *please.*"

Hairston couldn't explain the sensation that crawled across his skin, as if the air filled with invisible insects.

"Please, John!"

Instinct came to a boil in Hairston's gut, telling him Pollard spoke truth. He considered the problem. Bill wanted him to burn the place. Was there another way? He could stab them all, but given their bizarre half-alive states, such wounds might not be fatal.

He put the knife hilt in his mouth, double-checked his back pocket for his matchbook. Still there.

He dashed out to grab the gas cans. The largest man he'd ever seen filled the opening at the other end of the hall, draped in a white robe but no pointed hood. A huge smile puffed the cheeks of his pale, hairless head. He loped forward.

Pollard wailed. "The overseer!"

Hairston transferred his switchblade from mouth to hand and brandished it. He could take one man.

The son of a bitch had speed. Before Hairston could block, the giant seized Hairston's coat collar and with a moist giggle lifted him in the air. His other hand grabbed Hairston's throat.

Hairston stabbed the overseer's left eye, and when that didn't loosen his grip, stabbed out the other. Then he buried the blade in the brute's throat.

The overseer hurled Hairston against the wall, then clutched oddly at his face, not even trying to remove the knife from his neck.

Head ringing, back bruised, Hairston snatched the backsaw from where it had fallen. He scrabbled across the floor to draw the full length of the saw's teeth across the Achilles tendon of his opponent's right ankle.

The overseer toppled. Hairston scurried back on all fours into the torture room, pushing the gas cans before him. Pollard said, in his ear—in his *mind*, Hairston comprehended now—"Hurry, he ain't down."

Hairston stood, poised to pour the first can of gas into the pillory.

"No! Get the book! Without it you'll never get out!"

"Damn, Bill, make up your mind." He reached between those mutilated faces, the hair on his arms standing on end with the strangeness of the air down there. He peeled the book off the floor, took in that the runnels formed a star shape, each of its seven points terminating beneath one of the heads.

When he looked up, the room was full of people, naked, most of them brown-skinned, flesh sagging from their bones, bandages stretched over their faces. He knew their still forms stared at him, though he couldn't see their eyes. He *could* see the symbols etched on the walls through their translucent bodies.

"John, finish it."

He stood, lifting the book out of the circle. The crowd vanished.

He tossed the heavy tome toward the exit, dumped the first can all over the heads and the strange pillory. Gasoline-thinned blood swirled and splashed. The prisoners opened their mouths to scream, exposing the charred stumps of their tongues.

With the second can he soaked the seven bodies, efficient and methodical, using the last dregs of gasoline to draw a trail to the door. Scooping up the book, he hopped outside.

The overseer had vanished from the hall. No trail of blood gave away his whereabouts.

No time to wonder. The match blazed on first strike. He set it to the damp floor and jumped back as flames leaped jubilant.

No mistaking Pollard's real in-the-flesh scream. The same sound he had once made under cover of rice stalks halfway around the world, as Hairston wound a tourniquet above the blood-spurting hole in his arm.

"Sorry, brother," he whispered to his old friend.

A tongueless keening scorched the air, though what direction it came from, Hairston couldn't sense.

The torture room combusted, flames cascading up the walls. Hairston backed away but didn't run. Lord knew what he'd be running toward.

The book was like a stack of bricks under his arm, cover sticky with blood. Maybe he needed it, like Pollard insisted, but it wouldn't do for a weapon. He spied the backsaw, reacquired it. The teeth had scraps of the overseer's flesh lodged between them. How the fuck could there be no blood? Was he fighting a vampire?

Under the rumble of the flames, a series of thuds from the tool room.

The overseer, so tall he could prop a bare leg on the workbench, was using the twine from Hairston's escape to brace three short slats around his gimp ankle in an improvised splint. Slime drooled from the pits of his punctured eyes.

The overseer completed a knot, swung his splinted leg off the table and turned his eyeless gaze toward Hairston. The switchblade still protruded from his neck.

Hairston immediately forgot whatever plans he'd formed for what to do next.

Attention fixed on Hairston, the overseer casually lifted a three-foot hacksaw from the workbench. Gripping its handle with both hands, he dragged the blade across his chest, shredding the robe. Smiling, he drew it next across his forehead, meat and bone spraying like sawdust from the wound. Then he slashed his own throat, twice, carving a bloodless X, grinning all the while. Hairston's knife fluttered loose to clack on the floor.

The huge man's mouth moved. No sound came out, but Hairston distinctly heard, "Your turn."

Hairston sprinted out the hallway's open end. He banged out onto a steel mesh balcony that overlooked an assembly hall full of people. That inhuman keening returned like a bat shrieking past his ear. He actually ducked before he registered that nothing was physically attacking him.

Behind him the overseer emerged into the corridor, silhouetted by flames, for which he showed no concern at all.

Hairston pounded down the spiral stairs, until the horrendous stench rising from below, worse than a corpse-stacked battlefield, stopped him cold. He took in the white-robed mob waiting for him, seated around rectangular tables like you'd see at church pot-luck. The only light came from a bulb on a chain, suspended from a tall stepladder that loomed on the opposite side of the room.

The overseer clanged onto the balcony.

The forty-some people at the tables weren't wearing hoods, like he had first thought. Bandages wrapped their heads, like the ghosts he'd seen upstairs. Only their mouths were uncovered, and they were using forks and knives to shovel their faces full of the reeking meat piled in sloppy gray mounds on the tabletops. Eating and chewing without pause, the soft slobbering and smacking like a thousand tiny creatures hopping through mud.

Those closest to him sat splayed in metal chairs, their legs missing below the knees.

"Christ Almighty, soldier, run!"

Pollard's words, the same shout from across the hills that saved him in Kunu-ri, shocked him into bolting just like it had then. Yet he drew up short because he saw no way out.

"They won't touch you!" Pollard barked. "They eat for our owner, that's all they do. Keep going!"

He charged through the middle of the feast, gaining speed as the overseer clang-clunked down the stairs.

The inverted V of the ladder hid an archway in its shadows. Just inside it stood bins of silverware beside a rack holding stacks of large porcelain trays, the same ones from which the eaters were slurping their mounds of meat.

While Hairston delayed in the doorway, the overseer again fixed on him, advancing with a grin. Whatever his powers, he was blind for sure, or else he'd have seen Hairston fling the tray, or at least have tried to duck as it spun toward him. Will of the Lord or sheer dumb luck, the tray smashed the brute edge on in the forehead, shattering at the same time bone cracked. The overseer dropped.

Rather than plunge into the pitch black with its rotten flesh smell thick as fog, Hairston groped for and found another light switch.

Anchored in the ceiling of this long, low room, rows of hooks suspended skinless corpses. Pigs, cattle, people. The red ichor that coated them wasn't blood: too bright, too rose-hued, as were the wisps of steam wafting from its surfaces.

Behind Hairston, the clunk-clomp renewed.

He sprinted, eyes fixed on the open area beyond the flayed sacks, desperately wanting to raise an arm to cover his face against that reddish vapor. But he dropped neither book nor saw, though he couldn't fathom how either would do him good.

The overseer's footsteps changed timbre as he thudded into the slaughterhouse, the same moment Hairston emerged from the rows of corpses. Before him loomed three more workbenches like the one upstairs, their boards blood-drenched, piled with hides, skins, entrails. Here, clearly, was where the bodies were cleaned before hanging.

What the hell is this place?

He forced himself to think, even though the overseer had almost reached him. His success with the tray provided hope. He tiptoed quickly to the furthest of the benches, out of the overseer's immediate path. Holding his breath, he set down book and backsaw as the white-robed man bulled out of the hanging corpses and kept running.

Hairston carefully pulled himself onto the bench and crouched down beside a mound of what looked like pig's guts. He squatted right in plain sight, but his opponent had no eyes. If demons' magic gave him sight, there was no hiding anyway.

The overseer stopped. Turned. Sniffed the air. Amidst the overwhelming stink, it had to be damn near impossible to pick out one frightened human.

The overseer mouthed words. Hairston continued to hold his breath. His lungs started to burn.

Slowly—but not looking at him—the overseer ambled in his direction, still snuffling. He rounded the end of the next bench over, came up the aisle that would lead right to Hairston.

Moving as if underwater, Hairston gently lifted and tossed the book so that it plopped on the floor between the benches. The overseer lunged at the noise. As he bent to grab at the object, Hairston leapt onto his broad back, executing the maneuver he'd spent the past four seconds rehearsing in his head. He clamped one arm around the giant's neck, used the other to press the teeth of the backsaw against his spine, put all his strength into a stroke that tore meat and grazed vertebrae.

Strong as the overseer was, Hairston's leap knocked him prone. He heard Pollard's voice, repeating syllables he didn't understand.

The star symbol on the saw blade glowed.

The overseer rose beneath him, grabbed at the arm squeezing his neck to pry it loose. Hairston stuffed his hand into the wound in the man's throat, seized cold tubes of flesh with adrenaline-jazzed fingers, and kept sawing.

The overseer flipped onto his back, squashing Hairston under his bulk, crushing his testicles, squeezing the breath from his lungs. He gripped Hairston's forearm with such pressure that skin and muscle parted. Hairston screamed and used the agony as fuel for his own attack, ripping the blade against bone. Its teeth tore far enough through to bite his own fingers as they clutched inside the overseer's neck.

The head came free like a cork jerked from a bottleneck. No wine poured from the wound.

That horrible keening returned a thousand times louder, dynamite inside Hairston's skull.

The overseer's headless body sat up, arms outstretched like Frankenstein's monster. Then it slumped sideways and sprawled, releasing Hairston from the worst of the crushing pressure.

But Hairston didn't squirm away. He clutched his ears in a useless attempt to block the keening. A desperate call swelled within the noise, a baby's squall, something that could only be quieted if you gave it what it wanted.

He had to give in to its demands. It wanted *him*. Its need flooded his veins.

Whispers fought the flood. "I can protect you but you need the book. I can help you read it, John. John!"

Hairston crawled to where the book lay, pages open to that same staring eye. Every motion brought stabbing pain. The overseer's head had come to rest against a sawhorse leg. Its mouth twitched.

"Just what that ape deserved," Pollard growled. "Was him hauled the rope that pulled Beddows up into that tree. That poor soul was the sacrifice that got all this started. If that hell-bound mob knew it would come to this, I still don't think they would have cared."

With a snarl of disgust Hairston kicked the head away.

"Those pages," Pollard said. "I can read them through your eyes. Repeat what I say."

Insanity. Hairston cradled the *Necronomicon*, staring into that star-pupiled eye, repeating the sounds Pollard made. Of its own accord his gaze moved in circles, following the symbols that sur-rounded the eye.

The keening dampened to bearable volume. When it did, Hairston perceived his own name, wrapped repeatedly inside that endless wail.

"My owner wants you to take that gorilla's place. If you hadn't freed me from his yoke, you'd have no choice but to obey. But you gotta keep reading. There's no getting out for either of us till we end this, buddy."

Hairston nodded. *Let's do it, then.*

Sometimes the Lord's work and the Devil's are the same. Korea was like that, and what Hairston did in that pit deep under-ground was like that too.

Pollard's ghost talked as they descended further into the bunker tunnels under Grover MacCutcheon's plantation, where Pollard said they'd both been brought as prisoners. "That wasn't me who answered your letters," he whispered. "He's had me since they killed Beddows. I learned how it all works, trapped inside his disease."

The old man who lived here had made pacts with things worse than the Devil. It had been easy for him to whip up the townsfolk, to carry out the things he needed to open himself to the fallen angels, strange creatures with stranger names that lived outside human time. When Pollard whispered those names it was as if his spirit spoke in tongues.

Hairston understood only a fraction of what Pollard struggled to explain, but when he found the plantation owner one thing be-came plain. Pollard's assertion that "he got what he wanted and it overwhelmed him" was one hell of an understatement.

What had once been a man lay on a pallet, frame shriveled to bones draped in flesh gone the texture and color of pus. Purplish mold had sprouted from the remains of its skin and spread across all the surfaces of the cellar.

Hairston took in these details only through peripheral vision, his gaze still tracking the symbols inked around the center pages, the vocalizations coming out of his own mouth turning his throat raw. The creature continued its keening and calling, though the energy—it wasn't truly a sound—radiated from its swollen yellow eyes, protruding tumors with pinhole pupils. The chant that Pollard led him through kept it from digging claws into his mind, but Hairston felt those claws probing, like bayonets stabbing the underbrush.

He didn't dare set the book down, so against his better judgment he waded into the sprouts of bruise-colored mold. A red vapor rose as his shoes broke the stalks. Still reading, he stepped onto the pallet, shouting Pollard's syllables against the rising shriek.

He set a foot in the creature's putrescent belly. It burst like a puffball, more of the vapor clouding below him. In the corners of his eyes, figures in white robes with faces suffocated by bandages rose from the floor, vapors themselves, watching.

He stepped on the creature's chest. His legs started to go numb as more dust billowed. The creature's shriek at last became true sound as he took another step and his shoe descended on its face. The head crunched flat, no stronger than an eggshell. The horrible keening didn't stop. Rather, it slowly faded, as if it were a water ripple, dissipating in all directions at once.

Hairston lost all feeling in his legs. He toppled off the pallet, the book splayed in front of him.

The white figures faded away.

"What now?" Hairston asked, but Pollard's ghost no longer answered. And though he screamed Pollard's name, again and again, some part of him knew all along this was how it would end.

The horrors in the cosmos that Pollard had yammered on about with such tremulous fear held no candle to the fate he'd abandoned Hairston to face.

He was on his own, not knowing how far underground he was, or where to go if he even made it to the surface with no legs to carry him, in a place where anyone he called to for help might just decide to string him up and burn him alive.

The earth above and below longed to swallow him whole.

THE PAPER BOY

Ghosts almost never harangue their killers. It's those who can actually feel guilt and shame who draw a ghost from hiding, regardless of whether they had anything to do with the death that spawned the haunting.
—Aaron Friedrich, *These Bloody Filaments*

alley behind our house
car parked against the fence, a beat up four-door compact
dead teen folded on the tiny back seat

all his blood emigrated through the new doors
moved out into the upholstery

cop had a laugh, said the boy came up short
owed someone meaner, had to pay exact change
no pennies left for his eyes

sure we didn't hear nothing?
struggle must've gone on for a while
he could've called for help

guy at our church owns a jewelry store
he grins around his reading glasses
they catch the one who did it, that's two thugs gone, he says

they towed that car off weeks ago
but the boy, he doesn't know

we've seen him draped on our chain-link gate
like he tried to climb over and couldn't make it
flimsy as the paper that shared his death
in four short paragraphs

no moon, nothing's waving
when we peek through the blinds
just a piece of trash tortured by the wind
so it looks like a face

A DEAF POLICEMAN HEARD THE NOISE

Icy fingers gripped my wrist. Even though I'd lain awake for hours waiting for this moment to arrive, I yelled in surprise as the ghost tried to yank me out of bed. She tugged hard enough to lift my sweat-slicked back from the mattress.

"Stop," I pleaded, and this time, to my shock, she listened. Though she didn't let go.

I opened my eyes to find her hunched by the bed, the edges of her body bright without casting any light. Her long black hair drifted like seaweed stirred by currents I couldn't feel. A gray sheen glazed her brown skin. Huge dark eyes flooded her broad face with urgency. Her egg pale gown flowed and drifted like her hair. No scent of marsh or sea or riverbank accompanied her, no such thing ever does.

I twisted my arm against her frozen thumb. She responded by gripping with both hands. I hissed as the sting of the cold redoubled. She started to sink into the floor, pulling me with her.

"I know," I said. "I know you drowned. You don't have to show me again."

She's not strong, but I'm a small woman—"stealing size," my stepdad's macabre joke—so the force she applied was more than enough to dislodge me. I put my hand up, palm flat, hoping she understood the universal warding gesture. "Stop! Please!"

Again she paused, which through all the months of this awful nighttime routine she'd never done before, not at this stage.

One of my pillows tumbled to the rug, incongruous beside her bright torso. She stared at me, chest deep in the same rug as if it were the surface of a pond, the rest of her somewhere beneath the floor. I had wondered more than once, if I could've cloned myself

34

and commanded that clone to lie in wait in the basement, would she have witnessed the bottom two thirds of this ghost suspended from the ceiling, gown rippling beside the hot water heater?

"Okay," I breathed. "Please hold still." With my free hand I groped for the steno pad I deliberately positioned in easy reach on the corner of my night stand, a pen wedged into the metal spiral. I waved it slowly above her, watched her eyes follow its progress the way a cat's do. "I want to try something new. Can you hold these? Can you write?" Since she began appearing to me, she had not spoken a single word. I presumed that for some reason, some rule of her existence, she couldn't. I lowered the steno toward her. "Take this please."

Her gaze stayed on my gift, but then her mouth opened in a soundless gasp or scream and before I could finish shouting "No, dammit!" her head vanished under the floor. She nearly pulled me completely off the bed, but as always, as soon as her face descended from my sight the rest of her disappeared.

A year ago—seven months before my private haunting began— I took up cycling to get to work, though my adopted city's notion of a bike lane took some getting used to.

My parents moved around a lot for a couple of career academics, which maybe contributed to their divorce. The town where I spent first and second grade had honest to God separate asphalt bike lanes. The next town didn't—too teensy, I suppose—but it was fine for kids like me to ride on the sidewalks. In the city where grown-up me found employment, a haphazard jumble sprung from a long-dead railroad boom, bike lanes were created only recently, using lines of paint to cordon off outside lanes from roads that aren't quite wide enough. I hate pedaling along the railyard fence while cars whoosh past just a couple feet away, but the trek to my office is a mere three miles across mostly flat ground, and lately, the pleasant muscle strain and rush of air across my face helps make up for my lack of sleep.

To get from my neighborhood to the main artery that takes me downtown, I coast down a gently sloping side street past regiments of aging mansions built in the 1920s, many divided into apartments by skeevy landlords. I can't go too fast because of the T-intersection at the bottom of the street. If I ever wanted to end it

all, pedaling pell-mell into the perpendicular rush of heavy, trac-
tor-trailer laden traffic zooming along that main road would get
the job done.

I'm not exactly sure when the roof party started to stalk me,
though I *am* certain the phenom got going a few weeks after my
drowned ghost started wrenching me awake every night.

They only ever manifested in the mornings, with the sun still
low in the east, backlighting them as they ran. I'd never seen them
on the strenuous return pedal up the same street. They'd keep pace
with me as I rolled downhill, leaping from roof to roof.

I never stopped to observe them. I deciphered what they
looked like through a kind of peripheral vision osmosis.

The three of them always stayed single file as they ran. First would
come a pale blonde woman dressed in black, her sleeves covering her
arms, her long dress flared as if it concealed hoops underneath; followed by a tall man in similarly antique clothes, the upper half of his
head wrapped in stained bandages; followed by a withered, blackened,
humanoid shape that never drew completely into focus.

When I first noticed them, I started picking up the pace
through the shortcut, dangerous though it was. They didn't ever
overtake me. The clearer their forms became to me, the more my
dread of that short segment of the route grew. Yet a knot of stub-
bornness inside me refused to loosen. I couldn't save myself from
lost sleep, but I wasn't going to give up the quickest bike route;
detouring would add a full, inconvenient mile.

So I continued, accepting the spectral chase as routine.

The morning after the introduction of the steno pad, after I'd
gotten the drowned ghost to veer so far out of her pattern, frustration stuck in my craw. I craved progress, though I lacked a plan for
it. As I turned down that haunted street and the corner of my eye
detected the party's rooftop dash, I squeezed the brakes.

The house they seemed to have originated from squatted
wider than others in the row, originally built square with a porch
fully encircling its girth, its symmetry marred by later additions
designed to cram more apartments inside.

The procession had already alighted on the next roof in their
path. They sprinted and leapt, the woman's silhouette wavering as
she blotted the sun, her followers or pursuers rendered even less
substantial for the instants they hung in the sky.

The blonde landed on the next roof, and swerved toward the street, dropping to the porch awning, then the front yard.

They were going to intercept me. A spike of fright burned away my curiosity. Warm air whooshed around me as I slammed shoe soles to pedals and something low to the ground, dark and furred, maybe a rat or squirrel, charged out from under a parked car inches ahead of my front tire. My swerve saved its life, my accompanying scream climbed higher as a spindly black limb stretched across my field of vision.

No fingers grabbed me. I screech-squeezed the brakes at the bottom of the street as a van blared its horn, the decal on its flank—CRIME SCENE CLEANERS—close enough for me to reach out and scratch.

Without a look behind—even though the impulse gripped my head, struggled to twist my neck—I continued on to work. Much as I hated cold calling recalcitrant sponsors for our nonprofit consulting firm, I plunged into the task with gusto, anything to ward off the memory of that withered arm reaching across my path.

That night, the drowned ghost changed things up. Instead of grabbing my wrist, she plucked at my night shirt, brushed cold fingers down my bare shoulder, insistent as a hungry cat and equally articulate. Her wide eyes implored.

"Can we talk?" I whispered, more softly than intended. She gave no indication she heard. I repeated the question, louder. She tilted her head in a way that suggested a question, though the desperation on her face remained unchanged.

I reached for the steno pad. Her hand darted toward my arm but drew back as I froze. I held up a palm in what I hoped was a steadying gesture. Whether or not I'd made my intentions clear, she focused on my palm as I snagged the steno pad with my other hand. I brought right and left hands together, separated pen from pad and held both out to her. "Can you hold these?"

She reached, with both of her slender brown hands, toward the pen, not toward my wrist, I'm certain of that. Her mouth opened, and I thought she was about to shape a word, but the attempt at speech became a silent howl, and she sank at speed through the floor as if something pulled her from below, too quickly gone to wherever the next step in the ordeal took place.

My lack of sleep the rest of that night I attribute to excitement rather than resentment.

Even if it ended up never doing any good, even if it took years to teach my ghost to communicate, I resolved I was going to keep trying.

I wondered if I could also redirect my morning bike ride in some new way. I determined I would do so. I wanted change, and damn the consequences. I decided to increase the odds of that by breaking routine.

When I could no longer abide my stepdad's "stealing size" joke, I showed him a Y strike, pulled it back an inch from his stubbled throat. I punctuated the gesture with a girly laugh just in case, but, nowhere near as dumb as he always looked, he got the message the first time.

I admit, just like when I finally got one over on my stepdad, I was punch-drunk. Unlike back then, I had no certainty as to what message to convey or how to convey it.

Still, since I couldn't sleep anyway, I packed my bag for work and suited up in helmet and Lycra well before dawn. If the trio emerged without the sun to reveal them, perhaps I wouldn't even see them. The jitters that possibility gave me fired up my resolve instead of undermining it.

Yet as I approach the turn, leg muscles pleasantly straining, I considered forging on toward the detour. For once, I had the time.

"Not the plan," I said in my mother's sternest tone to the waiting specters and to myself, as I veered into the shortcut.

My head swam as I made the turn. A darkness hung before me that didn't belong to the pre-dawn sky. A cloud of ink or a hole to another world or both, it filled rapidly with constellations of pale hands, dozens upon dozens of them, all waving at me to turn back. At the center of those clusters of fingers and palms the drowned woman's desperate gaze implored me.

I had pedaled into the midst of the mirage before I could fully process what I'd seen. The inky murk faded as I reached it, the way fog seems to fade away as you walk into it. Out the other side, the sudden brightness forced me to squint, and I squeezed the brakes.

From the east the sun peered over the rooftops. I stared back at it, dumbfounded and risking serious retinal damage. Somehow, in the time it had taken me to turn the corner and swerve into the inkblot full of hands, at least two hours had passed.

I was the one who had been given a message: not to risk that stunt again.

My trio of pursuers emerged from their rooftop. I did not let them intercept me.

Early on after the drowned woman's visits began, I had tried sleeping in other rooms. The results were much the same. At least the carpet beside the bed was plush, not so bruising to land on if she succeeded in dislodging me. Getting pulled off the living room couch onto the hardwood floor hurt something fierce, with an extra dose of coffee table corner adding injury to injury.

You might wonder why I didn't try sleeping on the floor. But a lizard-brain level fear kept me from attempting that—the floor was always where she was trying to pull me, and where she always vanished. If I was already there when she appeared, would I vanish with her when she pulled me down? I didn't want to find out.

Tonight, though, I planned to learn whatever I could.

My drowned woman had saved me from *something*—a gratitude, a rosy warmth in my gut, that I had been protected from whatever that something was, carried me through an especially dreary day on the job, full of: tedious exchanges with co-workers determined to focus on anything other than their duties, even though their responsibilities, if carried out as delegated, would genuinely bring aid to those less fortunate; project requests packed with minutia, all of it insignificant to the task of improving a city that never thought to build bike lanes or adequate storm drains or to escort its homeless with psychiatric disorders to a clinic instead of a jail cell. The fact was, if any truly worthy initiatives escaped the grind, you could bet you'd see them smeared with caca as soon as elected officials laid hands on them.

Maybe my ghost kept coming to me because there really was something I could do, if I went along with what she wanted. Maybe for once I'd get something done that mattered.

I had a difficult enough time sleeping on a firm mattress even before I became a haunted woman, no way I was getting any shut-eye while lying on the rug beside the bed, so I had to come up with a way to pass the time. I ended up lying on my stomach with the steno pad folded open in front of me, staring at the ruled pages I hoped the drowned woman would write upon.

I tried some automatic writing, a stupid exercise an adjunct professor once demanded of me in a college course. It turned into a kind of journal entry about how I'd lived in this city for six years and still didn't feel like I knew anyone well. I wasn't sad about this, as I had yet to meet anyone that was really worth getting to know. No one who liked the same books that I did the same way I did, no one who could comprehend that the ear-splitting ambience of the local bars was no way to get acquainted with anyone, no one who understood that coffee is a vile concoction brewed by the devil or that children are Old Scratch's emissaries, especially the cute ones.

I once read an old, painfully slow-paced ghost story, where the dude who's being haunted realizes gradually, even glacially, that he's hearing sounds like a series of notes plucked on a harp inside his house, though he's totally alone. It's at about that same pace that I became aware in half-conscious increments of a chill against my back, like a breeze had crawled under my blanket to caress me, even though I experienced no sensation remotely akin to the motion of air across my skin. I felt that nonexistent breeze in my hair, against my neck, my ear.

I grew certain that if I turned my head, her face would be there, pressed right against mine. I didn't turn my head.

I continued to write. Ice caressed the back of my hand, folded into the gaps between my fingers, pressed into my palm, squeezed my knuckles. I couldn't see the ghost's hand at at all, but the pen in my hand twitched across the paper like a spiritualist's planchette. I shuddered and another body shuddered against mine, legs against my legs, belly and breasts against my back.

Wherever her body lay, it must be cold, so cold. She longed with animal appetite for the heat of breath and a beating heart, but she believed I was governed by kindness and she willed no harm to come to me. She feared her desperation could hurt me if unchecked, could drive me away even when tempered. Gradually, glacially, I absorbed this cascade of desires and frets that didn't belong to me, didn't originate from within my own mind.

Neither did the words my pen scrawled in the steno.

An idea that did belong to me bubbled up from the lake bed of my trance, a eureka cry of celebration that I'd at last bridged the communication gap, that soon I would understand everything the

drowned woman was trying to tell me. That burst of sweet validation broke the surface and smashed the spell.

The lamp on my beside table illuminated nothing beyond
blanket and rug, wall and curtain. I grabbed the steno, held it to
the light, and made a noise that was both cackle and sob.

As when I encountered the inky cloud on my bike route, the
trance, which I had experienced as mere minutes, must have lasted
several hours. All that time I had been scribbling, and I'd never
flipped the page over to start another. The writing that I generated,
if it had been writing, had accumulated in layer upon layer until it
congealed into a mess of indistinguishable cross-hatches, as if I'd
set out from the start to color the entire surface black, pen stroke
by pen stroke.

Had the ghost manifested then, had I the power to do so, I
would have seized her by the shoulders, shaken her. *You could see
the page! Why didn't you stop?*

I threw the pad across the room.

A beat later, reflecting that the situation was hardly the steno
pad's fault, I stood up to retrieve it and noticed the clock read 4:58,
just two minutes before my alarm was going to sound—in time,
were I foolhardy enough, to once again brave my shortcut before
the sun came up.

Yet my ghost had warned me. A sack of guilt settled on my
heart, growing steadily heavier. I could not deny, however difficult
it might be for her, that she was *trying*.

I deactivated the alarm, pulled back the curtains so the sun
itself would roust me and went back to bed. Naturally, I didn't fall
right into sleep, but lay there wondering how I might find the self-
possession to flip the page during the next ghost trance, or perhaps
break free *before* the ghost writing condensed to illegibility. The
chill of her presence, I told myself, half-joking, would at least pro-
vide some counter to the summer heat and humidity. When winter
came around again, the ghost and I would need to find a different
way to talk. Maybe by then I'd have means developed to convey
that information. I chuckled aloud at the thought.

I was going to keep trying, no doubt about it, and if I never
solved the mystery, perhaps the ghost, wherever her lost body lay,
could at least find some comfort in my persistence.

TICK FLICK

G reg jabbed Jeff's third shoulder, though he made sure he didn't hit hard enough to capsize the snack bucket. Jeff would make him pay if he did. "Quit hoggin' the candy. Trailer's almost over."

Jeff took his mouth out of his food long enough to ask, "What kind you want?"

"You know. A softy."

"None left."

"Liar! I know you ain't drunk 'em all yet."

Jeff shrugged all his shoulders and relented. "Here."

Greg clutched the softy with four hands to make sure it couldn't slip away. He used two more hands to open it so he could really sink his mouth in. It still wriggled a bit; he couldn't keep it under control and focus on the scenes projected across the dome at the same time. Thank God's hook-covered tongue it was just a trailer, and for a horror movie at that. He didn't much care for horror. He didn't understand why they'd put that kind of a preview in front of a comedy, anyway.

He did catch the very end. On the right side of the dome, a shapely girl gorged contentedly, her expanding flesh filmed from a flattering angle, a suggestive angle, showing no signs she was aware of the siphon-wielding maniac crawling into view on the dome's left. The image wavered in disconcerting fashion before fading to black.

Greg didn't even bother reading the title. As if this same ridiculous scene had not been played out over and over in one cheap slice-fest after another.

Jeff freed his mouth to chortle. "I saw you tense up."

"What?"

"You can't handle a little scare. I saw you tense up."

"Did not." Greg pounced on a quick subject change. "Gimme another softy."

"Outta softies. For real this time."

"The other kind, then."

Jeff drew out a full-grown and, in a rare show of courtesy, split it himself, a messy and noisy process. He did grumble, "I thought they put more suppression juice in these." Greg wondered, too— once the movie started, was that noise going to interrupt every time someone got hungry?

With a shrug of two shoulders, Jeff chuckled. "Maybe they can't help but wake up when they're gettin' eaten."

The flick was starting. "Shhh," Greg admonished before starting on his half. Not as sweet as a softy, but still rich and heady, a pleasant mix of salty taste and thick texture.

Greg wasn't prepared for the movie to open with a scene of lovemaking. No one had asked him or Jeff their ages when they bought snacks and tickets. They were both big for fifth instar, and the truth was Greg had never been asked his age before at the theater, but it had never occurred to him that the staff just didn't care, that they weren't even trying to stop him from seeing something like this.

The actress—she was so beautiful, and she was feeding and swelling even as her lover mounted her, the dirtiest and most decadently sensual thing Greg had ever seen in his short life. The view swooped around the couple, hugging contours, close enough to show the sensory hairs. Greg didn't realize he was holding his breath until he exhaled all at once with a big whoosh. He was afraid Jeff would laugh at him, but his friend was mesmerized by the panorama. The bodies of the lovers dominated the entire curvature of the dome, going out of focus here and there in a manner surely meant to further tease. The entire sight was so distracting and the view so close and claustrophobic that the long blade that scissored through the woman's head arrived with no warning.

Her mate continued his business, oblivious to the Host blood pumping back out through her wound, until he detected her body shrinking in his arms. He looked around, startled, and noticed the space where her head had been. "Huh?" he said, a stupid noise, all his eyes bulging—then the blade snipped his head away, too.

Aghast, throat constricting, it took Greg a moment to comprehend that the awful noise in his ear was Jeff's howling laughter. He jabbed his friend's shoulder again, this time not caring how hard. "You said this was a comedy!"

"It is!" Jeff gasped. "Shhhh!"

The splatter from the blood formed the letters of the title: *Love Reaper*. Which made Jeff laugh even harder.

Heat pooled behind Greg's eyes. He didn't like horror movies. He'd specifically asked Jeff to pick something *fun*. Not for the first time, he wished there were other kids willing to hang out with him. But Jeff was the only one, and Greg was the only one who hung out with Jeff, so they were both stuck. Sometimes he really wished he had someone else, anyone else, to spend time with outside school. He had no idea what Jeff thought, and was sure that if he ever asked, Jeff would just make fun of him.

The letters went weirdly out of focus, as if the membrane of the dome rippled. The shrill of the alarm drowned out all other sound.

The way the trailer and now the film had kept going out of whack—that wasn't the projection, that was the telltale tremors as the Host surfaced from its stupor and tried to move.

Jeff shoved him with all four right arms. "Stations are over there! Go on! Go!" The other members of the audience were already scrambling toward the walls.

Greg's innards burned in psychosomatic anticipation of what was coming. Whenever the Host resisted, every citizen had a sacred duty to join in the Suppression, exsanguinating the Host at every possible point, weakening its strength until a new flood of chemicals could send it back into stupor. They had to be careful, though: only stupor, not death. The Host was their home, the source of their sustenance, the center of their commerce, its flesh the walls of their cities. The Death of the Host was Death to the people. Greg had recited that mantra since he was tiny.

He pulled down the flaps at the first station he reached and plunged his mouth into the flesh of the Host. It was nothing like the softies—gritty, fibrous, its intense coppery tang dirtied with other metals and unidentifiable chemicals. The additives were going to make him sick, with throbbing aches in his joints and stinging acid burns in his throat and gut.

When he was little, he'd had a medical exemption, but the first time there had been an alarm at school with no teachers nearby to isolate him, the other kids had surrounded him and threatened to pull off one of his arms if he didn't join in the Suppression. He'd been sick for days afterward and his mother had scolded him nonstop, but he still had all his arms, and he understood that to keep them, he had to suck it up. So he did, literally.

Thank God's lucky quest that alarms were rare. Or at least they used to be rare.

The fluid from the Host filled him like motor oil. He fought against the instinct to yank out his mouth and vomit it all up.

The hallucination began. Greg want to moan aloud, *not again, not again,* as sensations overwhelmed him, of infinite mass, of vast, immobile weight, of many-limbed multitudes crawling through every cavity in his inconceivably huge body, the maddening itch of their bites by the millions. Sightless, he wanted to scream, tongue as paralyzed as the rest of his body, swarming inside and out with spiny invaders.

The alarm stopped—thank God, thank Her swollen belly!— and Greg sprang away, spitting Host juice. He hunkered down on his arms and trembled, praying for the visions to go away. Each time, they took longer to fade.

He still itched with itches he couldn't scratch as he clambered back into his seat.

The hallucinations shamed him—he knew of no one who had ever experienced anything similar. It was as if some perverse impulse compelled him to sympathize with the Host, which was the grossest possible blasphemy.

Next to him, Jeff fidgeted, unusually quiet.

The movie resumed, of course, with a quartet of randy youngsters descending to the lake for a weekend getaway—at least Greg's misery let him tune it out. He took spiteful pleasure in the notion that the flick had probably been ruined for Jeff, too.

His miserable delight lasted for about a minute, and then Jeff nudged him again.

"What?" he snapped, startled at the volume of his own voice. Jeff flinched, then reached toward him once more. A softy squirmed in his hand.

Greg turned to focus all his left eyes on the offer. "You said they were gone."

"I—"

Greg stopped just short of accusing his buddy of lying. Because, if he was lying, and hoarding one last softy for himself, why reveal the ruse now?

"I ... I was saving it for after the movie. I was going to surprise you." He nodded at the stations along the wall. "But I know the Host blood makes you feel bad. So I thought ... "

Someone shushed Jeff. He, also, was talking a little too loud.

Shame warmed the spaces behind and beneath Greg's eyes. Something else too, a tightness across the bands of his hearts that wasn't at all unpleasant. He forgot to say thank you as he accepted the gift, but he did manage a nod.

Jeff shifted uncomfortably, then nodded back and returned his attention to the dome.

This softy made a high-pitched little scream as Greg sank his mouth in, but he didn't care. Nor did he mind that he still had more than an hour of *Love Reaper* to go. Even the grossness of the Host blood in his guts didn't bother him.

He was having a great day, a really great day, and it was only going to get better.

THE CRUELEST TEAM WILL WIN

A spider with a leg span wider than my outstretched hand squeezed out from the space behind the light switch, and spread its wings.

I froze, my finger still on the toggle. Behind me the dust-draped ceiling fan hummed to life, the light bulb beneath it flicking on to paint the monster with my shadow.

The marks on its body formed a single staring eye above a screaming mouth. Two more false eyes glared red across its dragonfly wings. Another hideous little soul turned demonic, yearning to grow into something far worse.

I showed it my own spirit form.

It made good on its threat and lifted into the air, but its terrifying modification only made my task easier and my beak closed around it. The poison leaking from its crushed body spread warmth as it slid down my gullet.

The first time I ate one of its kind that poison made me quite sick. I underestimated how sick. I told my sweet neighbor across the hall that her three year old wouldn't wake up screaming any more, her apartment was safe again. Minutes later, I drove to work at the fabric store, nearly crashed my car just trying to park, staggered inside and barely made it to the bathroom stall, dry heaving over the toilet while my manager clucked behind me, *Leeanne, are you okay? You need the hospital?*

But when you eat a ghost, there's nothing to throw up. And the kind of poison a tainted soul puts in you, no doctor can help with that.

So I told her I'd be fine, it was just food poisoning, I'd be over it soon. I couldn't go home, I needed the money too much.

So I sucked it up and headed out to the sales floor. And then I found out something else about that poison. When the nausea subsided, a euphoria kicked in, not far removed from the time I mixed Flexiril and peach schnapps, a lava lamp glow oozing through me. All day I fought the urge to take my blue jay form right there in the store. My wings, slices of sky, would stretch longer than the fabric tables, and then I'd fly right through the ceiling like a ghost gone giant-size, meld my blue with the blue above.

I did that once, a couple years ago when I was less weighted with sad knowledge of the world: quit a job at a print shop by going blue jay right in front of my skeevy boss and flapping away through the cinderblock wall into the shimmering heavens of the spirit world. But when I returned to earth again, I still needed to pay for my classes, to cover my rent, to eat.

That sad weight kept me grounded that first delirious day of spider poisoning, but the sensation was addictive. The very next time I was asked to cleanse a house, I found another spiderling. It was strange that I found another right away, and not a run-of-the-mill, perfectly-human-looking haint, but it shot out at me from under a closet door, its mutation a second set of legs tipped with pincers, and I didn't hesitate to eat it. And the next one I found, and the next one, and the next and many nexts since. And this time too.

The urge hit my brain straight away, to stay as I was, shift completely into the spirit world and rise up through the floors and ceilings of this rambling house as if it were mere mirage, and soar at the noonday sky like an ocean dive in defiance of gravity.

But I had already collected my upfront fee from the charming elderly couple that lived there, and now I needed to collect the rest of it. Classes, rent, normal non-ghosty food. I didn't charge a lot, but it would at least give the debt dog a bone to run off with and chew on.

Emma Manderley was a frequent customer at the fabric store who knew about my specialty in clearing malevolent influences— the word gets around, you know, among those who care about such things—and the Manderleys had just enough sensitivity between them that they would know the thing that had bedeviled their sleep was gone without my even needing to say so.

They were waiting in their station wagon, sitting in the driveway with the radio playing. I had told them I only needed a few minutes. My magic never took more than a few minutes. I looked forward to their relieved smiles.

My brain buzzing pleasantly from the poison, I climbed the spiral stairs out of the musty basement, traipsed through the slightly-less-musty ground floor and glanced out the front window as I crossed the living room.

The station wagon was completely blanketed by a substance like dense strands of shimmering gauze. A slender woman in slate gray business attire, knee-length skirt and matching jacket, was striding up the front walk.

I didn't slow, didn't want to linger in the window where she could spot me. I leaned to spy through the front door peephole.

I've known since I was a little girl that there are other people like me. My parents weren't spirit folk but my father's sister was, not a blue jay like me but a raven. She taught me how to be who I am, and to be wary of others who do what I do.

See, you might wonder why I don't spend all my time as a bird, and this is why: our world of meat, metal and bone is a dangerous place, but the spirit world is a hundred times worse. Filled with predators. No laws, no one to make the cruel rein in their appetites. Ghosts are our natural prey in our animal forms and they can be dangerous enough (though before I started finding the spiderlings, it used to be that if I rooted out a ghost, I could just order it to leave and it would flee, because it knew what I was and what I could do). But there's many out there don't limit themselves to just ghosts.

I could tell right away this woman had a spirit shadow. It loomed dark around her in my second sight, even though the day was bright. White streaks flared from the temples of her pageboy to frame a narrow face split by sensuous, disproportionately wide lips. She could have been twenty or sixty, her features smooth but not youthful. Behind her a single strand of blue spiderweb rose straight into the sky, and behind that I recognized the same webbing, cocooning the station wagon and the poor couple inside it. The driver's side door was ajar, bound that way by the webbing.

I wasn't going to get my paycheck.

The woman stepped onto the porch, raising her fist as if she intended to knock.

Her dark eyes narrowed and I had a second to realize she was staring right at me through the door. I leaped back and stretched my wings. She changed, too, her fangs missing my head by less than an inch as she phased right through the wood.

A spider large as a minibus, legs longer than my wings, glared at me with eight eyes like black pearls embedded in coal-shiny hide. Her form flowed straight through the walls of the house as if they weren't there, just like mine did as I beat my wings in thunderous panic, shoving as much air between us as I could, my heart shrieking with fear.

I flapped fully into the land of spirits, leaving behind the world of flesh. Surrounded by the sourceless silver light of the spirit realm, I risked a look back and discovered the spider had followed me, clambering after me at terrifying speed on her single strand of blue thread.

I should have easily left her far behind, but the thread moved of its own accord. Its anchor point, somewhere out of sight high in the heavens, kept pace with me as I flew, matching my maneuvers.

I risked a plunge right at it, meaning to snip it in half with my beak. It dodged me, then sprang back, and I bet if I hadn't ducked so quickly myself it would have looped around me. And worse, the spider picked up her already impossible pace.

She called after me in a shockingly honey-sweet voice, "Birds eat spiders, but spiders eat birds, too."

She didn't have to run anymore. She was level with me, merely had to ride her magic thread until I tired out.

I knew what was hunting me, who she was. My Aunt Audra told me stories about the Night Queen in the Silver City, who savors drawn-out death, who only ever pretends to show mercy because she loves to watch her victims' hopes die before their final agonies begin. "She calls herself Lilith," my auntie said, "but she's not *that* Lilith. They say a couple hundred years ago she was human. But no one calls her one now."

And a few months ago I met a couple like me, good people like Audra. They were passing through Hagerstown, stopped in the coffee house across the street from my store. An odd pair: Kori's a bird person like me, a killdeer; Nathan, though, he's a panther. But one without claws: he had two prosthetic hands. I thought at first he'd fought in Iraq. They were both friendly, super-friendly, but they never told me what did that to him. I mentioned Audra's stories of Lilith, though, and they both went pale. "She's not a story," Nathan said, and they warned me to stay away from her. Nathan, it was like the words got stuck in his throat, but Kori told me what she looked like. And now I remembered her description, narrow face, hair white at the temples. "A black widow as big as a house. I hope you never look on her."

I would not live to tell Kori her hopes had come to naught.

Because I couldn't get away. Not just because I couldn't shake Lilith's magic thread but because out there in the ceaseless silver light, here and there and there, I started to see shadows suspended in the air. Things with too many legs, emerging from the physics-defying passages that, in the spirit world, are as numerous a mile in the air as they are a mile underground. More creatures like Lilith, at least a dozen, not as big as her, but bigger than me. Not close enough to catch me. Not yet. It was just a matter of time before my constant swooping to keep out of reach of the Night Queen put me in range of one of her clan.

I could only think of one thing to do. I didn't have to fake the quaver in my voice. "Your Highness, what have I done to upset you?"

"How droll that you know me," she said. "Someone of your kind should stick to acorns. You keep murdering my pets."

Pets? The spiderlings? Those strange mutant ghosts-things that invade the homes of the mundanes and drive them crazy with nightmares? My stomach lurched at the thought of killing anyone's pet, a terrible guilt twisting through me the instant before my rational side tamped it down. Lilith could not mean that term of endearment the same way as you or I would mean it. The Night Queen grieves for no one.

I continued to avoid her, though as the old joke goes, boy, were my arms tired. "Those weird little ghosts? Why would you care about them?"

"My dear, those weren't ghosts. Surely you could tell by the taste?"

But I had never eaten a ghost, before that spiderling across the hall attacked me. How many ghosts had Lilith devoured over her long lifetime? I couldn't imagine. I gave her a version of the truth. "I thought it was their mutation. I've heard of spirits changing themselves, mutilating themselves, trying to become demons."

Lilith laughed, the sound grotesquely emphasized with a waving of her fangs. "Stupid child. It's our kind who does that. Chooses to modify the forms we're born with. Ghosts have no such power." And surely Lilith knew what she was talking about, as the living, breathing, supreme example. "Tasty as ghosts are, though, I have found that the little human flies make for finer dining while they're still alive. I've been experimenting, indulging my culinary skills, figuring out the best method to sup from many of them all at once."

I couldn't help myself. "Oh, no."

Her voice brightened with mirth. "You have been eating tiny little pieces . . . of me."

I might then have simply folded my wings together, dropped like Icarus and hoped quick death on jagged rocks waited below.

I was so, so fucked.

I said, "Your Highness, I didn't know. I am so sorry."

"I am sure you are sorry," she said. "But perhaps you can make it up to me. Let me take you to the Silver City." Her pearl eyes glinted. "You are what you eat, you know. Let me study you, and see how your diet has affected you. I bet you've already changed in ways that will surprise you."

"I've never been to the Silver City," I said, vapid as a Kardashian. "I'm honored." More of her kind crawled through the air about me, awaiting the right moment to spring. "I'd like to go."

She stretched out her long, sleek forelegs in the most disturbing offer of embrace I have ever seen. "You'll have to let me bind you, I'm afraid. I promise I won't bite."

I flapped away again. I was starting to wheeze, my spirit form unable to stave off the sensation of swimming a marathon. "You don't need to," I gasped. "I'll go willingly."

"My promise only comes with cooperation." She said it so soothingly. I knew I would be better off forcing her to kill me quickly.

"Okay then." I panted the words, flapped my wings in a short, painful burst, then stilled them, let that thread drift closer. Easily within her reach.

She continued her ruse, reaching for me gently rather than snatching me from the air. It bought me the time I needed to pull my wings close and dart straight for her face.

Those of us whose spirit forms take an animal's shape can all do the things that animal does best, without need for a second's thought. Lilith proved herself learned when she taunted me with that "acorn" crack. Blue jays like to pin acorns with their feet and break them open with a single peck. We have very strong beaks.

Except my talons closed over her two largest eyes and my beak struck her hard as a jackhammer in the closest thing a spider has to a brow. Her oversized exoskeleton was thick as a brick wall and I split it wide open.

I dropped away but I still wasn't quick enough. No way could I ever have been quick enough. She didn't try to grab me—she was in too much pain, I think—but she struck out of sheer instinct, sheer hate, sheer vengeance. The daggers of her fangs pierced my stomach, and pain exploded through me, like she'd pumped magma into the wounds. I screeched as I fell, flapping my wings to escape the agony, but it was inside me, fire worming through every vein.

Lilith's magic thread came loose from its mooring in the heavens, and she dropped from the sky, vanishing the next second. I didn't notice where her followers went. I was being flayed from the inside out. Those shrill, pathetic shrieks, that echoed through all corners of the spirit realm? I was making those noises, so out of my mind with pain I didn't even know the sounds were coming from my own throat.

But the very thing that got me in so much trouble also saved me.

After untold miles, the pain began to fade. Before I had attacked Lilith I had played at being more worn out than I actually was. Now I really was that tired, probably a hundred times worse, and I had no idea where I'd flown.

But I didn't care.

All those exorcisms I performed, unknowingly chowing down on extensions of pure undiluted Night Queen, had built up my tolerance to her venom. Enough that even though a direct bite felt like flinging myself on hot pokers, it didn't kill me.

And when the agony faded, bliss took its place. A euphoria like no earthly drug could ever induce.

Thoughts of disgust crawled across my mind, that the substance I found so addictive was the venom of the Night Queen herself. But that realization made not a scratch on the joy that buoyed me. Nor did any worries about where I would land, or how I would rebuild my life. Nor did the certainty that I would spend the rest of my days a marked woman. I regarded my cares like an airplane passenger watching farmlands scroll by below. I was a piece of the sky, pure sun-painted blue, invincible.

I flew to the east, away from the encroaching dusk, and I didn't look back.

THE NIGHTMARE AVATAR'S
NIGHTMARE

with Christina Sng

Along the alley wall
it crawls, spider-like
and grotesque, face
like a child's, a murdered
child's, swollen and black
with coagulated blood;

It smiles, teeth sharp
as ice slivers formed
on remote mountains
where hearts and corpses
remain as cold as its
eyes, which glisten like

icicles in the storm-choked
night, where it climbs
without fear or slippage,
tiny hands at the tips of
each limb clasping silently
as it lowers itself onto

a balcony where the
scent of prey is thick:
a child whose fears are

ripe for manifesting,
who presses her pale face
hard against the screen

and grins toothily at
the dismayed visage
before her, staring with
unblinking feral eyes.
No fear clouds her mind,
no joy, no dreams, save

a hunger in her gaze
that echoes its own,
her soul parched, stunted,
starved even of nightmares.
Her visitor turns and flees
into the sewer below

as welts open in its shadowy
flesh, fear crescendoing,
rapturous hunger uncoiling;
with no nightmares to harvest
but its own, the abyssal
famine consumes from within,

leaving nothing
but a shell
of black dream dust,
banished with a laugh,
a cough,
an apathetic sigh.

TARDIGRADE

G unshots in the dark. One, two, three, four, five.

In the abyss, a flatscreen monitor lights up, as if awakened by the noise.

From the computer, loud chimes play "Turkey in the Straw" as a creature dances on the monitor, a bear-like thing with chitin for skin and a circular sucking mouth in place of a face. Needles protrude and retract from the orifice in time with the music.

Shuffling in the dark. Bare feet descending stairs. One, two, three, four, more.

A ghost appears, a woman in a pale night robe, trembling all over, pistol clenched in one hand, a snub-nosed, square device. Her wide eyes are moons, her breath coming in half-sobs.

Black stains spatter the belly of her robe. She stares at the monitor. One of the stains is moving, separating from the rest, inching up a fold of cloth over her ribs. She doesn't notice, but we do.

Hand shaking, she taps a key. The screen changes.

A window opens on a murky video. Voices speak in soft tones, a couple talking quietly, near-whispers, yet the playback is loud.

I think you need to look at this, the man says.

The woman replies, *I could lose my job. Hell, both of us could lose our jobs.*

The woman in the night robe sucks in air through her teeth. She flips on the desk lamp. The room she is standing in is the room shown in the video. She is the woman who whispers in the video.

The man in the video says, *Muriel, please, look.*

We shouldn't be talking about this here.

What, the man says, *it's not like they'd bug our house.*

Watching the video, our Muriel barks a loud, bitter laugh, then another, then a gale of them. She steps away and flips on the overhead light while the video keeps playing. The room is large, contains two utilitarian matching desks with matching monitors atop them, both surfaces stacked with printouts, neither desk noticeably neater than the other. The video our masters made plays on the monitor closest to the window that serves as our vantage point, just as it did when the recording was made.

How did you get this? says Muriel in the video.

They sent it through my secure protocol just like any other document.

Why did you read it?

There's nothing there instructing me not to. Then, voice higher, more defensive, *They're the ones who gave it that funny name.*

Our Muriel's pupils are pinholes in glistening gray eyes. In full illumination, her gown is a gentle turquoise defiled with dark red stains. The moving blotch we noticed earlier has crawled out of view.

She advances toward our window, guided by the angle seen in the video. Her face looms into close-up as she paws and pounds around the window frame. *Where are you?* she says, *Where the fuck are you?* Talking over the voices from the recording.

Do you believe that? the man says. *Do you think this is real, what's in this write-up here?*

In the video, Muriel says, *Are you sure our client sent that?*

Her husband clicks on the keyboard. *No, I'm not. I don't know who did.*

Delete it, now. We have to forget we ever saw it.

Our Muriel, intent on finding the camera, doesn't notice when the video changes, until muffled cries emit from the computer speakers.

There's motion on the screen. When our Muriel returns to her computer a new system window has opened and the scene contained in it hangs frozen, veiled behind a large button that reads

CLICK TO PLAY

Muriel does, releasing the video to keep playing.

In this video, a woman slumps in a chair, her wrists tied, a hood over her head. She's wearing jeans and a tank top. The quality of the recording saps the scene of all color.

We hope Muriel understands the transition, though if she recognizes this bound woman, she offers no sign, only watches without blinking as the subject twitches her head, jerks her shoulders. She might be mumbling: it's hard to decipher the sounds she makes within the unfiltered hiss of the soundtrack. A banner has appeared, blocking the captive's face:

CLICK TO MAKE FULL SCREEN.

Muriel clicks. Larger proves blurrier. Metal shelves surround this woman. They hold spray cans and bottles of blue cleaner, the image too grainy to render the labels decipherable. She lifts her chin. Something dark moves out from under the hood and down the taut skin of her throat, oozing like blood, sidewinding like a snake. The image pauses just as the camera moves closer.

WE APOLOGIZE FOR THE POOR QUALITY. THIS WAS OUR FIRST TRY. CLICK TO SEE OUR NEW VIDEO!

Muriel's laugh could double for a sob. But she takes the bait and clicks.

The room full of metal shelves reappears with new occupants. Bright light, harsh light, washes out the faces of the couple kissing. It's impossible to tell, honestly, if the woman is the same seen in the video previous. She's in a black T-shirt that exposes her midriff, has short dark hair, her face obscured. A head taller, the man in the denim jacket bends his neck at a right angle to keep his mouth in contact with hers.

He clutches at her. In their passion they lean too hard into a shelf. Bottles scatter and clang on the unseen floor. Glass smashes. The pair stays lip-locked.

They spin as if dancing, carom into another shelf. They appear to be pushing against one another, he shoving at her shoulders, she slapping at his chest. Their kiss never breaks. They lurch forward and jostle the camera, which falls, clatters on the floor, and ends up aimed at an out of focus gray object, perhaps one of the bottles.

Just before the video ends its runtime the camera view shifts, rolls toward what appears to be a face in close-up, the movement too quick to display clear details. The final pause obliterated by a new banner:

CLICK TO REPLAY

Fuck this bullshit, our Muriel says. *Fuck it.* But she clicks.

The last half-second plays again in excruciating slow motion. The rolling camera pans across a chin, a mouth hanging open, seen in three quarter profile, perhaps a glimpse of a person on all fours. A thin black tongue protrudes from between front teeth. A second tongue curls out at the corner of the lips. That there are two tongues can't be mistaken, as the movie becomes a still, held for a full second before the message appears:

SEE WHAT YOU DID

Fuck you! I didn't do this! Muriel shouts, and she's in close-up again, pounding on the wall, trying to find our recording device. She backs toward the door, picks up the gun on her desk. Her eyes scan for the source of our gaze, and the muzzle of the pistol waves back and forth in synchronicity. Neither eyes nor gun find a point of purchase.

I had nothing to do with that project, she says, more calmly. *Once I knew about it, I wanted to stop it. I did stuff to try to stop it, stuff you didn't see. You've done this—*her face screws up, her voice cracks—*you've done this to us for nothing!*

A new video starts automatically. Again, the view is familiar: this same room, the home office, at an earlier time, lit by daylight streamed through the window that always doubles as our vantage point.

Our Muriel's husband can be heard, somewhere beyond the open door, his voice raised, though he falls silent without the shouted words ever becoming intelligible.

He comes into the room, followed by a figure clad in black, face hidden under a dark balaclava. The figure is smaller than Muriel's tall, lanky husband, but carries a pistol.

Quiet, the husband activates his computer. Our Muriel, back to watching, puts a hand over her mouth as he begins transcribing from a piece of paper, typing the words into a chat window and sending the message. The messaged person responds. The figure in black, pistol pressed to the back of the husband's head, mutters, *Answer her like you always would.*

Muriel screams into her cupped hand. Now a dark blotch crawls on the shoulder of her robe.

Muriel's husband sounds like he's quietly hyperventilating as he types, watches the responses, types back.

Muriel keeps keening into her hands. The black clad figure seems to look right at her, mask stretching in what might be a veiled smile, one eyelid descending in a wink—though in truth the intruder must have been looking right at the recording device mounted in the window, able to see exactly where it was. As Muriel realizes this, she dashes back to us, pounding furiously on the window frame, still keening. We get a good look at the thing crawling in her hair, our brave, beautiful child.

She doesn't see how the black clad figure injects her husband— that must be what she's doing, and yes, now it's obvious, in profile, the figure is a she. There's a needle protruding from between her fingers into her victim's neck, though there's no hypodermic visible. She flexes her hand and the needle withdraws as if it were a tongue.

There's no way to tell if she's the same woman from the earlier video. Even we can't be sure.

Open wide, the figure says, then puts something in the husband's mouth.

Muriel misses all of this. She howls in frustration as she beats her fists on the window frame. Then she leaves the room. She misses all the minutes of footage that follow, what happens to her husband after he's been injected and then forced to swallow the thing his captor brought. We don't pay much attention. We watched his twitchy, drooling transcendence the first time it happened, we don't need to see it again. But we watch the door. We want to know where Muriel went.

She misses the best part, when the woman in black returns to the room, calms the tendrils wriggling between the husband's teeth, and explains to him what must come next. She misses the kiss full of interlocking twig-like limbs that follows.

Muriel comes back, doesn't even look at her monitor despite the sounds coming from it, fiddles with the back of her husband's computer where we can't see what she's doing. Then she sets a jar down beside his monitor. Inside it our beloved child wriggles and twists. It keeps trying to escape as she sits at her husband's keyboard as if she's up in the early morning hours trying to beat a deadline, her fingers clacking at keys, her gaze focused on the rapidly changing screen that we wish we could read. She ignores the form the size of a thumb leaping against the glass on its many legs, making the jar clink and shift.

Audible from the video on our Muriel's computer, her husband calling out, *Oh, hello, sweetie pie, how was school?* Then after an indistinct answer, *Now, I need you to be my best little girl, just like you would for mommy. We have a visitor and I think you're going to like her.*

A growling starts in Muriel's throat, as if there's a wolf spirit hidden somewhere in her lungs. Our precious child keeps trying, maybe meaning to knock the jar over so it rolls, hits the floor and breaks, but it's too heavy and our child is too small. We don't dare intervene.

Muriel leaves off what she's doing to grab the cord of her computer's power strip and jerk it out of the wall. Of course, her computer continues to play the video. Our masters anticipated such a move. But she disappoints us by taking the jar, setting it on the floor where we can't see it, and resuming whatever she's started on her husband's computer.

She doesn't even react to the distant sounds of her daughter's transformation, no louder than whispers on our recording.

She turns her husband's monitor to face us. *I know who you are*, she says. She unplugs a tablet from her husband's computer, placed where we couldn't see it all this time, collects her gun and leaves the room. We listen, but she must be moving so quietly.

She reappears, dressed in jeans and a sweater, black hair tied up in a ponytail. She picks the jar off the floor, and we learn it has a small hole in the lid as she sets it on the desk again and pours bleach into it.

Our child pumps legs wildly, slashes with the spines that sprout from its back, stabs with its mouth needles, leaps and leaps. Our child is doomed.

Her husband's monitor displays a woman's picture. We recognize her but we're disappointed in Muriel. She is correct. The woman on the screen is the woman who visited her house. But she is not who *we* are. Her assumptions about her enemy are as false as her claim that she had nothing to do with Project Tardigrade.

I know who you are, Muriel repeats, as our child screams and dies. *I know where you are. And this is the last time you'll know where I am.*

And she leaves. Some part of us may have reason to fear her. For now, we all mourn.

With Muriel and her rage out of range, we dare to detach ourselves from the window frame. We are still recording what we see in this room, but we are much more than the task appointed by our masters.

We descend to the floor and circle around the jar where our child lies murdered, partially intact spines floating atop liquefied remains.

Muriel's computer is still playing the message our petty creators made for her. We alter it; change the sound it makes to one that is both a cry of grief and a call to the other children placed in the house.

After a few minutes, there's movement, stumbling, shuffling, from the upper floor. The sound of a heavy body dragging itself down a staircase, across a carpet.

Muriel's husband pulls himself through the doorway. His legs are not working. His bare torso is riddled with holes, the ones in his back larger than the ones in front. Even we can see his spine is severed. It will be hard for him to do what he must do for us.

New blood from his mouth and nostrils joins the tributaries already dried there. He grimaces each time he puts weight on his elbows and pulls himself forward. Each time he grimaces, our children flick their antennae from between his teeth.

As he struggles to position himself in his chair, we can see there are only four holes. Their absence is explained when the remaining child, our child and Muriel's child, joins us.

If only Muriel had waited. She would have seen that there's no cause for vengeance. What she believes lost, what she believes she was forced to do—none of it is true.

Muriel's husband slowly, painfully uses the crippled flesh of his first body to navigate his own computer. He must tell us, if he can, what Muriel found out, where she might be going. He glances once at his daughter, whose pink pajamas are bloodied by the debris from the single wound in her forehead. She smiles back, several of her baby teeth dropping free to make room for the antennae snaking out between them.

Her gaze moves from his to ours, and her smile widens.

We soar close to deliver a loving kiss.

BURN THE KOOL KIDZ AT THE STAKE

Michelle says, "Nobody's going to die tonight." She puts her squat silver revolver right up against Darren's temple. "And you're nobody."

Haley lets the video proceed uninterrupted. Darren dies. The shot, the wound, the fall look real. They almost always do.

Haley believes those names are the right ones, the originals: Michelle and Darren. They devolve over time, then reset. This combination Haley has seen before, Michelle as streamlined blonde Valkyrie, eyes marbles of blue malice, Darren curly-haired, oily-skinned, blinking terrified behind glasses that his executioner ordered him to put back on his face after he made the mistake of trying to hide them. Haley has seen the roles reversed, too, Michelle with long dark hair full of split ends, nose too long, horn-rimmed glasses perched on its bridge, and Darren a golden-haired Adonis become sacrificial lamb.

She finds more each day. Sometimes a new one appears within an hour of the last.

Kharmony, her assistant, keeps trying to put a smile on the situation, tells her, *It's because you have so many fans.*

The console that houses Haley's computer gleams in the artificial twilight, its boards of carved and polished mahogany fitted to resemble the helm of a fantastic riverboat, its décor a mix of scaled monsters and sleek circuitry. Flanked by fake gauges, the mock wheel to the side of the monitor allows her to raise and dim the lights. Above the devices functional and not, a bronze plaque reads Argo Celeste. The room beyond continues the nautical motif with a wooden frieze of merfolk and clawed leviathans, winged kraken and walking sharks.

65

Used to be, the fanciful props drawn from her own books empowered her at the keyboard. The videos distract her now. Her search reveals a new iteration. Always variations on the same title, *Burn the Kool Kidz at the Stake.* She finds them just as easily if she searches her own name.

She has never written a story by that title, but despite her vehement public protests, no one believes her. Or the ones that do stay silent while the ones that don't shout volumes.

The false excerpt with its fraudulent title appeared on her website almost two years ago, placed there by hackers unknown. Every public disavowal she made was answered by ten anonymous or pseudonymous responses sown throughout corners of the web bright and dark: Her publisher censored her. The controversy jeopardized her movie deals. She caved in to parents groups, to corporate pressure, she's a coward, she's too greedy, she's mentally unstable, she's still working on the book in secret. The most entitled of her fans were more than willing to argue these points directly *with her,* so scandalized and captivated they were by this single scene. She took her attorney's advice and stopped talking about the forged excerpt altogether. By that time the fan videos, based on screencaps, had already started to pop up.

Though the evening is young, the winter sun has long set. It wouldn't matter a jot—nothing compels Haley to honor a diurnal regimen—but soon she's due in her home studio for a vlog recording. Enough time to watch yet another iteration of Darren's murder.

Her phone plinks at the same moment that a message bubbles at the bottom of her monitor screen. *Remember your vlog in 30,* types Kharmony. *Put some pants on.*

Voice-to-text conveys Haley's reply. *Yes mother.*

From the video player: "And you're nobody." The gun fires.

Kharmony types as if gifted with telepathy. *Is the shooter blonde or brunette today?*

A pang of guilt, and anger, as if her assistant were trying to spy over her shoulder. *In this one she's albino, that's original. And he's African-American.*

Ugh. So morbid. Catch you in the studio.

Her obsession with the videos snowballed after one of the murders turned out not to be fake. The clip, despite the best efforts of many major online platforms, has been watched by hundreds of millions. Yet the dark-skinned woman playing Michelle, with her bleached hair and feverish stare, has never been identified. True but astonishing, as the corpse of Bobby McCloskey turned up almost immediately after his death was offered to the world as entertainment. In honor of Haley's supposedly suppressed story, one she never wrote. One she never would have considered writing. Her novels are elegant labyrinths steeped in myth, her heroines smart and determined, essentially good souls who might at most have horrible choices forced on them by the societies they traverse. Unfunny high school satire falls so far beneath her that rage twists her in knots if she dwells too long on her fans' conspiracy theories. How could they read every book she's written, absorb every film adaptation great and mediocre, and still misunderstand her so profoundly?

Enough of this. She has an appointment to keep, with those very same fans. Ruefully she thinks #notallfans.

She leaves the video feed open and heads to her walk-in closet. In the passage from fifth-floor writing den to bedroom she skirts by Arachne, a maquette from Maze of Dreams, the movie made from her first novel. Seven feet tall, the spider-goddess's svelte torso rises centaur-like from the black teardrop of her abdomen, her legs long, graceful arches. She guards Haley's most private chambers.

A wash of jasmine incense greets her. Her clothes closet is larger than the bedroom she and her sister shared in the rundown farmhouse where they grew up, on land where their grandfather had been a sharecropper. Her father had been white, a student from New York who'd joined the protests, and the Ku Klux Klan burned a cross on their lawn when she was three years old. She remembers the holy shape searing against the night, her parents' hissing whispers as they retreated into the mud-caked cellar to hide.

She smiles, surveying a hundred wardrobe options.

The wheezing, drawn-out death of the farm industry has allowed her to gather hundreds of acres to her personal kingdom, bounded on one side by road and security fence, by river on the other. Souvenirs from her imagination lurk within the woods and atop the rolling hills just as they do in her house. At the exact center of the grounds stands her husband's mausoleum.

The colossal absurdity of Kelvin's heart giving out during one of his lengthy pre-dawn runs still stabs and twists. His perfect, steady heart turned traitor inside his chest. A starry-eyed fan and shrewd agent all-in-one, then a sleek-bodied lover. His eyes wide and mouth open in something like rapture when she found him in the shadow of the Three-Faced Witch, where he'd been lying for hours. Haley could never know how much time had elapsed between his collapse and his death, all of it spent staring up at the steel colossus, three thick legs bent and three long arms outstretched in dance, three mouths opened to sing a spell to slay armies.

The shrine she had built for him took no cues from antiquity. Modeled on a Frank Lloyd Wright design, the elegant cone of concrete and glass stands in the midst of a level field, the mirrors around its peak reflecting the sun. She has not ventured out to meditate beside it in many months. Not since the boy in the video was murdered.

The jeans she selects, ripped in fashion-strategic places, would have fit her in junior high had her family been able to afford them then. Much more importantly, they fit her now. So does the $200 sleeveless black turtleneck she picks to go with it. Sometimes the things she wants and the things her fans want to see *do* coincide.

Her in-home studio takes up a quarter of the third floor. She takes the lift, steps out to confront the teeth of the Vampire Baron from *The Scarlet Crown*. She affectionately flicks a finger against the commissioned sculpture's oversized incisors.

The cameras in the green-walled studio already blink with life, activated remotely by Kharmony and her tech assistant Jennah. Working from the office she rents for them in town, they'll record her vlog entry from multiple angles and add appropriate backgrounds generated from the movies and games in real time as she speaks.

"There you are," chirps Jennah's syrupy Southern voice from the speakerphone.

"What, were you worried? I had to get presentable." She mock-flips a curly bang away from her forehead. Her assistants laugh, because they know that's a joke. Cameras love her, always have. The speakerphone renders their laughter tinny, like a cheap synthesizer effect.

The laughter stops. "Ready to go?"

"Of course." Her eyes focus on the teleprompter just below the central camera lens.

"Rolling in five," and the countdown begins.

Haley arms herself with a smile that could dispel a thunderstorm. "Hey, there, Children of the Seven Sigils, so glad you can join me again—"

As she recites with an ease that blends nerdy excitement and breezy candor, an alarm goes off in the house, faint through the studio's soundproof walls. She doesn't let her surprise ruin the take, nor does she alert Jennah and Kharmony to what's going on. When she first installed the system it was oversensitive. Rain buffeting the perimeter fence could set off an alert. Since that problem got fixed, silence has reigned, her kingdom undisturbed. The only threats that she's had to fend off have come from the World Wide Web.

The security company will call, she'll miss the call because she's recording the vlog, she'll have to call them back to stop them from sending sheriff's deputies to her gate.

"... so that wraps up what I'll be doing next month," she reads. "Thanks for watching, and remember, don't worry who the cool kids are, because if you're my kids, you're the cool kids."

Even as the last bit of script rolls from her mouth she blinks in surprise. Surely she didn't write that, and surely Kharmony knows better. But she has no time to ask questions, because the alarm is still pulsing. She proffers just enough winning smile to conclude the shoot, then leaves the studio.

Her writing room on this floor is across the hall, its walls decorated with a mural that comprised the artist's interpretation of the tomb carvings from *The Diamond Dagger*. Tall humanoids with owl wings and round eyes watch as she flips on the computer, clicks on the desktop icon that accesses the security camera feeds. The screen divides into quarters, with the views cycling through the feeds in staggered intervals. No sign that the security firm has tried to call.

She doesn't process the figure approaching her husband's grave until the second time the view appears. She freezes the feeds.

Recurring dreams have been rare for her, but of late she's developed one. In this dream, she's a future archaeologist leading an excavation of the ruins of her mansion, digging out rock and sifting through sand to uncover the strange artifacts buried there—the bric-a-brac made from her books, all bizarrely, completely unfamiliar, and a source of growing frustration, because every object she uncovers dissolves into graceful streams of multicolored dust on exposure to open air.

Only one object pulled from the debris remains intact: a golden death-mask. A distant portion of her always recognizes the face, with its hard eyes and lush yet severe mouth. The never-identified suspect in the murder of Bobby McCloskey, who played the part of Michelle to his Darren. Oddly, this knowledge never wakes Haley up. She sets the mask aside and continues to sift, until the dream ends under its own arcane rules.

But her heart jumps now, at the thought that the intruder on her property might bear that same face. Under the moonlight, her skin is dark, her hair black, her eyes hollow. She's dressed too warmly for the temperature, in white shorts, pale sandals, a paler tee with a printed logo across the chest. She must have come in over the riverside embankment, a steep climb, and through the brambly woods atop that. How she did it without getting covered in mud and scratches, Haley can't fathom.

The woman pauses at the switch that activates the night illumination for Kelvin's monument. The lights come on, and the camera inside the mausoleum sees the intruder in full. Haley sucks in a breath.

It's not the murderer from the fatal *Kool Kidz* video, whose face Haley has been studying for months. Nonetheless, she recognizes the intruder.

Deepa had been a student at an intensive summer writing workshop Haley taught more than twenty years ago, during that anxious time when the buzz for *Maze of Dreams* had begun to build yet the book hadn't appeared on shelves. Deepa was the reason Haley had vowed she would never teach another.

Older, yes, with gray in her hair, made white by the mausoleum light, but little about her has changed from what Haley remembers. A heavy jaw, eyes slightly bulged in their sockets, mouth naturally turned down at the corners, giving her a perpetual surprised frown. Everything about her a little too long, too thin.

Deepa lingers, circling the mausoleum, reading the verses from Maya Angelou inscribed on the walls. Betraying no reaction, she starts toward the house. The walk will take her at least twenty minutes.

The alarm no longer sounds, Haley must have inadvertently deactivated it.

She should be afraid. Instead outrage boils behind her eyes, anger constricts her chest, contracts her fingers into claws. Deepa had resented Haley after just a week of class, because Deepa wanted to be Haley but Deepa wasn't Haley. She had not wanted to hear that developing her talent would take time and further success would depend on perseverance and luck. She had wanted to be told that she was at least Haley's equal, that she was Haley's best friend, even though they had barely met. And when Haley refused, she transformed into a stalker.

Haley can follow Deepa's progress through the video feeds. If her pathetic need remained so strong after all these years that it drew her to trespass on a freezing night, then let her see all the things she'll never be. Invisible, with eyes everywhere, Haley will savor her reactions.

During her rage-fugue she's somehow lost track of the time. Deepa has reached the house, stands by the swimming pool, regarding the tarp covering the water, which undulates as if breathed upon. Highlighted green, the pool is long and narrow, perfect for two people to practice laps. The thought that Deepa might be connecting the mausoleum and the pool made for two slashes Haley deep. Her grimace bares her teeth.

In no hurry, Deepa circles the house, which is as much a marvel as the career souvenirs it contains. Different wings partake of difference architectures: neo-classical, gothic, post-modern. Haley had not simply orchestrated the construction of a palace, but one that could be mistaken for no one else's.

In the spring Haley had Jennah and Kharmony stay under her roofs for a week. They knew her as well as anyone ever had in the wake of Kelvin's death, and still they'd been unable to stop gawking. Haley spotted them in peripheral vision many a time, glancing furtively at halls or walls or grounds or even her, and whispering to each other.

The cameras reveal no alterations of Deepa's expression as she completely circles the house, ending up at the same spot by the pool's shallow end. Near her looms the glowering, gaunt, five-armed figure of Gigenia, the taciturn guardian of the dream maze.

The video feed skips.

Haley jerks her hands away from the keyboard. The house monitor program has opened the patio doors that let out beside the pool.

One feed shows something immense thrashing in the pool, wrapped in the tarp, its weight bearing it down to the bottom. The next feed over, Deepa stands inside the house, next to an eight-foot high sculpture of a ten-headed monster, given no name in book or movie, though Haley thinks of him as Ravana.

Another look. The pool is calm, its tarp undisturbed. Gigenia is missing from her pedestal, so it seems on quick glance. Haley doesn't have time to be sure. Another video skip, and Deepa strides through the main hall of the first floor.

In the foyer, Ravana's shape has changed. Given the camera angle and the dimness, Haley can't be sure of more.

In the hall, a high gothic space with a glorious spiral stair that rises all the way to the fourth floor, Deepa tips her head up to study the phoenix chandelier, its flurry of wings spreading in an oval thirteen feet wide.

Haley's father came from New York, but not from the city like everyone instantly assumed, especially given his academic background and the arrest record he earned from protests. Raised on a farm upstate, he once took Haley to a traveling fair. The stares and frowns aimed their way became something else when he bought a token for a shooting gallery and proceeded to hit every single target in the booth at least twice.

He wanted her to know how to hunt. He wanted her ready if the cross-burners came back. He trained her with a rifle and a pistol. They spent hours, weeks, years on poetry, on the delights found in great books, but he wanted to make sure that wasn't all he left behind. He told her that disassembling, cleaning, and reassembling a revolver had a poetry of its own. Cancer had its own poetry, too, he told her, when he faced that ordeal. *Everything should be something to write about.*

She has her gun safe concealed in her walk-in closet. She runs there now, up a set of back stairs. Taking the lift would generate attention-drawing noise.

On the fifth floor, through the door to her writing room, she hears, "And you're nobody." The firecracker pop of a gun.

The statue of Arachne has been moved. Did she bump it on the way out? Even if she had, she could not have shifted it so it blocks the entrance to the walk-in closet door, it's far too heavy. She has to press up against the latex-rubbery spider abdomen to open the door and squeeze past, her pulse thumping against the unpleasantly moist surface.

She emerges with a jet black semiautomatic 9 mm. She keeps it pointed at the floor as she walks toward the sound of soft footsteps.

They come face to face in her library of treasures. The walls are nothing but books. Stories she loved in childhood, works by admired mentors and talented rivals that she pored over as an adult, volumes with covers that struck her fancy, others recommended by publishers, agents, managers, and most of all, copy after copy of her own babies, in hardcover, trade paperback, mass market, in dozens of languages, in special signed editions. Her most prized curio, the printing of *Maze of Dreams* that unfolds into a real maze, preens on a central pedestal. More sofas, love seats, and recliners than one person should ever use fill the space between pedestal and shelves.

All the reading lamps glow. The overhead light blinks out. Deepa allots Haley a brief glance before turning to peruse the books, as if she's an invited guest with all the time in the world to indulge her curiosity about what a bestselling author reads.

The intruder removes a book, Haley can't see which one. Nor can she see Deepa's face, only a cascade of graying hair that spills past the waist.

"So did you come here to see me, or just to wreck my property?" Haley tightens her fingers around the grip of the gun. Her heart flutters, her jaw clamps, her teeth grind. An ache blooms behind her left eye. A strange pressure squeezes her from all directions.

"You told me that if I did what you said, I'd be the cool kid all the other cool kids envy." The voice doesn't come from the figure in front of her. "After what you did to me, I haven't written a word."

You fucking stalker, you did it to yourself, Haley wants to shout, but the force coiling around her holds her jaw closed, her arms pressed against her sides.

Lips against her ear. "Calling me crazy in front of the entire class. You broke me in front of them for entertainment. You broke me to turn your own luck around."

The figure of shadow, hair, and long limbs remains in place. The lies it tells are the least of Haley's worries. Instead of screaming a denial, Haley mouths a plea without words, the sounds she makes getting no farther than her throat. The tightening coils crush her fingers and squeeze the gun out of her hand. Her knees forced together, she loses her balance, but the force that holds her trapped keeps her upright.

"After what you promised me."

Her mind vomits memories. The range of expressions among Deepa's classmates, from mortification to lascivious smirks. Lying on the bed in the cabin the night before, Deepa's light, lithe weight atop her, her hands slowly sliding up onto bare skin beneath Deepa's blouse, Deepa's lips kissing the underside of her chin. No such thing ever happened. She remembers it as if it's happening now.

The books are falling from the shelves. Her vision fills with black spots, round accusing eyes.

There is a skip.

She's staring at a line of hieroglyphs. Golden symbols woven into the rug.

She picks herself up. Her library of dreams remains pristine. She's alone.

She was always alone. She sits cross-legged on the floor, moaning in a kind of panicked anger, as real memories wash away the hallucinations outside and inside her head.

Those images of mockery and rejection—they came from the most creative work Deepa ever produced. Her suicide note.

No memory in a life afflicted by aggressions macro and micro would ever descend lower than the cracked and seeping voice at the other end of the phone, switching from quiet sobs to calm anger. Haley's own gut had twisted tighter and tighter, but she couldn't make herself stop talking, though it was clear Deepa's mother would never, ever believe her. *Nothing like that ever happened. I swear to you. I swear.*

All of it, lies. She's absolutely certain.

No sign of the gun she fetched, but surely it was never in her possession. She dreamed all this, some sort of unprecedented waking nightmare. Did she even record the vlog? She has to contact Kharmony, make sure she really made the message for her fans, and then ponder the next steps she needs to take.

As she stands, the abruptly cold air conceals the faintest whisper, or it could be a trick of tinnitus: *Nobody's going to die tonight.*

PUPPET SHOW

The colosseum lights went black and the opening riff soared and growled, slamming down a head-pounding beat. At the front of the audience, crammed against the rail by the forward press of bodies, Ken Rosemonde still managed to check his watch, raise his eyebrows: So the rumors were true. Another concert started right on time, down to the minute. No other band held such a reputation for keeping to a clockwork-tight schedule.

Everyone was already on their feet, bouncing heads and thrashing necks to the heavy guitar crunch; the snare burst in, time to mosh. Bodies smashed into one another, sweaty flesh slapped against sweaty flesh. The drummer jazzed up his rhythm, quick-shifted to a military march, and the mob bellowed approval.

Ken did not share in their joy. The squashed rock critic plotted his revenge: *I'm going to pan them tomorrow. Zero fucking stars. Tell parents never to let their kids come back—*

A voice sounded from the darkness: "Let the world bleed, friendsss."

The lights came up and the show was on.

The boiling Cesspool dominated center stage (the infantile press kit capitalized the names of all the props). Its bubbling depths glowed through thick panels of transparent glass, the light source somewhere beneath the roiling muck, the gurgling fluids refracting liquid oil colors, blues and purples and reds, swirling together and whirling apart. A dagger-shaped pool, its point facing the crowd.

The band, nowhere to be seen. Gaping at the spectacle, Rosemonde had to admit, despite his vow of vengeance, he found the intense multisensory assault perversely persuasive—

The lighting changed hue, and changed, and changed, and each time it did the boiling bile altered its spectrum, now to hideous churning browns, now to neon lavender. The drummer ditched his frills, paring down to snare and bass: *whack-thump whack thump WHACK-thump WHACK!-thump*

"And now, friendsss," came the voice, "I would like to intro-duccce . . . the Scream Queen!"

Psycho-soundtrack shrieks from the amps and she appeared, lowered by a pole from the ceiling girder-rigging, animatronic eyes wild with fright, hair electrified blue, feminine physical features immensely, grossly exaggerated. Her legs pumped up and down, running in place above the pool of oil.

Over the sharp beats of the drum, the unseen host addressed his audience: "Behold, friends, the Scream Queen, forever doomed to be fed to the beassst . . for your pleasure!"

The percussion expanded and sped into a jungle rhythm, huge and hollow and insidious. That moment, the Scream Queen's mouth opened unnaturally, impossibly wide as something rose from the muck beneath her: the air filled with scream samples across all octaves, overlapping and echoing. A monster arose from the Cesspool and unfolded itself, a hydraulic construction of epic dimensions, with six eyes veined by fire and seven rows of laser-lit fiberglass teeth. The Scream Queen's neck twisted so she stared straight down as the beast reached for her with three scaly limbs, the talons at their tips unhinging, extending.

All to aware what was about to happen, Ken Rosemonde braced himself against the rail. Of all the rumors so far confirmed, he seemed to be headed for first hand validation of the truth behind the one most circulated. He desperately hoped it wouldn't prove as awful as he'd heard.

All sound cut off, save the Queen's hundred multi-layered screams, jacked up to earsplitting decibels.

The beast lunged and dug its talons through her belly, ripping her latex flesh wide open, and a thick glob of red spilled out into the pool. With a sound like cannon fire, blood-coated confetti sprayed over the audience, gushing from the Scream Queen's open bowels.

Her legs still kicked. Her mouth still screamed.

She threw her arms out to the audience in a mechanical plea for mercy, and that horde went berserk, cheering on the creature to finish the job. With a modulated roar it detached her from the pole, dragging her down to its mouth—her electronic screams accelerating to ridiculous speed—then she disappeared head-first through the beast's open gullet.

The thing closed its jaws and her legs dropped out, still kicking, to splash into the Cesspool. Still visible as they sank, they continued to twitch.

The drums slowed down, took on a new beat, and the beast slid back into the churning colors of the deep, eyes glowing, gloating, hunger for the moment sated.

Plastered in gristle and the sticky concoction used for blood, Rosemonde fought to translate his disgust into his review's opening sentence: *Using a vomitous blend of ear-shattering sound and simulated violence, Bloodbath Jubilee's deplorable antics left this reviewer—*

A glimpse of a shadowy man-figure moving along the rim of the pool spurred the crowd to surge with a deafening roar that derailed the critic's peevish trains of thought.

The figure's amplified words sliced above the cacophony. "Predator and prey, friendsss. The nature of the beast!"

Unable to move, unable to think, Rosemonde became by forfeit part of the fandom tide.

Beams of light struck all around the pool's perimeter, and there at its dagger point, solidified in a spotlight flash, stood the star of the show: the man known to the world only as Bloodbath, his salt-white locks curling down his shoulders, his face painted in a too-wide, red-lipped clown smile. He raised his arms, spouting jets of fire from the palms of both hands. He laughed; his hands spun on his wrists, showering blue sparks; he jumped down from his perch on the Cesspool wall, and bowed.

The sweat- and ichor-drenched mob ate it all up, gorging themselves on smoke, mirrors, and blood.

"No one's caught me yet, friendsss," hissed Bloodbath with a flourish of his tattooed arms, "because I leave no one alive to speak of my deeds!"

And the crowd roared even louder as the band dashed out, instruments gripped in spiked gloves, and hurtled into "Spirit of the Ripper":

Lovely lady, take my hand
Walk with me to Death's dark land
I came from a forgotten time
To sculpt your flesh, to make it mine

Toniiiight
Sacred blood will spill
Toniiiight
I will drink my fill
Toniiiight
I shake with the thrill
Toniiiiiiiight
I revel in the KILL
Tonight . . .

I've travelled far from times before
To stalk you on this barren shore
To carve flesh with a surgeon's knife
Tonight my art will end your life

From host to host through mists of time
I twist the wills of men to mine
Unspeakable crimes performed
By the Spirit of the Ripper

Beneath the Cesspool, pumps inhaled air, hoses vibrated as fluids squeezed through, watertight lights in the oil stuttered with the drumbeat, dazzling and dimming at remote control cues. Invisible commands infested the airwaves, directing props to flare, spotlights to dance, musicians to play. Backstage, in the command center, ever-evolving schematics pulsing before his mind's eye, the Engineer sat straight-backed, poised to broadcast new orders with flickers of thought. The moment neared for the next great spectacle—

When the guitar solos reached their rapid-fire arpeggio peaks, Bloodbath threw his mike aside, tipped back his head and spewed blue mist from his mouth. He stretched out his right hand— tongues of flame appeared at the tips of his fingers—and when he touched his fingertips to his blue-mist breath, the gas stream erupted in a column of fire. As the audience howled in amazement, the singer whipped his head to sweep the stream of fire-breath in a scorching arc across the stage, chromatic arrays of fireworks detonating along the path his flaming breath traced. His fans hooted and whistled and pumped their fists.

The Engineer cued Bloodbath to take another bow. Thirty-seven wires jacked into his skull with long acupuncture-style pins kept him synced to the mechanisms on the stage; he redirected three to measure audience reaction.

Image-inputs split his vision into multiple fields, made him master of all surveyable: beneath the stage, pistons fired, gears clunked; behind the scenes, some Roadies locked custom-made girders into place, supervised through a vox-capable camera-eye; from the colosseum floor, the ebb of enthusiasm clued the Engineer to rev up the next song in the set.

He ran a mechanical stress test; when numbers came back satisfactory, he flipped a toggle on one of the consoles stacked before him—turning gears that raised a titanic Chinese dragon mask up from the boiling Cesspool and out over the crowd, loosing gasjets from its nostrils that ignited in brilliant red firespouts. He flipped another, triggering Bloodbath to rave out a spiel about the dark forces of the past returned to destroy, every light fading and blazing with his booming syllables. The dragon mask lowered. The Engineer waited.

Bloodbath's rant culminated in a high shriek that blended into the first psychedelic licks of "Delusions of a Dragonslayer"; the great mask's mouth opened, just before submerging, and a *basso profundo* bellow came over the amplifiers: "HIDDEN CHILD OF MINE, COME FORTH." The Engineer flipped a third toggle.

A second dragon of latex-and-steel, miniature version of the first, burst from the bass player's chest, opening its many-fanged maw to shower the front rows with fake blood.

A thin smile played across the Engineer's face, as he registered more reactions: horror, delight, fascination, frenzy. He let the fans sink their teeth into the song's acidhead madness; then he ran a vitals check on Bloodbath. His smile faded. Not good: this Bloodbath's vital signs were fluxing too fast; he would short out, maybe halfway through the concert. For the show's hair's-breadth timing, very bad indeed.

He patched a line through to the Propmaker. The chubby fellow appeared in the lower left quadrant of the Engineer's vision, jowls highlighted red beneath hot tungsten bulbs.

In the converted dressing room, the Propmaker peered up from his operating table as the closed-circuit monitor hummed. The wired Medusa-head of the Engineer materialized on screen. "You got the new lead man fixed up yet?"

"Lord, man," replied the Propmaker, "the answer is no." In the corner of the Engineer's vision, the Propmaker's brow knotted, his eyes narrowed; his thick purple lips pursed. "I just got around to installing the vox co-ordinator—"

The Engineer's lips curled in a tiny smirk. "Don't make me recommend a pay cut. Put ou some hustle."

The Propmaker's scowl radiated deep creases. "I've told you time and again, these tours through the backwaters leave us short of stock. I tell you, stick to the cities, my supplies are endless, but you say no, gotta reach all the fans, take it on the road, and when a mess arises you blame me! This kinda thing is gonna get us caught!" He wagged the scalpel in his hand like an accusing finger; blood from the blade spattered his knuckles.

The Engineer's smirk cracked wider. "Leave no evidence, breed no suspicions." An alert light at the tip of one of his needles blinked red and the Engineer's expression flipped to blank. Bereft of priority, the Propmaker's visage shrank to a tiny square along the left edge of the Engineer's vision, embedded among spinning axles, screaming faces, a close-up of a power saw as a Roadie completed his work.

Unaware, the Propmaker continued: "They miss people quicker in the boondocks! Someone figures something out, and before you know it, they're coming through the trees with torches and pitchforks—" Recognizing the Engineer's empty stare, the Propmaker quivered with rage. "Quit wasting my time! I'll have him ready, alright?"

Ever so slightly, the Engineer nodded his head.

With a huff, the Propmaker switched off the monitor, returned his attention to the old wino laid out on the operating table. "Bastard, interrupting me like that." He completed the interrupted incision and peeled away the skin from the dead drunk's throat and face.

"Much improved," he chuckled, before spraying preservative over the exposed muscle. From the rack beside his operating table, he took a tiny wireless receiver capsuled in blood-caked plastic and fastened it behind the loose bone just above the larynx. A custom-made clip locked it into place.

He nodded, pleased. The real work was yet to come: two bristles of wire leads, one for the left side, one for the right, that when properly attached would deliver jolts to the proper nerve centers and cause the face of this new Bloodbath to scowl and smile in perfect sync with the voice broadcast.

One by one, deft as a watchmaker, the Propmaker hooked each color-coded filament into place with a fiberoptic probe, his eyes fixed not on his hands but on a second monitor clamped on the corner of his table, which, through its tiny blue screen, showed him the tissue greatly magnified as he poked through it to find the facial nerves and fasten down the leads. Optic, olfactory, auricular, portio dura, submaxillary, hypoglossal . . .

"*Voila!*" he cried, whipping out a supple Bloodbath mask. "Your makeover is complete!" Smearing paste at the crucial junctures, he laid mask over muscle, carefully aligning lips and eyelids.

But still, so much to do—hydraulic joints constructed with capabilities for unnatural rotation still to install, exhumed from the last burned-out Bloodbath. Squibs to wire up with hidden pouches of fake blood or flash powder, fireplugs to insert in the fingers.

Wheels rumbled outside the dressing-room: a young blond wisp of a Roadie slammed an aluminum cart through the door. "Got it," the Roadie wheezed, "I got it all, man, I brought it—" Dark tracks veined his trembling broomstick arms. "God, I gotta have . . . I gotta have a . . . "

Shuffling over to the cart, the Propmaker passed him a rubber strap and a syringe. Panting, the Roadie seized the offerings and used them. Within seconds his tension eased. He sighed in deep relief.

"Potent stuff," clucked the Propmaker, swiveling one of his operating spotlights over the contents of the cart. "Doesn't last, though. Let's see what you brought."

Bugged-out mechanical eyes, hip-joints, shoulder-joints, massive wobbling silicone implants, wide-hinged jaws, all spattered red with viscera: "Salvaged the pieces from the Scream Queen, good, good! This saves time!" The Propmaker pointed at a nude woman stretched supine on the dressing room make-up counter. "Open her up for me and clean her out, I can jump right in when I finish up with Bloody B here."

The calming haze of the Roadie's buzz started to fade. His eyes widened, pupils still dilated:. "You want me to cut—?"

"Yep, cut. You don't have to be too precise, I'll finesse it when I wire in the implants." The Propmaker returned to his newly converted derelict. Wielding his scalpel like an artist's lightpen, he drew another line in the meat over the old man's ribs before he realized the Roadie hadn't budged. The boy gaped at the body on the counter, a new supply of sweat slicking his forehead.

"Listen," the Propmaker growled, "I got to prep that dish for the Final Sacrifice at the end of tonight's show. They bring her in, I'm about to get started, then the Wire Octopus calls and tells me to build a new Bloodbath, and they literally drag this guy in from under the overpass at the back of the parking lot, so I'm at square one. I don't got time to start the Sacrifice on my own, so you help me out. You cut and I pop in what she needs when I get to her."

The girl on the vanity might've been college age but looked younger; her skin pearly-white, her black-dyed hair cut in the now-again-fashionable mushroom style, her lips rouged pink, her breasts small, barely developed. The Roadie swallowed visibly as his buzz lost all hold and shell-shock locked his joints.

The Propmaker slit the old man's armpit open.. "Boy, she came in kicking! Tried to put some eyes out before they put her under. Told me they flashed a backstage pass to get her in the car—" He traded his scalpel for a saw. "What I heard, she said she always wanted to make out with B-B here." He thumped the dead wino's chest. "So, looks like she will."

With a few saw strokes and a tightening of clamps, he had the first shoulder implant in place. When he looked up, the Roadie still hadn't budged.

"I don't think I can do it," the boy stammered. "Not without another hit."

The Propmaker set down his tools. "New boy, huh?" He jabbed the air with a bloodstained index finger. "You get nothing, kid, nothing at all, till you've done your job."

Trembling, the Roadie nodded.

"Shouldn't be so hard," the Propmaker said jovially, "I made some quick scratches to show where to cut."

So he had. Straight down the belly, across the underside of each breast, beneath the armpits, across the eyelids, inside the thighs, behind the knees, underneath the jaw.

"Go on, man, the knife's right there."

Stress driving his deprived veins to feverish thirst, the boy picked up the blade and cut. The Propmaker watched a moment to make sure the Roadie did it right; satisfied, he put on that hustle the Engineer demanded. Decisions, incisions, bone connections, blood drainage, liposuction, skin lifts, quick circuit tests, latex strips to paste over wounds stitched shut . . . the Propmaker's hands flowed as they reshaped flesh—

His junior partner threw down the knife with a cry. "Man, man, can't take this. I'm gonna hafta have . . . I gotta have . . . oh, man, why we gotta *do* this?"

"It's so cheap, that's why we do it," chortled the Propmaker, musing that the boy needed longer-lasting doses. "Good business, good show business. We satisfy the fantasies of our fans," and here the Propmaker licked his purple lips, tasting the beauty of it, "and we don't have to shell out for new props and robots every show. We just recycle the implants." The hand-held stitch machine whirred as the Propmaker closed the last incision. "*Bon appetite!* Push this out to—"

The mirror above the counter was the classic Old Hollywood kind, a rectangle rimmed with incandescent bulbs. The Propmaker could see the boy's face framed within those glowing yellow orbs: eyes closed, eyelids inflamed, cheeks tear-sticky, trickles of spit down his chin, nose running, shoulders heaving. Not withdrawal; the kid was crying. Crying!

The Propmaker aped a paternal tone. "Hey, it's rough, kid. I know. You'll get used to it." His finger tapped on the operating table. "This is done. You push this thing out to the Tekkies, they know what to do with it." He detached the surgical monitor from the operating table. "Leave the sacrificial virgin to me."

The Roadie nodded, ran a hand through his dirty-blond hair, took hold of the operating table and wheeled it out the dressing room door.

As soon as the door closed, the Propmaker switched on the main monitor. The Engineer reappeared, strobing green from some unseen indicator light.

The Propmaker addressed the screen. "We got a problem."

O ne of the table's wheels squealed loudly as the Roadie ran down the corridor, underscoring his runaway train of thought: *I gotta get outta here. I gotta get outta here. I gotta get outta here—*

He moved at a sprint, pell-mell down the hallways. *This job's not worth the fixes. I never should've joined up.* Careening through the maze beneath the colosseum, wheel screeching, feet pounding tile, he rounded a corner, plunged past a burnt corpse propped against a wall, its metal-framed wings rustling . . . another corner, some arms and legs hanging in a rack, tubed and wired to blood-banks and batteries . . .

Distracted, he nearly crashed head-on into a pair of fellow Roadies bearing a coffin-sized cooler on a stretcher. The three Roadies stared at one another, mutually stunned, before the coffin-bearers recouped and scurried away with their cargo.

Beyond the site of near-collision, the door to the Tekkie lab stood wide open. Despite the need screaming in his arms, the Roadie forced a calm demeanor. *Maybe I can leave this and sneak away, mingle with the crowd, they'd never find me then.*

A Tekkie clad boots to headband in shiny black vinyl spotted him at once, rushed up to relieve him of his charge. "Hah! Glad to see *him!*" the Tekkie crowed. "Wire Octopus's all up my ass about this guy!" He seized an edge of the cart while mimicking the Engineer's orders in a parrot-squawk: "Ready to change out? Ready to change out? Ready to change out—"

A muffled noise from the speaker plugged in the Tekkie's ear, and he touched a finger to his collar, switching on the mike suspended before his lips, voice instantly respectful. "Yeah, he made it . . . running with it now, man, I'm set up to do the switcheroo . . ."

The Roadie shook from the yammering in his veins. He could get fixed here, he knew, but he had to hold out. Quietly, he backed away, aiming to escape.

"Hey! Where ya goin'? Bassman's on the fritz, we need another hand." The Tekkie pointed to three Roadies in street clothes halfway across the equipment-cluttered conference room, two of them holding open the Bass Player's ribcage while the third tightened something inside. Another Tekkie supervised them, this one a massive man, shirtless, wider than the Propmaker and three heads taller.

"Well, ya gonna move, or do I need to get a shock-prod?"

The Roadie tried at gambit. "Look, man, I'm really hurting, I need to go get a hit so bad."

The vinyl-clad Tekkie smiled. "Yeah. I know. Move."

Gorge rising, the Roadie stepped toward his next task. When he turned his back to the Tekkie a needle pricked his neck.

A whisper. "Here's your fix, sweetie pie."

Sleep juice pumped into the Roadie's head, swirled black in his brain. The Roadie gasped once in futile protest. Next thing—

—agony wrapped his face, like he had sandpaper on the underside of his skin, abrading nerves with every muscle twitch. He could move his eyes, but his corneas scraped on razors, every part of him compressed, the very flow of blood pushing up against the new skin that swathed him, spiking signals of pain from every contact point.

A scream caught in his chest, and stayed there, unable to climb into his throat. Bright lights blared, whirling (*oh man, Oh my God, they*) twirling overhead, thick blasts of color sweeping out into the darkness, shining down on (*they put me in THE SHOW!!*) a sea of ghastly faces, laughing, cheering, jeering, howling, stoned and blank-eyed . . .

Bloodbath boomed, "Come join usss."

Something else controlled the Roadie's body; an electric tingle at the base of his skull forced him to move—

At the front of the hoarse-throated throng, one face stood out, grimacing in distress. In desperation the boy focused on that face. *He's gotta see, this isn't what he thinks . . .*

I'm alive!

Ken Rosemonde recoiled in disgust; the grotesque new puppet shambling onto the set kept its eyes locked on him. Some sick joke by the band? Did someone up there know who he was?

Pale, starved, bone-jutting frame sheathed in a plastic second skin, face a rubbery Harlequin mask, half-black, half-white, it stared straight at Ken even as it lurched to center stage, led by Bloodbath's beckoning finger.

Washed in the rippling glow of the Cesspool's murky color mix, Bloodbath raised his arms, drawing all stage lights to shine on him at once.

Rosemonde groaned. An unannounced encore, more excuses for ear-bursting music and play blood-letting, now this. He ground his teeth. He wasn't going to sleep tonight until his revenge was written, revised and uploaded to his editor.

"Friendsss!" hissed Bloodbath. "I would speak with you one last time tonight, with no fanfare, no fireworks, no grand effectsss. I know there are thossse who accuse my Show of being a bad ex-sssample for the young!"

Rosemonde stiffened. Maybe they really were on to him. The starving harlequin continued to stare at him, working its jaw like it meant to speak.

"Tonight, I've decccided to answer those criticsss."

The reviewer's mouth dropped open.

"To do my civic duty . . . My own way!"

"FIX ME!" The interrupting croak came from the plastic-wrapped Harlequin, clutching at Bloodbath's studded jacket with both hands. "I NEED A FIX. A HIT. NOW, OR I'LL KILL. OR IT'LL KILL ME. NOW. FIX ME UP, NOW!"

Bloodbath's eyes widened in mock shock as the Harlequin-junkie clawed the singer's vest, scratching, searching for something to fix with. "WHERE IS YOUR STASH? I KNOW YOU'RE HOLDING. I'LL TEAR YOU APART, I WILL! WHERE IS IT? GIVE ME, GIVE ME!"

Ken gawked, his stomach in knots.

"I'M BURNING! BURNING INSIDE! HELP ME!"

Two men dressed in black leather rolled a huge prop out from backstage: a massive metal pump, made up like a titanic hypodermic, its wicked needle more than four feet long, tapering to a gleaming point. They wheeled around the Cesspool to the front of the stage, positioning the hypo with needle-end pointed at the junkie, Blood-bath standing between them. Immediately the Harlequin struggled to reach it, the singer holding it back with a hand on its chest.

"MINE," the Harlequin croaked. "MINE!"

The junkie's lips moved. Rosemonde blanched, because they shaped different words than the raspy tirade crackling from the amplifiers. *Help me,* it mouthed. *Oh God, please help me.*

"Ssso simple," whispered Bloodbath, gesturing at the Harlequin's prize. "Ssso sweet. Is thisss what you want?"

"*YES!*" the junkie shrieked.

No, mouthed its lips. *No, no, no, no, no . . .*

"Then hhhave at it!" Bloodbath stepped back.

Drumroll.

Stumbling toward the gleaming needle, the Harlequin's eyes never left Ken's face. Rosemonde wanted to shrink away, but this crude creation's range of expression astonished him. Pleading, begging . . . then, a horrible, horrible sadness. Ken desperately wanted to escape that stare but could only stare back.

The Harlequin impaled itself on the needle, a full foot of its length sinking into the junkie's belly. The drumroll heightened, tightened, a sigh of pleasure breathing from the loudspeakers. A guitar note struck, tremolo-wailing, as the Harlequin's head snapped back. "FIX ME!"

The hypo plunger glowed green as it depressed.

Fiberoptic tracks lit up all along the Harlequin's body, worming blue down its arms, pink across its chest, purple through its legs, twisting gold around its head, illuminating the path of the drug. The tracks spread, wove together. The Harlequin, a circulating, human-shaped web of light, snapped back its head again. "MORE! GIVE ME MORE!"

The hypo reached its limit.

The Harlequin drooled rivulets of blood across the white side of its face.

Red splotches burst beneath its second skin, spreading like paint poured on glass as the web of color blinked. The second skin filled, swelled. The background axe crunch jumped an octave, higher, higher, an eardrum piercing shrill.

Rosemonde threw his arms over his head seconds before the sticky red shower gushed across the front rows.

All sound cut off. From the darkening stage: "Remember, friendsss, what you've ssseen tonight . . . and when you face the needle, asssk . . . Do you want thisss?" The last phrase, digitally delayed *ad infinitum.* "Do you want this? . . . Do you want this? . . . Do you want this? . . ."

When Rosemonde looked up, a drop curtain hid the stage. The show was over.

The reviewer inspected his neighbors. Stunned, shocked, quiet, milling about uneasy . . . for all their bloodthirst, hit hard by Bloodbath's message.

Amazing.

B right and early next morning, an internet review appeared, blasting the Bloodbath Jubilee for its "skin-drenching showers of gore and fake blood." But the reviewer confessed to admiring the production's "unprecedented creative anarchy"; sang praises for the "brilliant dark turns of Bloodbath's demented musical style"; and finally proffered glowing words for the Jubilee's surprise encore, a "stunning, stomach churning depiction of the destructive power of addictive drugs."

THE BONE BIRD

I set out in the night to slay the great bird,
across the clear-paned lake with ghost stars in the deep,
my blood and my breath the world's only heat.

I set out in the night to slay the great bird,
and I thought of the faces waiting back home,
small forms wrapped shivering in tattered wool,
shivering in fading ember light,

and the beak struck before I ever lifted my sword,
and the beak pierced my skin and my heat and my light,
and the bird feasted well while the moon watched round-eyed,
and the bird buried me with my soul still inside
my clean-picked skull.

And the water eddied through my bones
as I wept with no eyes and cried with no tongue
and silt became my blanket as the sun lingered longer,
while at night the bird watched,
silent, unblinking, vast feathered cruciform,
my sole constellation through thaw and freeze,

it watched as small forms bundled in tatters
skated across the clear pane under moonlight,
frolicked on the lake after dark,
shadows above my murk-shrouded grave,
slow specks beneath the bird's lowering cloud.

And my jaw flapped to warn
and my arms rose to ward
and silt billowed before me
as I flowed, as I floated, pressed myself to the ice,
and my driftwood fists pounded,
as shadows stopped sliding, as faces turned down,
as small wool-wrapped forms gathered into a circle,
as stomping feet mocked my urgent tattoo,
as tiny mouths laughed and tiny hands pointed,
as the bird dipped its head
and its beak daggered down,
pierced through the deeps,
plucked the spark from my ghost
like a mite, like a liver,
its appetite only for me.

Mud filled the swirl of my screams.

Starved to pinions and bones,
it still hangs in my night,
with its emptied sockets
that call to my own,
awaiting my rise
to feast as I drown,
its appetite only for my sickly light,
for my rage that feeds it still.

LONGSLEEVES

*D*on't do this, *she said.*

   There's nothing for it, lovely one. A shame you won't be so lovely once we're done.

Merav drifted between white hot pain and blissful shock until a voice lifted her to consciousness, its timbre akin to creek water rushing over rocks.

Her mouth burned as if she'd kissed a boiling kettle. The world smelled of blood and char. Branches partitioned the haze above her, dangling fruit with red, shivering skin.

"I can help you," the voice said.

A slender man leaned over her, his shoulders too broad and too knotted with muscle for his tall frame. As she stared, dazed, through the mask of agony fused to her face, she pieced together that she still lay in the ruins of the cabin where Uethorn's men had dragged her, deep in Dium Forest. Light shone through holes in the rotted ceiling.

The branches she perceived were in fact antlers, sprouting from the head of the man studying her. Four round, bloody objects hung in those antlers, spasms contorting their surfaces.

She remembered Uethorn's armsmen in their reeking leather. The blade heated by the torch. She touched fingers to her mouth, cried out at the pain that touch triggered, made a thousandfold worse when she flexed her jaw.

When her vision unblurred, the shapes on the straw beside her resolved into a gruesome stack: four leather-armored bodies, the stumps of their necks seeping.

"They pay still for their transgression in Olderra's wood," the antlered man said.

Even through the pain, she knew that name, whispered in Cal-charra with the tones of awe reserved for floods and earth tremors. The stories: that Olderra's wrath once inflicted a year of saltwater rain on the ancient city. That she had rearranged stars to spell a message. That the last House to cross her, countless years ago, had been con-sumed in their manse by fire so hot it blinded all who witnessed it.

The man leaned close, and Merav discovered he had the face of a stag, long snout and tawny hide, though the dark beads of his eyes turned forward, human-like, beneath a blunt brow ridge. When he spoke he revealed incisors like ivory petals and two long rows of molars in his lower jaw. "I'll take you to Olderra now."

She started to scramble away and fell back with a croak.

"I understand your fear," the creature said. "You're hers now. You were hers when your blood touched the soil. There's noth-ing for it." Hearing him repeat the words of Uethorn's men as his strong arms gathered her for a cradle carry, she screamed, only to faint from the pain.

Her sight fluttered through the fugue that followed, witnessing high shrubs, mottled leaves, a wolf pack scattering into shadows.

Sometime later her bearer paused and shivered, the tremors in his oak-solid muscle stirring her awake. A pale serpent drifted across the trees ahead—a ghostly banner winding between the trunks. A second one soon joined it, weaving closer in the same sinuous way.

The antlered man shouted, though Merav didn't understand his fear. Was this not the witch Olderra come to claim his burden?

The long white limbs whipped in a frenzy beside Merav and the antlered man as he broke into a run. The sudden jostle opened wounds clotted shut, driving her back from consciousness.

When she regained her senses she lay on a table. A dry husk of a face floated above her, brown as a chestnut, shriveled as a dried apple. Lips pursed in a starburst of wrinkles. *You are almost mended.* The mouth didn't move to shape the words.

Ochre eyes flicked to one side. *Help her up.*

The antlered man leaned in, offered a thick-knuckled hand that Merav didn't want to take.

She lifted her head. The pain was gone. She touched her jaw, jerked her fingers away from coarse, misshapen flesh.

Above her a vertical tunnel spiraled into darkness, its walls like the underside of peeled bark.

A wooden platform drifted into view, hovering in mid-air, no means of support visible. Startled, Merav scanned the chamber, discovered more shelves and trays of various sizes suspended all around the table, stacked with vials, jars, bottles, books and other objects not immediately identifiable.

She turned to the wrinkled face, named its owner. "Olderra."

The witch's smile creased her cheeks. "That is a name I use, yes."

That this tiny woman stood at the heart of so many tales of woe and terror—Merav wanted to laugh, to wake safe in her bed and cackle at her own folly.

The deer-headed man's hand remained extended. Merav told the witch, "I don't want him touching me!"

His expression didn't change, but he lowered his hand and backed away.

The witch reached up as one of the shelves floated toward her fingers. She snatched a small pouch from the shelf without looking, shook it between forefinger and thumb, rattling its contents.

Merav sat up. "What is that?"

"I've not quite finished you yet," the witch said. She flicked the opened pouch at Merav's face. A puff of darkness billowed into wrestling foxes made of smoke. Merav recoiled—

And blinked, the apparition gone. Olderra curled the pouch into her palm, shook her hand as if she'd gotten it wet. The shelves started to retreat.

Merav touched her jaw again, felt skin and bone and hair where none should have been. "What have you done?"

"What I could," Olderra said. "What had to be done." She inclined her leathery face toward the antlered man. "Show her."

The shelves were attaching themselves to the walls in a series of clicks and scrapes. "Show me what?" Merav demanded, but Olderra was gone.

The antlered man stood by an exit, a crude arch bitten out of the spongy bark walls. He bowed his head and stepped through. Merav looked for another way out of the roughly cylindrical room; found none, other than a forbidding climb up the detachable shelves and into darkness.

Her bare feet touched warm earth. She no longer wore the skirt, corset, or undergarments she'd had on when Uethorn's men abducted her from Rosepike Market. Her clothes had been replaced with a tunic and breeches of identical brown. She shuddered as she stood, wondering who had done that.

Beyond the arch lay a chamber shaped exactly like the one she'd just left, with an identical bark-tunnel ceiling—except there were no shelves on the walls. The air changed from dry to dank. A pool in the center of the floor brushed the room in wavering light.

Across from her, the antlered man pointed at the water. "Best you look."

The reflective surface permitted no glimpse of the pool's depths. The creature staring back at her possessed her eyes but wore the rust-pelt mask of a fox.

She opened her mouth, and the fox mirrored her, exposing a narrow tongue, incisors like curved needles. She curled her lip. The fox's muzzle wrinkled in a snarl.

"What . . . ?" She couldn't finish the question. Her voice sounded no different.

The antlered man's mouth twisted. "Milady healed you."

"What have you done?" she shouted. The fox-woman in the pool flashed her fangs. "Change me back!"

Behind her, Olderra spoke. "You were already changed. This healing is the best I can offer."

So often her father had shouted her down and worse, when anger moved her to speak. She had a swift, sharp tongue that resisted all containment and had learned to counter his physical savagery with verbal jabs that left scars of their own, she was certain. Yet at this moment, though the rage came, words did not. The brute snarl that issued from her throat shamed her.

The old woman peered up at her, impassive. "Hitch your cart to that anger, you're about to have need of it. Hundeil?"

The antlered man sighed. "I feel them, milady."

Behind Merav's eyes a searing urge took hold, an itch deep in her skull that craved scratching. Though nothing about the chamber altered, she noticed shadows moving around her, noises seeping through the walls, harsh male voices and a girl weeping, a stench of heated copper.

"Again, our peace is broken," Olderra growled.

Hundeil flared his nostrils, clenched and unclenched his fists. "Open the way."

"You'll have company this time," she said, and laughed at his snort of protest. "You have no more choice than she does."

Merav found that she lusted to open a belly with claws, to crush a throat between her teeth.

"So be it," Hundeil said. *"The way."*

The arch no longer led to the chamber of shelves but out into the night. Rain spattered at the threshold but did not cross.

As Hundeil's form blocked the muted moonlight, panic rose in Merav. She could not have said why, but she craved first blood. She had to reach the prey before Hundeil.

She plunged into the drizzle after him.

They emerged by the ancient cottage where Uethorn's thugs had marred her face. Even through the storm, rot fouled the air. She registered fleetingly that Olderra's home was nowhere to be seen.

Three horses stood outside the cottage threshold, eyes flaring to expose the whites as they fixed on her and Hundeil. A lump of flesh lay crumpled by the front hooves of the closest horse. Blood drained into the soil from the fallen body. Through the soles of her feet Merav sensed how the earth thrummed with the transfer of precious energy.

Torchlight flickered inside the cottage. A man raised his voice in alarm—prey giving away its place.

Merav didn't understand the covenants of Olderra's forest, but she knew they had been broken, the offenders' lives forfeit. Hundeil circled to a side window and reached through the way a bear grabs fish from a river. A man screamed. The window was wide enough to pull the screeching prey's head through but not his shoulders. Hundeil gripped the man by the hair, bending his neck backward over the sill.

The horses bolted as Merav leapt over the bleeding body and through the front door. With a shout, a bull of a man charged toward her, swinging his torch like a club. Her response took no thought. She caught his wrist and dragged him off balance. He stumbled into the wall. The leather and chainmail he wore gave her easy purchase as she sprang onto his back and bit at the base of his neck. He howled as her teeth hooked his spine. She clamped and twisted, thrilled at the sensation of cartilage separating, bone breaking.

Iron seared her side.

She tore loose from her prey. Another armsman faced her, and though the torch had guttered out she could still perceive his scarred and bearded face. The knife he had stabbed her with glinted, no blood on its blade. The burning stripe across her flank faded. Behind the armsman lay the stack of headless bodies Hundeil had left when he had retrieved her for Olderra. Their soft parts teemed with insects.

Merav yearned to lunge, but the man kept the knife before him. That iron blade had burned where it touched her.

The man gagged. Merav shrank back, not comprehending—it looked as if a tree had reached through the cottage door and snagged him around the neck. Then Hundeil stepped fully inside and straightened. The armsman lifted from the floor, neck hooked in the upper reaches of Hundeil's antlers.

Hundeil shook his head once. The armsman's spine snapped. Though his body went limp, his mouth continued to move.

Merav's attention whipped back to her own kill. She clawed at his head until she tore it from his shoulders. As he stared up at her, terrified, his mouth working silently, she recognized him. Jintien. A sergeant of House Lohmar, leader of her father's personal guard. She had enjoyed Jintien's company. He had a broad, kind face, stretched often by a gap-toothed grin.

Without understanding why, she hooked Jintien's head to her belt. The head disappeared, but she still felt its weight against her hip. It felt right. It felt *just*.

"We tend to the wounded one now," Hundeil rumbled. Two new heads had joined the ghastly fruit suspended in his antlers. "She still has blood left."

"As I did," Merav said. With this prey—the men, her father's men—vanquished, her hunger for blood slid away.

"Yes," said Hundeil. "This is the way of the forest. If it's her fate to live, Olderra will heal her."

"As she did for me," Merav said. Then made a leap. "And for you."

He left the cottage without acknowledging her words.

Outside, the rain had thinned to mist. Hundeil scooped the dying girl from the muck, and as her head lolled, Merav recognized her, too. Kaediya. Two years younger than Merav, one of Uethorn's grandnieces. They had crossed paths at three of the four harvest banquets Merav's father had made her attend the previous fall. Scions of rival houses, she and Kaediya had exchanged no more than diffident pleasantries at each occasion.

Mud plastered Kaediya's raven-black hair across her long face. Her already pale skin had been bled to white. Her wide mouth hung open. Her wound wasn't visible, but the flow of her life rolled out like a tide.

Questions swirled in Merav's mind—why had she and Kaediya been brought to this place, marked for slow murder?

A moan rose over the patter of the storm and the rustling of the leaves. Hundeil's scent soured with fear.

He ran, Kaediya clenched in his arms. Merav followed his lead without knowing why, but she soon enough spied the cause of his flight.

She remembered a serpentine length of white cloth, seen in delirium as Hundeil bore her to Olderra's lair. She now learned what the object was: a sleeve.

The hooded figure flowed toward them from the shadows. The white robe that shrouded its emaciated form gleamed bright against the overcast night. It floated with arms raised, the sleeves of its raiment outstretched to either side, longer than human arms could possibly be.

When Merav was only five she had traveled with her mother and father and eldest sister to the keep of Dreygim, far to the south of Calcharra—one of the few memories Merav had of her full family, before they lost Mother and Sister both to the yellow pox. The prince of Dreygim kept reptiles in immense cages, their scaly visages a fixture in Merav's nightmares for months afterward, serpents who could swallow a man whole. These sleeves were longer than those serpents, waving slowly as if trailed through water.

The figure lifted its hood and moaned again, as a grave exhaling rage.

Hundeil quickened his sprint. Merav hesitated, and without appearing to gather speed, the figure halved the distance between them. The sleeves extended between the tree trunks like slow chameleon tongues, sinuous white arms curving together to embrace her.

Merav tore her gaze from the fluttering white and bolted.

Never before had she run with such speed or such fear, caroming off trees, tearing through brush, ripping loose the roots that hooked her feet, stumbling again and again until she caught up to Hundeil. Both were wheezing with exhaustion when they reached the gnarled behemoth of a tree that proved to be Olderra's dwelling. Its bark parted like curtains to admit them.

Merav doubled over, gasping, pulse pounding in her chest and sinuses. Inside the hollowed-out tree trunk, the interior had changed yet again, a hearth improbably embedded in the wood opposite the entrance. In the chamber's center stood a round table ringed by benches, set with three bowls.

Olderra pointed through the arch behind them, now opening into the room of floating shelves. Hundeil carried Kaediya there. "Put her on the table," Merav heard Olderra say from the other room, even though the witch was still hunched by the hearth fire, dipping a ladle into a kettle hung from a spit. Merav peered through to see a second Olderra at Hundeil's elbow as he placed the girl's body on the medicine table and shelves detached from the walls.

Hundeil returned to the dining hall and the arch behind him stretched shut. He sat as Olderra used the ladle to fill the bowl before him. A smell of mutton and spicy roots overwhelmed Merav. Her stomach growled.

Hundeil took up a spoon and supped. "Wonderful, milady," he said, as if he hadn't just run miles carrying a body while a long-sleeved specter pursued.

The witch filled Merav's bowl. Merav remained standing, despite her hunger. A slight frown made not-so-slight creases on Olderra's brow. "Have some. You've earned it."

The more Merav became aware of it, the more the invisible weight at her hip disturbed her. The weight of Jintien's head. A new part of her, a piece of her psyche that hadn't existed before she woke up on Olderra's table, insisted that this new accessory provided comfort, that its presence was right and just, but that part did not rule her, no matter how persistently it snapped its jaws.

She was a beast now. A monster, like the thugs from Uethorn House who had mutilated her, like this murderous antlered man and the awful witch who was his master. And *her* master now. The death of gentle Jintien was on all of their hands.

Gentle Jintien, who had spilled a harmless girl's blood. Merav couldn't fathom why he would do that. Had her father ordered it?

The question gave strength to her repulsion. "Take it from me," she said. "His head. Take it, I don't want it."

Olderra regarded her with bushy eyebrows raised. "The price is paid. The bounty rightfully belongs to you."

"I don't understand any of this and I refuse. Jintien was kind to me."

"Not to the child on my table."

"Then give what's left of him to her, once she's half-monster like me."

Hundeil flinched. Olderra's glower intensified. "You cannot make a gift of your trophy, especially not to her," she said as the arch in the wall reopened. "But I will do as you wish. I will take it from you."

Merav followed her into a chamber that shared the same tunnel-ceiling they all did, filled with rows of freestanding wooden racks not unlike the bookcases in the library at Garthand Palace. Tall glass jars crowded the racks.

The room was silent, yet full of subtle movement. Each time she blinked, the jars altered their configuration, as if the racks were switching places the instant her lids closed.

At last Olderra snatched a jar and opened it. The weight vanished from Merav's belt. Something spun in the jar, a tiny man formed of pale smoke, the gray circles of his eyes huge with horror. Then Olderra closed the lid, and the effigy of Jintien faded. She replaced the jar, immediately indistinguishable from its brethren as they shifted places. Merav could not have found it again on threat of death.

"Now will you eat?" Olderra asked.

Merav would never before have enjoyed such a gristly, fat-filled soup, but it proved ambrosia on her tongue. Her joints twinged, finally admitting aches from her exertions.

Olderra sent her to the moss-lined chamber that would be her new bedroom. It too had the same tunnel-ceiling. Contemplating its shadows, Merav drifted to sleep, and dreamed of bringing down a stag with her tiny teeth and dragging the corpse home to her kits.

D ays and nights coursed past with little to distinguish them, their hours marked off by meals before the hearth, slumbering in soft moss, chores of cleaning or retrieval carried out through the dozens of rooms confined within the tree, most of which served no obvious purpose. In one, dried leaves spun forever in a slow cyclone. In another, glass windows honeycombed the walls, but Merav could make no sense of the roiling chaos of color outside the panes. In another, slabs of wood grew together into stairs that rose to the trunk's upper reaches, but an immovable trapdoor at their apex barred further exploration.

At first Merav and Hundeil spoke little at their shared suppers, but gradually he proffered carefully measured tidbits. "All milady's chambers exist in one place," he said. "Beneath this same roof. But they never merge. Only milady can move between them freely."

Merav asked him to explain. He tried: he and Merav could go only where their host allowed, he said. Yet in his experience, once permitted access to a room, he needed only to think of it to summon an arch that led there, until Olderra chose to once more bar his access.

After learning this, Merav tried repeatedly, without luck, to summon the chamber of floating shelves. She wanted to know what had become of Kaediya, who had not reappeared. Olderra, too, eluded her.

Hundeil talked of the workings of their home but would not discuss its history. He did confirm with nods and strategic silences some of Merav's suspicions: that Olderra never left the tree and yet could travel far beyond Dium Forest. That the tree held so many rooms within its unnatural dimensions that it was possible for many to live inside it and never cross paths.

He talked least about himself, until Merav finally asked him, "Who were you, before?"

In the middle of serving her soup, he dropped the ladle, slopping red sauce across the tabletop. As he cleaned with head bowed he muttered, "Milady prefers we not speak of such things."

Merav spread her hands. "I don't see her."

He snorted. "You believe she can't hear us?"

"I'm sure she can, but does she always listen?"

"Not a gamble I will make."

She couldn't stop herself from laughing. "What could you possibly say that would worry her? We are both trapped. Helpless as kittens in a sack."

His narrow jaw flexed, cords bulging in his neck. "We are not trapped. We are saved."

The rage her father so often inspired, that spurred her to call him coward and monster, reared its head. In retaliation for that rage, her father had more than once pinned her down and beat her, careful not to leave visible bruises—but that never stopped her. Hundeil was a sheep by comparison.

"You?" she mocked. "Saved from what? The arrow of some hunter who spied your horns through the trees?"

"The first time, an assassin's garrote," he said evenly, "when I commanded merchant ships for House Leursind."

Merav stared. House Leursind was only a story, attached to a burnt-black ruin of a demesne in Steermast Quarter, uninhabited for centuries.

His deep voice quavered. "Longsleeves, the second time—" His eyes widened in surprise at his own indiscretion, and he turned from her, head tilted in shame.

He had to mean the entity in the woods, its sleeves ever seeking prey to strangle.

"Is it a ghost?" she asked. "Longsleeves?"

He summoned an arch and left before she finished the final syllable.

He successfully avoided her for several days, until Olderra called her into the apothecary chamber with its hovering shelves, to reacquaint her with Kaediya.

"You friend returns to us from a far distance," the witch said. Behind her, Hundeil loomed, impassive.

A thorn-studded heap of vines sprawled atop the table, its foliage adorned with violet flowers. Their sickly-sweet scent flooded the room. Olderra opened her fingers, trickling powder into the heap.

The botanical mass coughed. Leaves and petals arranged themselves into a face. Kaediya's gray eyes stared out from it.

Merav burned with questions: why had her father's men brought Kaediya to the woods, why had Kaediya's house abducted Merav, why were House Uethorn's men ordered to mutilate her face? But Kaediya's expression held no recognition, no acknowledgment of her surroundings. Merav's hopes drained away.

Kaediya sat up, her form winding tighter into human shape. Olderra demanded, "Tell me your name."

Mute, the flower-woman regarded the witch.

Deprived of one set of answers, Merav aimed for another. "What is Longsleeves?"

Hundeil started.

Olderra seemed unsurprised. "Longsleeves is what it chose to be."

Some part of Merav, the same part that had enjoyed the weight of the ghost hanging from her belt, tried to keep her jaws closed, but it could no more stop her than her father could. "Milady, that's not an answer to my question. What is that creature?"

The floating shelves began returning to their places. "Your enemy," Olderra said.

"Why? Because it's *your* enemy?"

The witch addressed Kaediya. "You at least will be more docile. Can you use a broom? Did your family ever require you to wash your own things?"

Kaediya nodded.

"Good, then I don't have to teach you. Help her up." Hundeil extended a hand and Kaediya took it, her new flesh rustling as she stood. Yet another door when none had been before opened into a room filled with huge, gnarled roots. A black substance crusted every visible surface. "Go in, listen for my instructions," Olderra said.

Kaediya shuffled uncertainly toward the root-room. The arch folded closed behind her.

"Such a shame," Olderra said. "One mercy, at least. She won't understand she's scouring her own blood from the heart of the forest."

Merav and Kaediya had never been friends in Calcharra. Still, witnessing the girl's existence as a listless automaton angered Merav more. "What have you preserved her for? She'd have been better off left for dead."

"You say that because you despise Uethorn House."

"Not true." The vicious rivalry between the houses Uethorn and Lohmar had been a fact of her life from birth, but she had always assumed it resulted from their competing spice and fabric trades, and thus a war of markets, not weapons. Blood had been shed in centuries past, so she was told, because the Uethorns had resorted to murder to undermine Lohmar's influence with Calcharra nobility.

As she had grown older, Merav came to loathe her quick-fist-ed father far more than any nebulous feud. She had expected no danger whatsoever when Uethorn's men approached her outside Rosepike Market.

She pointed at the wall where Kaediya had departed. "I don't understand any part of what's happened to her, or to me, any more than I understand that creature in the forest that your strongman runs from. But I am certain you understand everything."

Hundeil and Olderra both eyed her. At last the antlered man grimaced at the witch. "It does no good to spurn the questions of the curious, milady."

"You would know that well, wouldn't you?" Olderra said.

The antlered man's face stayed inscrutable.

Olderra sighed. "We'll see where your curiosity leads me, then. The one called Longsleeves arrived as you did, a wounded bird brought to me when the covenant had been broken."

"Someone harmed her?"

"Yes." Olderra fell silent, her mouth working as if her next words resisted uttering. Her demeanor grew strange, lips peel-ing back, eyes squeezing tight, arms shaking as hands curled into fists.

At last she took a breath, then spoke rapidly, in pained sylla-bles. "There are men of Calcharra who—who mistake their wealth for a . . . a license to defy the Ones I serve, the Ones Who Dwell Be-tween, the masters of the forest. The brutes from Calcharra seek—seek to curry favor from ancient things, forces . . . order sacrifices that—that the Ones cannot abide. I am charged with righting the wrong, as best I can." She sighed as if she'd just set down a sack full of bricks, gasped for breath and resumed. "When those I save from death spill . . . spill blood unsanctioned, they . . . they reject the gift the Ones give them. They will never, never again be right with the forest."

Merav twitched her ears. The talk of sacrifice and seeking favor from ancient things and defying Ones that rule the forest made little sense to her, but she believed she understood one implica-tion. "Longsleeves lived here?"

Another deep breath. "Once. Now it has no home."

This is not my home, Merav thought. She pointed a clawed fin-ger at Hundeil. "What grudge does Longsleeves have with him?"

"Its grudge is with me," the witch said. "For that, Hundeil suffered."

"Twice milady has saved me from death," the antlered man said. "I am grateful for it."

"Grateful for what?" Merav's hackles rose. "Are *you* grateful that the forest gifts you with slaves?"

The witch had recovered her composure. "The forest requires it."

"What are you to the forest?"

Olderra scowled. "I should have left your mouth unmended."

"If you don't want these questions asked, surely you can stop me!"

"I understand why the Ones chose this shape for you, with its snapping jaws," Olderra said. "Longsleeves resented the forest's price as much as you do, broke the bargain, and incurred a debt that can never be paid."

A new arch had appeared behind the witch, leading into a unfamiliar room where thick shoots grew from the floor to form pedestals supporting heavy books. "If you desire knowledge so strongly, seek it there."

Merav peered into the odd library. The closest tome was illuminated in letters she didn't recognize. When she turned, brimming with more questions, the witch had vanished.

"She's indulging you," Hundeil said. "She allows your insolence because she's fond of you. Don't squander that."

"Fond of me!" Merav spat. "Then why did she refuse me answers? If she indulges me, it's because I'm nothing but a child's toy to her. One insignificant slave in a line of many. Just as you are."

Hundeil went rigid. They stood in silence, eyes locked, for a long, tense time, before Hundeil summoned an exit.

"She's a monster," Merav said, watching him go.

The next day Kaediya joined them in the dining hall. Her leafy brow crinkled above a puzzled stare as Merav tried to remind her of the dinners and dances they'd attended in Calcharra. Hundeil glared over his shoulder as he stirred the soup, silently entreating Merav to stop.

Throughout the meal Kaediya shook her head in response to every question Merav asked. At last Merav accepted then that she had to find a different path for answers.

She regarded the heavy antlers branching from Hundeil's crown.

In tales, ghosts spoke. They warned the living. Exposed the wicked. Revealed things only the dead could know. "Your prisoners," she asked him. "Can you talk to them?"

"What?"

"The heads that hang in your antlers. Can you speak with them?"

His scent grew acrid with outrage. "Their voices do not deserve to be heard."

"Our voices do," she said.

He let his silence express his disagreement.

Merav again accepted a door forever closed. He would never be her ally.

D ays passed without a glimpse of Olderra's cowl. Merav spent as much time as she could polishing jars in the room of shifting racks, which she privately named the Chamber of Spirits. She had discovered that sometimes, when she laid her palm on one of the jars, the ghost sealed inside would stir. Usually this produced a faint twist of smoke and little more, but sometimes she could make out a face.

Jintien could explain why her father had ordered Kaediya's killing. Perhaps he even knew why House Uethorn had targeted Merav. She spent days searching among the jars for his ghost, until the morning her frustration peaked. She started removing jars from the shelves two or three at a time and rubbing them with her paws. Perhaps in every dozenth jar a face congealed, but never Jintien's. She pulled a dozen more from the shelf, intent on testing them all.

Abruptly she awoke amidst her cushions of moss. From then on, whenever she focused her mind on the Chamber of Spirits, the arch she summoned always led somewhere else.

M erav crouched by the reflecting pool. Her vulpine features bared fangs in synchronicity with a soft, bitter laugh. Behind her Kaediya used a broom of thick straw to smooth the floor. At the noise she glanced Merav's way, face colorful, expression blank.

As Merav watched in the watery mirror, Kaediya finished her work and turned to leave. An arch opened before her—

Into the Chamber of Spirits.

Merav sprang, tackling the other woman and falling through with her as the entrance closed. Kaediya shrieked as they hit the floor. The sound wrenched at Merav, but she bounded upright and dashed between the racks, determined to resume her hunt. She might have only seconds before Olderra intervened.

She picked up a jar, clutched it between her palms, watched for smoke to stir. A face appeared, not the one she wanted. She slammed the jar back, grabbed another. Nothing. Next one, a face appeared—the same one as the first time. The racks had tricked her. It was her turn to shriek.

Kaediya shuffled close, leaning on her broom like a cane, her fright apparently forgotten. She watched Merav snatch and curse, the leaves of her brow crinkling. In a jar by her flowering shoulder a figure coalesced, its mouth and eyes stretching in fury, its fists flailing.

Merav swiped the jar holding Jintien's ghost before the racks could steal it away. Kaediya stumbled back, her body emitting a hiss of leaves disturbed.

Merav shook the jar. "Jintien! Hear me!"

Her old friend's face filled the vessel, his silent howl vibrating the glass. She tried to pry off the lid but it wouldn't budge. She applied her fox body's full strength to it. Muscles tore in her forearm, her shoulder. In her elbow, the sensation and sound of a cord snapping.

The lid broke free.

The ambient light dimmed. Jintien surged out, paying Merav no heed.

Kaediya screamed as smoke whipped around her. Vines tore loose from her body.

An itch to murder had possessed Merav when Kaediya's blood first had been spilled in the forest. As Jintien's ghost strove to complete his final mission, rend Kaediya leaf from limb, that itch returned a thousandfold. Taking life unsanctioned abused the goodwill of the Ones, defiled the forest.

The knowledge that a killer strove to break the forest covenant consumed Merav. Bloodlust coursed through her limbs. Jintien's head was forfeit. But the ghost had no head to claim, no blood she could spill, no flesh she could rend. She staggered, her rage deprived of focus.

Leaves and petals burst from the smoke that twisted about Kaediya's body. Kaediya's screams stopped. Her gray eyes fluttered to the ground, petals plucked and discarded. A new pair of eyes took their place, their familiar gaze dark and cruel in a manner that Merav had never before recognized.

As Jintien's spirit filled the emptied vessel of his victim, energies drew taut through Merav's flesh. The desire to kill poured a river through her, drowning out the voice within her that wept for Kaediya's murder. Before Jintian's new form could even draw breath she leapt, the wet roots and stems vile in her mouth as she tore head from shoulders.

The head unraveled, leaving her no trophy.

All about her an icy wind blew, and that wind carried Olderra's voice. "You impudent little fox, what have you done?"

Hundeil's forest of antlers charged into view. Merav, ruled by her thwarted craving, pounced on him without thinking, knocking dozens of jars to the floor as she attacked.

His blow knocked her aside as if the earth itself struck her, but her reflexes recovered faster. She grabbed his arm and vaulted forward to claw his face. A long strip of hide tore loose from his muzzle. He bellowed. The heads dangling in his antlers emitted ear-splitting wails.

"To spill blood unsanctioned is to reject the gift of the Ones." Olderra's voice rose like a river cresting its banks. "You are expelled from this sacred place! Join our enemy in exile!"

The jars and walls vanished. Merav stood among withered trees in a part of Dium Forest she'd never seen. Light blared through skeletal branches, the noonday sun a merciless witness. Three cart-lengths away, white fluttered. Longsleeves drifted toward her, un-coiling its tapering arms, face veiled under its long hood.

Merav's urge to attack warred with her fear, leaving her paralyzed as the long sleeves slithered to either side of her.

She only found the will to move when the rough cloth brushed her skin. She clawed at the fabric, and it tangled her wrists. She savaged a sleeve with her teeth but it looped around her head. She thrashed and bit. The cloth stretched and ripped, but more replaced it. In moments she was completely cocooned.

She kept struggling as the wrappings tightened. Something forcibly caught her chin and lifted it, like her father whenever she

had tried to avoid and ignore him. The fabric over her eyes parted
to grant her a view of Longsleeves' cowl as it lifted, opening into
raw, roiling hunger.

The folds of cloth hadn't covered her mouth. They were *avoiding* her mouth, the place where Uethorn's men had wounded her
and Olderra had healed her.

She demanded, "Who are you?"

The wrappings tightened, as smothering serpents.

"Why are you doing this?" Merav gasped.

And the creature answered.

Tableaux came to life in Merav's mind, flat and faded like aged
paintings, and yet they moved. The same nightmare that Merav
had lived since Uethorn's men took her to the cottage played out
again, with a different cast.

A girl bound and slung over the back of a horse, armsmen laughing as they bore her into the forest, to the same cottage. The merciless bite of an axe; her arms chopped away, leaving agony behind.

Heads dangling from antlers.

A ceiling like a tunnel. A second girl brought to the forest, the
thrill of killing the killers, puncturing them with poisonous fangs
and crushing them with the snake-like arms the forest gave her to
replace the ones the armsmen had hewn off.

Those same arms, transformed to white sleeves, squeezed her
now. Merav fought back not with claws and teeth but with will.
"Tell me your name," she wheezed.

The creature stilled, as if startled. The tableau of violence
subsided.

Merav heard a word. *Maelina.*

She knew that name. A great-great aunt, she would have been;
vanished long ago. Merav's father had spoken of her murder as the
worst of the long-simmering grievances with House Uethorn.

More memories poured from Longsleeves. The other girl en-
meshed in the tragedy, the one Maelina had helped save, given fish
scales for skin, a long mouth filled with needle teeth, water seeping from her hair. A Uethorn woman, dragged to the Dium Forest cottage to be slaughtered, flayed alive by men from Merav and
Maelina's own house. She and Maelina had hated one another even
before their reunion inside Olderra's tree. They did not recognize,
as Merav did now, that they were the victims of a ritual.

They had fought. Hundeil had tried and failed to intervene. Maelina, victorious, was banished . . .

Maelina and her enemy, Merav and Kaediya; their misfortunes followed a baffling but undeniable pattern. Had it gone on even before them? How far into the past did these ritual murders go?

Longsleeves—Maelina—trembled even as she tightened her grip. Merav could no longer speak. She hoped her thoughts spoke for her, that her words could break through the monster's mindless bloodlust. *You and I are bound by family and bloodshed.* The pressure built in her lungs, her brain. She tried to share her own memories, scenes of Hundeil waking her in the cabin, of Kaediya bleeding into the mud. *Look what I'm showing you. Our fates are bound to this horror. To this atrocity inflicted on us by the men of our Houses! We must defy it!*

Her head went light as the blood stopped flowing to her brain. Then she collapsed to the forest floor.

Longsleeves had released her.

Wind breathed against them as the entire forest seemed to sigh, in sadness, in relief.

"I am sorry," Olderra said.

Merav craned her aching neck to stare at the witch, who stood among the withered trees. Longsleeves slumped to a kneeling position. Its shoulders hitched in silent sobs.

Eyeing Olderra warily, Merav croaked, "What curse will you bring on us now?"

"You are within your rights to despise me," the witch said. "The rules of the Ones I serve are complex and exacting, inscrutable to mortals, and more than one has found them as intolerable as you do. But I am not responsible for the pact between your houses that has been a source of screams and spilled blood for four cold centuries."

Merav's voice, still little more than a whisper. "Pact?"

"The sacrifice of daughters, made to curry favor with things more ancient than this forest. Made inside that cabin, long ago. The greedy men who first swore themselves to this arrangement did not want the blood of their own daughters on their hands. But to kill a daughter from the other house, that was acceptable, that absolved them of what little guilt they might have entertained. They tailor the manner of death to harm what each girl values most. In your case, your words."

Merav found herself bereft of them.

"They might believe this approach curries more favor, but in truth it's a sadistic flourish to no purpose. All that matters to the creatures they propitiate is the bloodletting. They care not how it happens, or who is killed. Those ancient things despise the Ones I serve and savor any act that defiles the forest."

For all the hate Merav harbored for her father, its seething core still revolved around the notion that he had chosen to teach her, shelter her, prepare her for her life amid the merchants and nobles despite her defiant tantrums because he loved her, stupidly, imperfectly, brutally, but nonetheless as sincerely as his malformed soul could manage. As her grip on that notion loosened, that faith drained from her heart, her anger pouring in to fill the hollow that remained.

"Why," Merav rasped, "didn't you tell me this before?"

"I couldn't. I tried," the witch said, eyes lowered. "The pact made by your bloodlines in that cabin defies the forest law. It bound my tongue. Even the half-truth I managed to utter brought pain with each syllable." She anticipated the question at the tip of Merav's tongue. "When you spared each other, just now—" she nodded at Longsleeves, who still trembled— "that freed me to speak."

"How do I know you speak truth?" But even as Merav asked, she sensed the answer she had for so long sought: the filament of blood magic stitched through her, connected to the quivering figure beside her, to the scattered leaves of Kaediya's corpse, to Maelina's twice-dead rival, back into the darkness of memory and time; dead women hanging from its string like the ghostly heads that hung from Hundeil's antlers.

Hundeil. He loomed at the edge of the copse, watching Longsleeves, his muzzle still bloody from Merav's claws.

"This must end," Merav said. "How do we stop it?"

Longsleeves raised her head.

"It can be done," Olderra said. "But it cannot be done in Dium Forest. Once you leave, you cannot come back. And I will no longer know what can or will happen to you, or how long the body gifted to you by the forest will last."

"I am willing to go beyond your knowledge, Olderra. Tell me what it will take to end this."

Though at one time she could never have imagined it possible, when Olderra finished speaking, Merav offered the witch her thanks.

*D*on't *do this,* he said.
There's nothing for it, honored one. A shame, father, that your honor was never real.

That night, in the great hall of Lohmar, two daughters thought lost by some, and disposed of for good by others, reappeared, one with sleeves as long as dragons' tails, one with claws and the visage of a fox. Lohmar was only the first manse they would visit that night, but it was fitting they called first at their birthhome.

The guards were unable to raise any alarms as white cloth tightened around their throats.

The sun would rise to find the Manse Lohmar and Manse Uethorn eerily silent. All the men of both houses, every husband, brother and son, beheaded in the night. Daughters, mothers and wives submerged in unnatural sleep would awaken to bewilderment and weeping, never to know why they'd been spared.

For a moment, once the most urgent deed of all was done, once her father's head hung from her belt, Merav's heart shrilled with grief. But given what he'd hidden from her all her life, the plans he'd made for her fate, her sorrow died just as fast, a candle flame snuffed out.

She and Longsleeves left Calcharra, moving south ahead of the dawn. Tales of their exploits would live on centuries hence, in nightmares, in fantasies of vengeance, in fever dreams.

"TOUJOURS IL COÛTE TROP CHER."

with C. S. E. Cooney

"In the time of Shakespeare, Joan of Arc was accepted in England as a symbol for everything vile. He makes her out not only as a sorceress, but a charlatan and a hypocrite; and on top of that a coward, a liar and a common slut. I suspect they began to whitewash her when they decided that she was a virgin, that is a sexually deranged, or at least incomplete, animal, but the idea has always got people going, as any student of religion knows. Anyway, her stock went up to the point of canonization. Gilles de Rais, on the other hand, is equally a household word for monstrous vices and crimes. So much so, that he is even confused with the fabulous figure of Bluebeard, of whom, even were he real, we know nothing much beyond that he reacted in the most manly way to the problem of domestic infelicity . . . I think, then, it is not altogether unfair to assume that Gilles de Rais was to a large extent the victim of Catholic logic. Catholic logic: and the foul wish-phantasms generated of its repressions, and of its fear and ignorance. He wanted to confer a boon on humanity; therefore he consorted with the learned; therefore he murdered little children."
—Aleister Crowley

1. GILLES

Once I slept on satin. Now it's rat shit and straw,
goose-down pillows now piss-stained stone.

112

They told me they'd hang me from hooks if I didn't
confess to those lies, confess to dangling those boys,
strangling those boys, slitting those boys
and pulling out their innards, treating them as toys,
making them watch as I pulled them apart,
sitting on their stomachs and turning them blue,
watching veins bulge and burst as I . . . as I . . . as I . . .
but none of it true! None of it! None! I am no sadist, no Satanist,
no pederast, I am none of these things, I am favored
of the King, Marshall of France, I have spilled the blood of
    filthy islanders
across mile after mile to restore the glory of the throne!
But they thrust prongs and heated tongs in my face,
told me, move my tongue or die without one,
promised me torture if I did not admit torture,
pledged to sever my soul from Heaven if I did not give the Church
the false perversions it demanded. The Bishop, in his greed,
wants my manse, my lands, my title deeds, and if I must lose them,
    let it be!
But You, whose light, whose holy glow is surely that
I see through the slat in this forsaken door,
You must know what truth beats in my heart,
which will drop with me through the trap door in the morn
and snap when my neck cracks from my shoulders. Yes, You.
This light that shows me every granule of dust in this cell
could never come from the moon, not down here, not so removed.
O, Father, if it is You, grant miracles, spring the lock,
or grant me last sleep and escape to Paradise!
Let this luster be the last I ever see in this place!

2. JEANNE

Chevalier, at ease! The Maid is here, your Jeanne
your friend, it's been too many years, monsieur.
Your beard is long, your skin is loose, you smell as rank as I did
after weeks in Vermandois. But never mind!
How sweet to see you, looking up at me like that, as if I were
a light, a torch, a corpse burned thrice to prove my heresy—
    but pardon me—

of course you were not there! One forgets.
Do you regret those days, Chevalier? Or did you cast my memory
like ash into the Seine? I've heard so much about you in the interim:
alchemy, sodomy, theatrical productions, an attempt or more to raise
a demon, and now—your own execution! Another thing
    we have in common.
Is it comfort you seek, my comrade, my companion in arms?
Absolution? Veneration? Shall I kiss these weeping holes that
yesterday were fingernails, these wounds that bled confession
to deeds so dark they must be writ in blood?
Shall I change your sores to jewels, promise you a life eternal
at my side, beneath my banner, haloed, holy
with cherubim to diddle daily while seraphic fiddlers play?
Is this what you wish from me, Gilles de Rais?

3.) GILLES

What mad sorcery curls its fumes before my eyes?
This light you wear, it shines, swims behind your skin,
your face a lantern . . . you shimmer like a stained glass saint,
which you, crazed witch, could no more be than I
Lord of the Fairie Mounds. No Christian prayer of mine
could draw *you* as an answer. For damned Jeanne,
no Resurrection! This is no alchemy, no silly piddling
in fool's gold, this is evil beyond measure—Father,
O, Father, sweep aside this creature,
this luminescent shade of a madwoman . . .
Fraud in life and death! Fell devils spoke in many tongues
on the stage of your broken mind, their fervor stoking that glow
so magnetizing in your eyes, but it was my lone voice
won your campaigns. One more whisper in your head
but this one in your ear, to direct a mind pliant as butter.
Those armies behind you, gullible men eager for divine favor,
but it was I that engineered all your battlefield glory.

Father! Hear me! I have always been Your hand.
My blade drank soldiers, not children, emptied only deserving men
and more deserving cowards. I know no angel stands before me.
'Tis a last wile of that heinous bishop, to send

this Jeanne in effigy, blazing brighter than she did even in death.
This cannot be a thing of yours, Lord. Make it not be!

4.) JEANNE

I cry your pardon, cher seigneur!
Of course *you* know what's holy, what is pure,
you who've muttered all the Mass of Saint Sécair
from aft to fore, who've drunk deep of the waters
of the drowned, and lit your aloes and your incense
in a dead man's skull, until the black glass bell
of midnight rang, and ringing woke the angels from their
    dreams of hell.
You're the expert on the sacrosanct—no prince or priest
or half-baked prophet girl revivified from death
would dare deny it—why, Christ Himself has often pined to
transubstantiate His little toe into a sou, and with it pay
admission to your passion plays, those revelries
that rival paradise: what, again, your asking price?
A peasant boy, perhaps, so pretty, flushed and tender
crying *kyrie eleison* in shrill soprano splendor?
You shudder now. Can it be you don't remember?
Strange what we neglect in pious self-reflection,
what truths we conjure or discard at whim
naked in the light by which all other lights grow dim.
But shade or demon, Bride of Satan, Queen of Heaven
here I stand, sole witness to your last confession.
Therefore, Chevalier, my saintly Gilles de Rais
Speak on! For it is almost dawn.

5.) GILLES

You corrupt creature! Baffle my eyes with radiance,
with every perfect-mimicked manner, yet I say again,
you cannot be Heaven-sent, for no thing divine could open lips
and spew those vomitous lies with such aching-sweet smiles,
speak with such moist sadness as you spin mockeries,
    the greatest of these
your usurpation of a simple girl's face. You exist

in my delusions, it must be so, else you're another trick,
I'm sure, a last ploy of the bishops to absolve their own black guilts
over the vile untruths they have twisted from my throat.
I deny their false power. You are not there. You are illusion.
As are all these movements you conjure in the shadows,
all mere figment, these crawling limbs, fleeting mirage.
The walls do not seethe with spidery and shriveled cherubim.
They are not there. No eyeless youth plays cat's-cradle
with his own entrails in the corner. The floor is not smothered
with faces, baby-fat faces turning black as they wheeze
for breath. These cruel giggles that echo, those disgusting
moans of ecstasy, that is not my own voice, it—is—not. *It is not.*
Those smells, seeping, septic—that taste—what is this—
on my tongue? Lord. My God. Stop this! I pray—Strip away
these traitor senses! Father. Father! Father! Save me!

6.) JEANNE

All right! Enough, I say! Stop gibbering! Really, Gilles,
a man like you, of influence, ignominy—aren't you ashamed?
How you do groan and foam and slobber—oh, don't start up again,
        you hypocrite,
apostate, puppet, shrieking *Father, take this cup from me!*
As if you were the Star of Morning!
No, you're right, you're absolutely right, I'm not your girl,
        the Maid of Orleans
your Jeanne—she's gone, she's atomized, at one with all the universe,
        and she
shall be a saint famed the whole world over.
Young damsels swinging wooden swords will hope
        her tongue of flame
will render them important. But for you, my doomed one,
        a different myth shall bloom:
dark of root, ruin for its fruit
Young girls will whisper when they speak of you: they'll say
        your beard was blue
Yes, and how you snuffed a new wife every night and never
        knew contrition.
All the little boys who swarm your rotten robes will vanish,

like their very bodies vanished
into cesspits, into ovens, into cellars, into ditches,
    the obscurity of history
shall erase them and replace them with a story and a moral,
    so delicious, Gilles!
So refreshing, Gilles! This reminds me I must thank you.
After centuries of boredom, no one living who remembered me
I wandered regions waterless and galaxies afar
Then, unlikely as an angel in an abattoir, sweet summons!
    You called. I came.
Some dabbler, some amateur, stumbling inebriate on mysteries
    beyond his grasp
You thought your tainted rituals as empty as your prayers
To lift you up in your despair, or just to lift you up in general—
    a problem, I recall.
A game. A spoilt child's game. But such a game!

Oh, Gilles, why do you scream so? You should love this kind of play.
These kinds of playmates. Just a sample, just a taste, in the dark
    before sunrise,
of what awaits when the rope takes all your light away.
How I hate to leave you, Gilles, but dawn is breaking, night is ending
Now the pigs to trough, the birds to branch, the king to his levee
Now the soldier must march forth, face the shadows of the gallows
face the gibbet, face his Maker, make his *peace*—

How sweet your face, suffused with hope at idle words,
how trusting, how absurd! Such delight you'll be
down there in the dark with me, for eons, for eternity,
    for however long
your torment stills my wanderlust, distracts and entertains—
but at last, Chevalier, my attention drifts,
my light withdraws. I, too, forget. I'll wander on
while you and all your broken screams remain.

> *Voyez, regardez, Cieux! L'échafaud, c'est le monde,*
> *Je suis le bourreau sombre, et j'exécute Dieu.*
> —Victor Hugo

BINDING

The little apartment fills with mocking laughter, the exact kind you'd expect from cynical college-age souls who've just been told their host knows a story that could scare their hair white.

And when Christian, their host and gamemaster, goes on, with a twinkle in his eye, "I swear, it's true . . . after you hear it, you'll never want to set foot in the library again," that laughter gets hurricane loud.

Christian's sly, almost imperceptible smile holds its ground until the jeers of disbelief die down. "Sure, students aren't allowed in the stacks," he continues. "But that doesn't mean the library can actually keep them out."

Beth snorts. "So someone's gotten past security. Did they steal a book? Like one of those," she made air quotes with her fingers, "'priceless grimoires'?"

"Oh, it gets way hinkier than stealing." Christian's eyebrows rise conspiratorially. "Kinkier, even." From his post on the love seat, he scans the apartment living room, the assembled lads and ladies, three of each, arrayed on couch, extra chairs, floor. "We're all adults here, right?"

Beth again: "In body only."

The hoots of derision start again, but Christian's smile doesn't waver. He looks from face to face, sees he has each one hooked. If he says, "Fine, I won't tell this story," they will demand he keep going, threaten to bleed him if he doesn't.

To some degree their skepticism is all sham. They're already a captive audience. They dared him to scare them.

They come to his apartment off campus because he delivers the goods. Role-play gaming runs at its best when storytelling drives the collective delusion rather than chance dice rolls, and he can spin a story. But usually it's understood that his stories are pure balderdash.

This new tale, not part of the game, might not be made up. "Couple years ago, I had a fellow sharing the rent with me, Derek," Christian says. "I've never heard of anything scarier happening on this campus than what happened to him in the library."

"Ooh, did he meet an eldritch horror?" Preity tries to emulate Beth's knife-sharp sarcasm but she only succeeds in sounding slumber-party giggly.

"Wait, let me guess," butts in Oscar, who always seems compelled to one-up Preity. "He learned something mankind was never meant to know!"

He doesn't get a laugh. Christian says, "Any of you heard of the Sixth Floor Club?"

Tyrell, the biggest and youngest of the players, ROTC, U.S. Marine Corps Scholarship, leans forward, eyebrows already raised in disbelief. "That like the Mile High Club?" When Christian just smiles, Tyrell emits a deep-voiced cackle.

All the others join in except newest member Vonda, pink-haired and bespectacled, who shouts, "What's on the sixth floor?"

But no one can answer over Tyrell. "No way," his burst of mirth concludes, "absolutely no way."

"Man, there's always a way," says Eric, edgy Beth's big-shouldered but mild-mannered squeeze. She smirks. "But wow. Sixth floor, that's the big special collection. That's the sealed vault."

Six to one, but Christian says "Hush, now," and they do. "Once you understand a couple things about Derek, you won't find any of this far-fetched. I almost said 'hard to swallow.'"

This time, Vonda snorts. "Perv."

"Guilty as charged. So was Derek. But unlike me, he was pretty to look at. He was super slender, and he had this rock video haircut and really big blue doe eyes and a pouty lower lip, even. Kind of like what Audrey Hepburn would have looked like as a man." Eric and Tyrell, both body-builder buff, exchange looks. Beth notices and swats Eric on the shoulder. They're a funny couple, crew-cut Chinese electrical engineer and short, zaftig, sharp-tongued artist.

"Women love that look." Christian raised his hand to solemnly swear. "He'd go to the Friday poetry slams and come back here with a stunningly beautiful girl. Every week, a different girl. Always gorgeous. A couple times, two girls at once."

That shuts the macho boys up. Oscar fidgets, takes off his glasses, wipes them with a napkin. Preity asks, sounding honestly concerned, "Were you jealous?"

"Of course. But, eh, he didn't rub it in my face or anything. But then there was a girl, this pale spike-haired brunette named Bonnie, that lasted multiple weekends. And started hanging out here weekdays, too. At first I thought Derek had switched gears and started going steady with her. But once I was around them enough I figured out it wasn't that. It was all physical, like they were addicts, to each other. A big part of it, I thought, was that in Bonnie he'd found a girl who had no boundaries. Whatever he wanted to try, she was up for it. I remember seeing bruises on her neck. And they weren't hickies. Hell, I saw bruises on his neck, too. And bite marks. Like, scabbed. On her shoulder, on her thighs, not kidding. But she always seemed happy to be here, they were constantly, constantly sucking face. That could be weird to walk up on, 'cause they even sort of looked alike."

Oscar shifts uncomfortably in the bean bag chair. The rest are rapt. Tyrell rubs unconsciously at the anchor, globe and eagle tattoo on his shoulder, black against the dark brown of his skin. Maybe he's thinking about bite marks.

"I confess," says Christian, "I'm the one who told them about the Sixth Floor Club. They were both sophomores, hadn't heard of it. But I've been here a long time, as you know. That's what being a professional student does for you. I've heard all the urban legends.

"I didn't think they'd go for it for real."

The next time Derek and Bonnie let themselves in late, there was another guy with them. He'd brought multiple partners back, but another guy was a first. Older guy, kind of hippie looking, long gray hair pulled back in a ponytail. John Lennon glasses. I didn't ask any questions. I figured it was just the next experiment, you know?

Then a week went by when I didn't see Derek at all. Nor Bonnie, who by then had her own key. I figured maybe they'd switched to her place. But eight days after that threesome, Derek comes home alone. He woke me up at two in the morning. He was shaking like a leaf in a storm. Those big blue eyes of his were eerie when the moonlight from the window caught them.

He told me that I should never, ever tell anyone else about the Sixth Floor Club. I started to laugh at him and he punched me. He was a welterweight but his fist hit my mouth like a fucking brick.

We all love to imagine that when someone attacks like that we'll spring right up and whoop some ass. But I froze. I couldn't process it. And he kept on talking like nothing happened.

So he and Bonnie were members of this closed chat group for . . . sexual adventurers on campus, I guess you could say. I'd never heard of it, but I guess I wasn't surprised to learn that it existed and those two were in it.

They queried about the Sixth Floor Club after I told about it and got a lot of responses like *Oh, I've heard of that* and *I can't imagine a creepier place to fuck* and some being really into that idea and some angry that the topic had even been broached.

But Derek gets a private email from this guy named Lloyd. *I work at the library*, he says. *I can tell you the schedule and loan you the keys you'd need. I'll do it if you'll let me watch when you and your girlfriend go at it.*

So Derek immediately pings Bonnie to let her know and it's something they haven't tried yet, and she's all for it. Turns out Lloyd was the gray-haired guy they brought here.

Once they were in the bedroom he just sat in the chair by the desk and didn't say a word, didn't crack a smile. Something about that just made the whole situation that much more intense, Derek says to me. *We put on a real show for him*, he says, *especially Bonnie*.

I couldn't believe he was sharing some of the things he then shared with me. How he started to get resentful, because he had to hold back, watch himself, so that the show could keep going, but she could . . . you know . . . as many times as she wanted. And the guy, they didn't know if he was an actual librarian or a custodian or what, not saying a word, not asking to join in, not giving any sign he's even into it.

But then, Bonnie takes pity on Derek and starts doing something that's going to bring a big finish, so to speak. And right at the moment of truth, this Lloyd stands up, throws the keys on the bed and leaves without another word. The guy scared Bonnie when he did it and it made her bite down.

Luckily, the injury wasn't serious. *I think the fucker meant to make her do that*, Derek told me.

They had what they wanted, though, and Lloyd had already told them all the whens and wheres.

The next night was a Sunday, when the library closes early. They could do what they wanted to do and still be out before midnight. Campus security sometimes comes in to do rounds, but they don't go to the upper floors unless they hear a noise or something, and sometimes not even then. At least that's what Lloyd said.

Behind the library there's a stairwell, at the bottom of it is an emergency door, behind that is a staircase going all the way up the spine of the building, and they had a key to that door, and to the emergency door that opened from the back staircase right into the climate-controlled sixth floor vault.

He and Bonnie were pawing all over each other, all the way up. She was commando in a skirt so she wouldn't have to strip, Derek said. They thought about just staying on the sixth floor landing and getting it over with there. But that would have been cheating. They wanted, you know, to go the distance.

The vault was cold and absolutely as creepy as advertised. That musty, acidic smell of old paper was thick as a fog. The shelves were so tall and wide that Bonnie and Derek could only walk between them single file. No light reached them, so they had to use their cellphone flashlights, and doing that they discovered that the reason why the shelves were so big was because most of the books, or as you put it, Beth, *grimoires* arranged on those shelves were the size of headstones. In the light from their cellphones they looked cracked and pink like dried-out hide.

It seemed like every turn they took just sent them in circles. But Lloyd had told them about a soundproof reading room that, if they left the door open, would give them a view of the main entrance to the vault, so they'd see if a guard came in. Supposedly they'd have enough time to slip out that emergency exit before the guard could reach them. Derek wasn't so sure about that once they found the place.

But it was in for a penny, in for a pound. There was a table in the room with a lamp, and a wide, plush chair. Derek turned the chair so it faced the door and the aisle that led to the vault entrance. He took a seat and Bonnie straddled him. It was wonderful and incredibly frustrating at the same time, he told me, how it was his job to keep watch, to stare out into that dark vault, and Bonnie's job to make it impossible for him to concentrate.

Because she did her job really well, he didn't notice there was another person in the room with them. He shut his eyes to savor what was happening and when he opened them again a woman was standing just inside the door.

He was so off-guard, he didn't scream, didn't do anything. Bonnie didn't even notice.

The other girl didn't make a sound, just stood there, watching. Like Lloyd had, except that guy was old and creepy and this girl was take-your-breath-away beautiful. She had dark hair, dark skin, dark eyes—"dusky" was the word Derek used, I guess that was his English major showing—but she had a round face that projected the kind of innocence you see in vintage photos. She was kind of clothed that way too, wearing this pale, frilly, multi-layered thing that looked like a Victorian dressing gown.

She kept quiet, looking right into Derek's eyes as he and Bonnie kept grinding together. He stared right back at her, and the more he did, the prettier she looked. He didn't breathe a word about it to Bonnie. Something told him that if he did disaster would follow. And he didn't want to tell her. He didn't want to share. He held that other woman's gaze until he couldn't anymore. He actually said this to me, that he never orgasmed so hard in his life, like his brain was blasted right out of his skull.

When it was over the other woman was gone. He wanted to go looking for her right then and there but that would mean he had to tell Bonnie what had happened. She was all triumph and mischief and nibbles and he didn't want anything more to do with her. But he didn't let on, he said, just hurried them back the way they came, knowing he was never going to answer Bonnie's calls or texts or instant messages again.

Because he was going to go back and find that girl.

He stayed away from the apartment so Bonnie couldn't find him. She never came looking, so maybe she didn't care as much as he thought. It didn't matter though, because he could not stop thinking about the dusky woman on the sixth floor. There was nothing rational about this at all. Just like he knew he couldn't say anything to Bonnie, he knew he couldn't tell anyone else, either, or he'd ruin it. He would never see her again.

He'd have gone right back into the library the next night, but Lloyd had warned him in all caps not to go in there after midnight, and even though it sounded stupid and Lloyd offered no explanation, he made himself stick to the rule.

He skipped classes. He stayed out night after night. The wait was agony. He didn't sleep until Sunday rolled around and he could go back to the sixth floor vault.

Walking between those stacks alone was ten orders of magnitude worse. He started looking all around my room as he described it to me, like he thought something might have followed him.

Once he was back among the shelves, the shadows made by his little cellphone flashlight warped in ways that didn't match the objects he illuminated, and he kept hearing a noise like pages flipping. Or shuffling footsteps. He couldn't find the reading room, though he followed the same path. Finally his light went out, though his phone had plenty of charge.

When something brushed his back, he *did* scream.

It was her, her gown and her skin just different shades of darkness.

His fear drained away. He asked her name but she didn't answer. Instead she took his hand, led him to a big wooden table at the center of the vault. Next thing he knows her shift has dropped away and she's climbing onto the table, graceful as a cat. Dark as it was, he could see every curve of her against the shine of the polished tabletop. She smelled like salt and honeysuckle.

He didn't have to be told twice. He stripped and crawled on top of her. She wrapped her legs around him and drove him in. Everywhere his skin touched hers, it was like an electric current fired up his nerve endings. The noises around them got louder, and he could see movement in the shadows, solid things with glistening skin and sharp scales, but he did not care.

They kissed, and her teeth were long, he'd kissed many many girls and he knew hers were too long and sharp, but he also knew she wouldn't hurt him. Her body pitched and quivered under his, and he let all control go. He didn't realize how lost he was until she met his gaze, and he became aware that he was watching his own body hammer against hers, that he was floating somewhere above, like in a dream, and it was *that* gaze that she was staring into, while things moved in his peripheral vision, circling the table, their forms like crocodiles, except they had too many legs, too many eyes. That certainty that he was safe started to waver, and he tried to look at one of the creatures straight on.

But then she squeezed him even harder with her legs and if he thought the time before was the orgasm of his life, it was nothing compared to what happened then. He thought he was going to die and he wanted it to be true, would have been happy had that been his last moment alive.

But it wasn't.

Next thing he knows he's alone on the table. He could still hear those noises in the stacks.

He wanted to shout *Where are you?* but he was too scared. Something like a big heavy box bumped his head when he moved.

He managed to get dressed, though, and when he tried his phone again it worked. He shined his light on the object on the table. Then he started screaming.

At this point, there in my room, his voice cracked and he shook so hard I thought he was going to reenact his screaming fit. He started speaking really loud, like he was yelling at me, but he was still telling this story. He didn't remember leaving the library, just that next thing he knew he was standing in that outer stairwell. His phone showed him 3 a.m., though he'd snuck in about 9:30.

And as he's talking to me, he's shining that very same cell-phone light under his face, like this, and he's saying, that book on the table, it was one of those special ones they whisper about here at our creepy little university. It was bound in human skin. But even though it was flattened, stretched and lacquered, he could make out a face on the front cover. It was the dusky woman's face. The book was bound in her skin.

Nervous titters gradually amplify into full scale laughter as the assembled unwind themselves from Christian's campfire tale.

"You're a sick puppy," says Tyrell.

"Thank you," Christian replies.

"Wow, that was stupid," says Beth. "Did you yank that out of your ass or what?"

"Baby, you were breathing just as hard as the rest of us," says Eric, who gets punched for his insolence.

"I'm going to have nightmares now," says Preity. "And I'm not going to set foot anywhere near that library."

"You're welcome," says Christian.

It's Oscar who asks, "Where's Derek now?"

"Couldn't say," Christian says. "I never saw him again."

Amid the gasps, Beth pounces. "This Derek guy wasn't even real, was he?"

Christian just shrugs.

A new round of jeers results. But they are happy jeers. Christian smiles. He's done his job well. They'll be back.

Eventually everyone files out save Vonda, curled feline on the couch. She pats the spot next to her. Christian doesn't need to be told twice.

She asks, "So was there a Derek?"

"Maybe. I might have taken a liberty or two."

"Tell me."

He touches her cheek, brushes a fingertip against her lips. "Maybe."

She kisses his finger, then sucks on the tip, slides her lips all the way down to the knuckle.

Many nights later, Christian, which is not his real name, switches on a lamp, violating the darkness of the sixth floor vault. Before him on the big oak table lies a massive book, big as a suitcase. He spreads it open, flips past one ghastly image after another.

He pauses at a contorted visage that fills an entire page, its distortions making it appear as if it is simultaneously an ink illumination drawn by a deeply disturbed artist and a flattened specimen somehow shellacked onto the leaf.

Not-Christian flicks the image dead center, right in the uvula ringed by a screaming mouth compressed and stretched to three times human size. "Long time no see, buddy," he says. "Your escapades sure make a great story."

He keeps flipping, past more flattened frights. "And now we see who took the bait." At the last one, he gasps, child-like, as if his next words will be, "I'm telling ... "

His fingers shouldn't be able to find purchase on the smooth surface of the page, but somehow they do, and he pulls up a flap that wasn't there the instant before, stretches it, the dark brown membrane expanding to reveal the eagle, globe and anchor. "Oh, Tyrell," he says, "who'd have thought it would be you."

He lets the flap snap back into place, flips through the few remaining empty pages, then shuts the book. Gently, he places a hand over the face that greets him.

"Not long now, love." He brushes his fingers across empty eye-holes, draws them down to stroke the desiccated lips. "Not long at all."

NOLENS VOLENS

S onja could not abide the man's bloodshot stare any longer. "Mr. Reynolds," she said, pointing, "who is that at your window? Do you know him?"

Reynolds stopped his spiel and swiveled his massive head toward his office's luxurious bay window. "Mrs. Delgado," the attorney said in his deep plantation drawl—stretching out the *MIZZ-zuhzz*—"I don't see a single body out there."

Sonja followed his gaze. No one stood at the window. The lushly seeded lawn gleamed green. Even though she had just watched a man in faded camo, dark brown skin offsetting hair white as fleece, limp from the street to the window across that very same lawn, his cane spearing the soil, fierce eyes fixed on her the entire time. In the instant she had spoken to Reynolds, the man had vanished.

"He must have . . . have ducked below the windowsill," she said, knowing how silly she sounded as soon as the words left her mouth. "He was standing right there, staring at me."

Reynolds glanced over Sonja's head at Ferguson, the PI in his employ: a short, wiry man with a face like leather stretched over a wooden mask. Sonja turned in time to see Ferguson shrug. "I'll go check it out," he said in a voice rough as pitted pavement.

Reynolds offered a non-smile and, as the office door shut, rumbled, "You all right with talking business while we wait?" From a desk drawer, he withdrew a sheaf of papers, dense with small-print paragraphs. Feverish sapphires in his wide pink face, his tiny blue eyes scanned her expression. Every bit of the wealth the man had amassed seemed manifest in his swollen girth, the bulge of his jowls. "I think you'll find it's an extremely generous contract."

"You've not even said what you want me to do. I'm not signing one thing until you tell me."

"Now, obviously, Mrs. Delgado, I'm requesting your services as an interpreter for someone whose spoken English isn't so good. I know what I'm offering you triples your usual compensation."

"Which makes me suspicious."

"Of the job or the person offering it?" His smile bared large teeth between the cotton of mustache and beard.

She ignored the thrown gauntlet. "What case is this connected to?"

"One we're gonna get tossed out tout de suite with your help."

He awaited her next question, but she chose to let the silence stretch. The man at the window had tipped her out of equilibrium. She needed to regain her balance.

She regarded the attorney's face, beady-eyed to the point of cartoonish villainy. *¡Que feo!* Behind the moon of his head, the shelves of alphabetized law books spoke to a fussbudget nature at odds with his rumpled suit.

To her knowledge, Reynolds's heart held nothing but loathing for her gender and her race. His crony Mickey Burkhart had won election to council yammering garbage about secret Muslims sneaking across the Mexican border. The fact that Sonja's father was a Cuban refugee would make no difference to his ilk. Yet he wanted to offer her a lot of money based on professional reputation alone, so he claimed. Strings had to be attached.

He finally said, "I've been retained by Jefferson Dalton III."

Dalton was a scion of old money with a huge brick rambler of a house in the city and an even bigger one out in the northern quadrant of the county. Mona Rae Hunsaker—Dalton's flamboyant, bottle-blonde, young-enough-to-be-his-daughter mistress—turned up dead beneath the I-93 overpass two weeks ago. Police had released damn near nothing to the press, but Sonja had overheard just enough courthouse scuttlebutt to know that a throat slit ear-to-ear and a disconcerting absence of blood spatter severely undermined any substance-abuse-fueled-suicide theories.

Of course, Dalton had hired Reynolds. "You were expecting me to gasp in surprise?"

"If you give this a moment's thought, you might instead jump for joy at this windfall I've brought you."

"Judge Golden's assigned me a lot of cases this month. I'll need to check that list, make sure there're no conflicts of interest." If so, Reynolds's offer was DOA, and maybe that was a good thing.

He smirked. "I know there's no conflict. There is *nothing* on the dockets concerning my client, and with your help, there never will be."

Ferguson leaned in to whisper in Reynolds's ear. Sonja jumped, her chair scraping backward, her hands leaping to her heart. "¡Puta madre!" She had not heard the PI reenter the office.

The men ignored her. Reynolds's bushy eyebrows lowered, but whatever the unhappy news was, neither shared with Sonja.

When the PI straightened, he said, "You told her what we want yet?" He turned to Sonja without a pause for breath, speaking over her as she tried to ask about the man in the window. "I bet you think Jeff Dalton the Turd is a douchebag, and I don't blame you, but he didn't kill that girl. I got a lead on a witness who can clear our client, but he doesn't speak the language so good."

Sonja bristled. "The only language you bothered to learn, you mean."

Ferguson shrugged. "I know how to speak money and drugs. That's what matters in my line of work."

Sonja had heard such macho-sounding claptrap before, mainly from police officers justifying the bruise-covered faces of inmates. She gathered up her purse, shouldered the strap, and gripped her attaché with the test of good intention it contained still unsprung. "Sounds like you don't need me."

"Hey, hey, hey, I meant no offense." The PI's tone softened to a surreal degree, this gentle immediacy a complete mismatch coming from his pinched mouth. "This is only about acquiring a reliable affidavit from a Spanish-speaking witness." His gesture included Reynolds. "We lack the skill set for that. You come highly recommended."

Sonja knew better than to buy into obvious performances. Still, she sat back down.

"There's no doubt in my mind that what Jorge Mercado-Guerra has to say will prove our client's innocence. But to be sure, we need you."

"You're a neutral party," Reynolds chimed in. "Beyond reproach. Rare in this town. Exactly what we need."

"What makes you think he'll cooperate?"

"We know he wants to." Ferguson put his hands together in imitation of prayer. "He's made some mistakes in his life, but he has a conscience. He's devout, and it's not just a show."

"Uh huh. And what did you offer him?"

"A trustworthy translator." Reynolds again proffered the sheaf in his meaty hand. "Will you at least review the contract?"

She took it, noted the template it was drawn from, flipped straight to the page that specified payment. More than four times her standard court-appointment fee.

"I want to think about this," she said. "In the meantime, may I talk to you about something else?"

"You mean whatever's inside that sharp-looking briefcase?" His amusement grated between her shoulder blades.

"Yes," she said, keeping her voice free of inflection, a skill she'd honed over four years laboring in this city's hick-run legal system.

Even as she withdrew a pair of pamphlets, he went on, "I think I can save you the trouble of a speech. You're planning on a song and dance about that Erasing Barriers Foundation and what a help it is integrating the folks here who don't speak English."

Sonja stiffened, knowing full well how Reynolds viewed "Mexicans."

He reached out. "Lemme see."

Sonja passed him a pamphlet. He glanced over it and opened another desk drawer, retrieving an old-fashioned, extra-wide checkbook bound with thick metal rings. He flipped past a couple dozen carbon stubs to a blank white form and scrawled across it, handing the filled-out check to Sonja with a flourish. "A worthy cause."

Sonja had anticipated the attorney's refusal as the excuse she would need to end this conversation. Instead, she gasped despite herself. She was staring at a $200,000 donation.

"I'd prefer my support stay anonymous," Reynolds said.

Sonja had not completely lost her head. "What are you expecting in exchange for this?"

Reynolds waved a hand at her. "What a cynic you are, Mrs. Delgado. I expect nothing whatsoever. I'd have done this a long time ago if anyone had thought to ask."

Sincere or not, he had just given the EBF enough funds to hire two more instructors.

"And it's yours whether you take the job or not," Reynolds said. "Whatever you're of a mind to do, I need to hear by tomorrow noon."

By the time she left, she'd completely forgotten about the blood-shot-eyed watcher at the window.

T he microwave clock changed to 10:11. She stared at her cell-phone (which read 10:09), willing Ferguson to call.

She reread (yet again) the text message the PI had sent at 9:15: *off 2 get jorge will txt when en route 2 office stand by*

Nothing about this meshed with normal standards and protocols. It even violated that bedrock axiom: no attorney liked to work after 5 p.m., especially not a plush tomcat like Reynolds. Contrary to television farces, nothing that involved attorneys ever unfolded in a hurry.

For Reynolds to make arrangements to collect an affidavit at midnight, Jefferson Dalton III must have paid exorbitant cash up front. He had to be terrified that the long arm of the law was actually going to touch him.

She waited in silence at her kitchen bar, her phone the only object on its polished, faux marble surface. She could have clicked on the radio to help time pass but didn't. When Eduardo was still alive, before the cancer sprouted in his stomach and tore him apart from the inside, he would have scolded her to relax. *Staying wound up won't make this go faster,* he would say.

In the bleak moments, when she and the bedroom clock locked gazes at 3 a.m., she's wondered if his "que sera, sera" attitude was what sent him to the crematorium, his determination to light the dark corridors of her life so great that he refused to acknowledge the ball of agony growing inside him.

The house she once shared with Eduardo had reflected all his eccentricities: indoor brick facades and gardens of white pebbles, an abstract painting of a spiny red-and-black orb that he insisted was a portrait of Eleggua. The duplex she lived in now was bland beige and showroom neat as if she could abandon it at any moment, even though she had lived there three years. Eduardo would never have stood for it, but he had no mouth and no say.

The phone shook with an insect wing buzz, and the screen lit up. It wasn't Eduardo's voice that came to her just then but her mother's. *Sacude todo el dinero que puedas de ese comemierda, mi Luz. Y no confíes en él.*

Oh, mama, I know, she thought. She put Ferguson on speaker-phone. "Yes?"

"He's with me, and we're on the way. See ya at the office."

"My billable hours started with your text at 9:15."

The PI barked a laugh. "That's the fat man's problem, not mine."

W hen Sonja arrived at Reynolds's law office, Ferguson's scare-crow form awaited her, silhouetted in the open front en-trance. Goose pimples rose on her skin as she pushed past him, moving from the muggy night to a mausoleum-cold interior. The PI clanged the doors shut behind her.

Jorge sat across from the moon-sized lawyer in the same yield-ing leather chair Sonja had sat in for her audience. A small fellow: shorter than Sonja, skin browner, hair gelled in a pompadour, he wore a black T-shirt printed with an image of a nude woman em-bracing a skeleton with angel wings. His mouth hung open. When his gaze alighted on her, his lips stretched in an almost-smile.

Reynolds nodded his ponderous head in greeting.

Ferguson handed her a sheet of paper smudged with photo-copy toner. "Before we record anything, we need you to read this to him."

Sonja glanced at the paper—some sort of poem was printed on it, lines grouped in couplets—and studied Jorge's slack jaw. "Is he stoned?"

"He's doing great," Ferguson said. "He's waiting for you to read him that."

The poem was written in English. "You want me to translate *this* for him? Why? It's gibberish."

Reynolds harrumphed. "It's code. He won't utter a word until he hears it."

"That makes no sense—"

"It's not supposed to," Ferguson said. "Like Mr. Reynolds said, it's a code. It's gang-related. A nonsense rhyme makes a way more complex password than one word alone. I got this from a DEA source who slipped it to me from a sealed court file. But I don't know how to say it in Spanish."

Sonja shook her head. "You can't be serious. I can translate that, but it still might not come out the way he's expecting to hear it. If you're not just shitting me."

"I'm paying you," Reynolds said. "Quite well. That's all that matters."

Ferguson touched her shoulder. "Mrs. Delgado, I know you ain't got nothing in common with Jorge here. You never ran with a gang in your life. Gangs though—hard life, hard knocks—those are things I'm up to speed on. It won't hurt you to do this, and we won't get anywhere until you do. You'll see."

She glanced over the poem. It was strange, but wasn't poetry always strange?

Split my tongue and I become the serpent
Slice my heart and I become the vein
Pith my mind so I become your servant
Pierce my eyes and I'll embrace the pain

She took a stab at the first line. The translation came easily, as if another mind moved her lips and tongue, breathed through her throat. Her voice adopted a sing-song cadence. Reynolds was speaking in the same cadence as if he was reciting it with her except the basso syllables he uttered were neither English nor Spanish. She made out a phrase, unfamiliar syllables: *nolens volens.*

When she finished, she had no memory of the words she'd just recited. Jorge stared at her with glistening eyes, his lips stretched into a four-cornered rictus.

"Ask him if he's ready to talk now," the attorney rumbled.

Sonja intended to do nothing of the sort. She intended to demand an explanation from Reynolds, but instead she obeyed his order.

"Si," Jorge answered in a monotone.

"Please tell him that we're going to start recording."

She relayed the message, hardly registering her own voice. Jorge's head jerked as if he struggled to nod or struggled against the gesture. Ferguson took an eon to place a finger on the tape recorder perched on Reynolds's desk and push the record button down. *¡Qué raro! ¿Quién usa cinta de casete en estos días?* Sonja thought, a junk thought.

"Mrs. Delgado, this is where you earn your keep," Reynolds said. A dark, freezing cloud bloomed from his mouth.

* * *

"*D id you drug me?*"
　　"*Now, Mrs. Delgado, when could we have done that?*"
"*What's 'nolens volens'?*"
"*It's just Latin. Lawyer-speak.*"
"*Something happened . . .*"
"*Something wonderful. You were perfect. I cannot thank you enough.*"

The conversation took place in a dream for all Sonja knew. The nightmare of her husband's return blazed many times more vivid.

Lying atop the covers of her own bed, she had no memory of how she got there. Eduardo crouched naked between her bare legs, his weight distorting the mattress. The beautiful brown of his skin had blanched under the twin assaults of cancer and chemotherapy, but even in death, he'd never drained so pale. His bones strained against his skin. His bloodshot eyes fixed on her crotch.

He raised an arm. The skin of his hand had molted at the wrist, an empty flap like a rubber glove peeled loose from rot-moist, asphalt-black flesh and new fingers twice as long as before.

He touched the inside of her thighs, and each fingertip was a red-hot skewer searing into her fat and muscle. She screamed as he pressed down, her flesh boiling out around his acid palm.

Again she awoke screaming. This time, she resisted the exhaustion that kept dragging her back into sleep, only to frighten her awake with the same dream.

She blinked into curtain-filtered sunlight that banded the room at the wrong angle to signify morning.

She wore the camisole and pajama bottoms she always chose for sleeping. Her purse slouched atop her dresser where she never ever put it, a white envelope tucked into its side pouch that turned out to contain one of Reynolds's elongated checks, an amount scribbled across it that more than satisfied the terms of her contract. Her phone perched on her nightstand, fully charged.

Words glowed across its screen from a number she didn't recognize: *your handiwork is all over the news*

She grabbed up the phone and called the foundation, reached the after-business-hours automated response. Then she noticed the date on the display, which couldn't possibly be correct. She called the court clerk's office, again an automated response. She half-staggered, half-dashed, downstairs to the den. The Spanish newspaper sat in a neat stack atop the coffee table, the way she always positioned it. She grabbed the top copy: *Sábado, el 22 de Marzo,* the same date on her phone display. She had no memory of placing the papers there. She had no memory of anything beyond the interview with Jorge five days ago. And it was after 6 p.m., according to her phone. She never slept that late in her life.

all over the news

She scrolled through her social media feeds on her phone. A tingling like the jabs of hot needles spread from her chest and neck as she found the first relevant headline: "Authorities probe apparent suicide: man charged in Hunsaker slaying found dead in jail." Before she even read his name, she knew the "suspect" would be Jorge Mercado-Guerra.

He had turned himself in to the police Wednesday morning. No mention of Reynolds or even Dalton in any of the articles or video clips.

That pricking sensation descended her spine as she finally thought to check voicemail and found none. Not even missed calls. She had lost five entire days, missed a week's worth of meetings, classes, court appointments, and not one person had checked on her?

She wondered if television news might tell her more. Idly she regarded the screen, shiny and black as Eduardo's hand in her dream. Behind it, beyond the curtains that draped the sliding patio door, a shadow moved, a blurred silhouette of someone framed in sunlight. The figure took another step to the side and jumped.

Sonja recoiled toward the stairs with a shriek, but her eyes had deceived her. Nothing slammed against the glass doors.

¡Dios mío! ¿Qué caramba fue eso? But it could only have been a trick of the eye.

She yanked the curtains aside. The patio furniture gleamed happy colors, the unoccupied deck immaculate.

Head spinning, she rushed to the kitchen, threw open a top cupboard, and seized a bottle of Kahlúa that had sat unopened for more than a year. She downed half its bittersweet contents in a single desperate swig.

The last drops were disappearing down her throat when the doorbell rang.

"¿Quién está ahí?" she croaked.

It rang again. Mind swathed in woozy warmth, she squinted through the peephole. A black man with white hair leaned on a cane, his red-rimmed eyes looking back at her.

A swarm of angry flies buzzed in her brain, driving her to speak before her fear could stop it. "I saw you at Reynolds's office."

"And I saw you," he replied evenly, his voice like moist honeycomb.

"Are you part of what they did to me?"

"I might be your only hope of fixing it." His lips curled in a sad smile. "But first you'll have to help me figure out exactly what it is they did."

She tottered, caught herself against the door. "Why would you help me?"

"That lawyer's people once did me a wrong, but they didn't finish what they started. That's all you need to know." That smile widened, and she mirrored it. She couldn't help herself.

Sitting at her kitchen bar, still wearing his threadbare camo jacket, he introduced himself as John Hairston, "But my name don't matter one damn bit. That asshole Reynolds has a pact with the Boneyard, but I got one of my own. Now tell me what happened 'cause I have a hunch, and I wanna know if I'm right."

He spoke nonsense, but a compulsion to hang on every word kept Sonja rapt. In the back of her mind, her mother's voice repeated with increasing urgency, ¡Corre! ¡Corre! "Carter Reynolds hired me to interpret for that man who killed himself—"

"I don't care about that. Tell me about the incantation."

Tipsy, bewildered, angry, she wanted to tell him off for talking over her, and at the same time, she needed, for reasons not at all clear, to voice everything he wanted to hear. She resisted both impulses. "What do you mean, incantation?"

"Was there a song? A riddle?"

"Yes!" At once, she felt better. "They made me translate a poem."

Hairston leaned in, his breath reeking of something that wasn't alcohol. "How did the poem go?"

She shook her head, furious with herself. "I can't remember!"

"Did it start with splitting tongues and serpents?"

A shadow memory of her mouth moving while some other force spoke through it. "I . . . think so."

"And the patsy was compelled to confess. And a poor man died in a rich man's stead." She had her hands clasped on the bar, and he placed his atop them, engulfing them to the wrists in furnace warmth. "Was there anything else?"

There was. "He said Latin words. 'Nolens volens.' Said it was legalese."

"It sure is. Means 'willingly or unwillingly.' The right words for this situation." He squeezed Sonja's wrists. "You live clean, don't you? Like a nun?"

"What? I have a husband . . . had a husband . . . "

"That's just fine," he said. "I think the fat man finally fucked up. I think I can restore your mind. If you want me to. If I do that though, you're gonna understand what got done to you. That might save your life, or it might make its ending even worse."

An ending. An escape. The thought pushed against the compulsions that held her fast.

"You have two ways out of the mess you're in, ma'am. The quickest way is the most painful. Do nothing—what's coming for you will find you, and it'll be over. The other way, your life will never go back to what it was, but you get a chance to live. Not a good one but a chance."

That growing urge to flee finally found a voice. "I don't want to die."

His smile glowed from an abyss. "You accept my help then?"

"Please."

"Then listen." He recited a poem of his own.

She clutched the strings of Hairston's words, permitted herself to act in ways that made no ordinary sense. Throughout, she retained consciousness and clarity.

She drove to a crumbling slum she'd never been to before, parked by an alley too narrow for a car, and followed it into an empty courtyard lined with windows like plucked-out eyes. She whispered, "Nolens volens," three times. When she left, a shadow trailed her.

She went back to her duplex and watched television, the images passing the time without coalescing into meaning. The black thing stood behind her, reflected in the television screen every time the images went dark. Whenever she got up to relieve herself, she was alone in the den.

After midnight, she selected the longest knife from the kitchen and a small screwdriver from near the furnace and went for another drive, a shiver of pleasure tickling her spine as the shadow climbed into the car behind her. More joined it, crawling onto the roof, clinging to the undercarriage, even running beside the car on two legs or four as she led them all out into the country.

She had never driven that stretch of road, never seen that driveway burrowing through the trees, but she killed the headlights as she reached it and navigated every subsequent turn in the dark. She killed the engine before the tree line thinned. She emerged into an immaculate yard, moonlit silver, that encircled a luxurious plantation house, the columns of its full-surround porch proudly gleaming, its gables arched in condescension. No lights shone from the windows.

One of the shadows returned from a foray, projecting a picture into her mind, a guest-room window with the inner sash open, outer screen loose. A voice in her mind, her own, shouted ¡Esto esta chiflado! ¡¿Qué estoy haciendo!? but she popped the screen out with the screwdriver. The gap beneath the sash was narrow. Lucky that she was such a tiny woman.

As she padded through rooms and halls and up the stairs, a horde moved with her, their presence sending joy through her veins.

She found the bedroom door ajar. Beyond, a huge shape pulsed under floral comforters.

She wanted to run down the stairs, out the door. She pushed into the room. Heavy breathing filled the stuffy space.

Like a would-be parlor magician, she ripped the covers from the bed in one swooping flourish, exposing the monsters beneath.

A pale, quivering mountain covered with hoary down, Reynolds lay stark naked and erect, his tree-trunk-sized thighs spread wide. A woman that Sonja didn't know was squeezed between them, using both arms to push up his belly, so she could suck on the organ it shaded. She was older than Sonja but much younger than the lawyer.

Sonja struck with the knife, drawing a dark, liquid line into the fat above his groin. She spat, "Nolens volens." Adding after a moment, "¡Muera, comebola!"

Reynolds's lover sprang upright as he bellowed, propelling herself straight into the arms of the shadow-thing crawling up behind her. Her skin sizzled and boiled as soon as it contacted the creature's black flesh. Her scream didn't stop when the creature shoved a hand into her mouth. Red ichor gushed out around its wrist. Five more creatures joined it on the plush bed.

Somehow her muffled, gargling scream grew louder until the creature's acid flesh eroded the roof of her mouth, and its fist punched through into the bowl holding her brain.

Reynolds too was repeating the phrase, "Nolens volens," just as she had in the courtyard, but the creatures, already claimed by her incantation, ignored his attempts to conscript them to his will. The strings of Hairston's willpower guiding Sonja imparted this knowledge to her, what Reynolds was trying to do, why it wasn't working.

Tendrils of joy coiled through her belly.

The shadows corralled his mass, their limbs clamping around his and eating into his adipose like hot knives into marzipan. His chant became a howl.

The lead creature discarded the woman's limp body and crawled toward Reynolds's blood-streaked groin. It dipped its glistening head, and Reynolds screamed ten times louder. The creature kept crawling forward, the skin of its scalp dissolving the flesh it contacted, its head disappearing inside the attorney's belly. It continued, relentless, its shoulders burning against his wobbling thighs. Reynolds shrieked, a giant infant experiencing the reverse of birth.

Liquefied innards sloughed onto the mattress. Sonja marveled that the attorney was still awake, still shrieking, the creature hidden to the waist inside him now, and as before, she just *knew*, rejoicing in the revelation, that the shadows knew how to inflict hideous damage without triggering death, prolonging the cruelty to sweeten the sacrifice.

Reynolds's voice went silent, but his mouth kept working as if his cries had shifted into frequencies beyond human hearing.

He slumped, and the shadows went still.

The phantom ecstasy faded from Sonja's bloodstream. Her nerves thrummed with terror. She was alone in an unfamiliar bedroom with two corpses and a platoon of shadow-creatures, their slate-blank faces all turning toward her. She had been meant to die as a result of Reynolds's curse, as doomed a lamb as Jorge Mercado-Guerra. With Hairston's intervention, the attorney had died in her stead, but now the spell was at an end, and the shadows had no more compulsion to obey. They were free to act as they pleased.

Yet unlike Reynolds, Hairston had left her memory of all the spell's words and workings intact. She repeated, "Nolens volens," and the creatures stilled. Wisps of ecstasy stirred at the base of her spine.

She had not eaten since Hairston called at her duplex. Still somehow, she doubled over and vomited green bile until she couldn't breathe. The creatures, which did not breathe, remained huddled in the growing lake of Reynolds's blood. The vice compressing her lungs wouldn't release.

Outside, a car engine puttered to a stop. The creatures relayed to her mind the sounds of soft footsteps, a key clicking in a lock, a need for new sacrifice.

"Carter?" Ferguson called. "Penny?"

Perhaps the attorney and the PI had a link beyond employment, a bond extended by the unholy arts they trafficked in. Surely Ferguson had seen Sonja's car, must have driven around it. The eagerness of the creatures expanded through her body, their desire overcoming her revulsion.

Sonja wasn't alone as she descended the stairs.

Ferguson realized much more quickly than Reynolds that the creatures would ignore his command, and as he fled through the house, they gave chase. Sonja fought the temptation to follow the creatures, to indulge the pleasures worming through her and exult in the hunt and impending feast. When they were out of eyesight, she instead dashed out the front door, across the lawn, and into the woods, fumbling for her car keys as clouds hid the moon.

If she could reach the road, she would drive as far from the city as her gas tank would let her. Headlights blazing, she began the painstaking back-and-forth turns to swivel her car around. She hoped Ferguson could fend the creatures off a long time because if he died before she reached the end of the driveway, she knew she'd never get away.

She glanced in the rearview mirror and shrieked at the sight of her husband's death-paled face, anguish twisting his mouth, red-rimmed eyes bulging. But the back seat was empty, and when she checked the mirror again, he was gone.

SAD WISPS OF EMPTY SMOKE

Every time I split your lip I leave a ghost.
Dark stairs spiral down your throat, each step built
the day I crushed you to the wall,
fresh planks hammered down with each new blow
until you begged and I punched harder
while your mother cheered.
Shutters latched behind your eyelids
rattle loose each night.
Wind howls through your broken nose.
X-rays will show
even once your candles gutter out,
this house is haunted.

Funny—
in my husk years,
as tumors suck my innards out,
when your noises roust me and I scurry
to your boot, bite through to flesh,
each time your heel hovers
above my wheezing carapace,
your guilt stays the killing thud,
at most you
nudge me with a scrape of sole on tile
until I scuttle back beneath the floor.

Then I hear the specters,
the ones with open ribs like jaws,
resume their tearing at your eyes.

I dry to cinder in the crawlspace,
eclipsed by the wraiths I've left you.

BLUE EVOLUTION

The dark blue sea stretched to the horizon, flat as a drum skin, calm as the dead, a tinted mirror reflecting the cloudless sky.

Parrish, a beanpole-thin biologist, bellowed from the crow's nest, "They're coming! Dozens of them!"

Asad leaned on the forecastle railing, squinted past the bowsprit, seeking in vain whatever hints of motion spurred Parrish's alarm. Beside him, Dishita adjusted her goggles. She sucked in a sharp breath. "Hundreds," she whispered.

Asad's heart kicked double bass thunder. With a deep breath he turned to stare down the gun barrel pointed at his head. "Listen, this situation has gotten—"

Dishita spoke over him. "You have to let us get the instruments, or we're all going to die. Our crew, your crew, all of us."

The double-pommeled gun was extraordinary, the being that held it even more so. The depths of its obsidian body possessed a translucence that broke light into prismatic flows, as if rainbows pumped through its bloodstreams. It had four legs that splayed out from its torso like the legs of a bar stool, and four arms crowned with eight-fingered hands, two of which gripped the exotic weapon aimed at Asad and Dishita.

Its face a mask of crystal facets, its long eyespot shining crabapple green, the Pirate King irised open the coppery aperture it used for speech. "I detect no threat."

"Go to the rail and look down, then," Dishita snapped. Though the King did not react, Asad winced at her provocation. That strange bellows-like gun had turned Dr. Jensen, owner of the vessel, into an avalanche of slate blue slag, his remains scattered across the deck like someone had overturned a wheelbarrow full of colored gravel.

The King's mercenary crew, some four legged and iridescent like itself, some more humanoid if not exactly human, all carried similar weapons. For every one of the nine still-living expedition members aboard the *Argonautilus*, there were at least two pirate invaders. Epperly, their blond, nervous nanobiologist, knelt beside the wheel with his eyes shut, the guns of his two guards pressed against each of his ears in a dictionary definition of overkill.

The gleaming golden *Argonautilus* need not have taken the shape of an antique sailing ship. Dr. Jensen could have directed his engineers to press combinations of buttons that rendered the vessel into a streamlined yacht, or a hovering hydroplane, or a gaudy amber submarine.

Disconcertingly, Jensen chose the sailing ship shape, citing how it would look in drone footage and social media posts as it gleamed on the surface of the Dream Sea, with no regard for how it might impede the scientific mission, an especially frustrating development for Asad, who signed on in hopes of escaping the grotesque commercial ambition that infested the lab where he used to work.

In what Asad could only process as a cruel cosmic joke, seconds after the *Argonautilus* emerged from the hyperdimensional hole in sailing ship form, the pirate vessel emerged right above it and rained pirates like hatching spiders onto the golden deck.

Asad had assumed they were here to steal the *Argonautilus* itself, or the precious treasures it transported, the "instruments" Dishita had so rashly revealed to the Pirate King. But the pirates displayed no interest in either, not so far.

Above them, Parrish screamed, "We need to go below decks!"

"Kill that one," said the Pirate King.

"No!" Dishita sprang in front of Asad, a head shorter than him and sixty-four times fiercer. "He's right. We all need to get inside the ship. All of your crew, too!"

Motion past the starboard rail snagged the corner of Asad's vision. He turned his head. At once Dishita's death-defying panic made absolute sense.

In the distance, a tower-like structure rose from the waters, colored the same deep blue hue, as if the ocean extended a finger into the air to test the direction of the wind. Asad couldn't precisely gauge the dimensions of this sudden column—perhaps the size of a ten-story office tower, taller than any building in the Mid-western American town where he'd grown up. Points of glitter appeared on its surface, studding the tower base to tip with windows of all colors, irregular ovals all illuminated from within, dark spots at the centers in the shapes of diamonds, portholes, stars, symbols of infinity. Eyes, more than any living creature could ever need, staring in every direction.

The column continued to ascend from the depths, soon taller than any skyscraper Asad had ever seen.

Other massive blue columns breached the ocean surface, eye mosaics opening on exposure to the atmosphere. Five of them surrounded the ship, as if a titan's hand reached up from beneath, poised to close fingers into a fist and pull them under. Asad's mind spun faster as the illusion dissipated, the blue columns of multicolored eyes extending up and up, their proportions that of giant sequoias, then larger still. Dozens more surfaced, transforming the sea into a fast-sprouting forest. Water bulged portside within fifty meters of the *Argonautilus* as another creature emerged. This close its diameter was wide as the ship's length from prow to stern.

"The panopticons," Dishita said softly. "That's what Jensen called them."

How many fathoms deep did these creatures stretch? If one followed them down in a submersible, would they turn out to be the pseudopods of a single inconceivably vast creature? The inane tumble of questions stalled Asad from taking action. He wondered how Dishita had spotted them at all, goggles or no, as their epidermides so perfectly matched the ocean blue, and he wondered how he'd noticed *nothing*, as they were *so* immense, the inhabitants of the ship mites by comparison.

The pirates, too, had gone still. None had acted on their King's command to kill Parrish.

He contemplated tackling the King, wresting that gun away. By no means was he helpless in a fight, he'd enlisted in the solar navy to escape his tiny hometown, been lucky enough to serve in years of relative peace, plunged straight into collegiate science after his discharge.

He concluded that if he attacked, he would die instantly. Instead he tried for reason, astonished he could string together words at all, adrenaline and panic making him a motormouth.

"The owner of this ship told us all about these creatures, and he was the biggest expert on them that there ever was, but now that he's gone our crew is the best equipped to deal with them because of what he tried to teach us. See, their ancestors used to be human-size, and even sort of human-looking, but they weren't like us at all, not biologically, and they were intelligent, mean-tempered, cruel, always slaughtering each other but not to extinction, practicing this horrible self-inflicted natural selection, and time passes differently on this sea, much faster compared to other seas, so every time an expedition visited they'd find the inhabitants evolved by hundreds of years, and they've evolved even more now because in the records from the last expedition they weren't this big—"

The King interrupted. "What did you say they were?" Nice to know a being that fearsome-looking could betray befuddlement.

"We have equipment on board and procedures we're trained for that will protect us, *all* of us, but you have to let us do that work, you have to or we're all going to die. Keep your guns on us if you want or whatever, but you have to let us *move*."

Parrish shouted, "Oh my God, what are they doing?"

The Pirate King aimed its green gaze at the sky. The pirate vessel still hovered up there, its somewhat ludicrous design an amalgam of muscle car and teapot. The panopticons, a living nightmare city of blue flesh and prismatic eyes, had reached and surpassed the vessel's altitude.

The vessel blasted a bolt of green plasma from its spout, into the nearest panopticon. The substance of the creature wavered and wobbled in the vicinity of the impact, and a multitude of eyes blinked out, but otherwise it didn't react. No, wait, it did—the eyes on the side facing the vessel all brightened.

"Tell your crew to stand down!" Asad shouted, his words drowned out by the noise of the pirates' next attack. The vessel fired again and held the new beam steady, trying to slice through the panopticon like a monofilament through a tree trunk. The creatures immediately behind the target bent their ponderous stalks to avoid the energy beam. Their eyes, too, glowed most intensely in the direction facing the pirate vessel. None of that was as extraordinary as the manner the intended victim employed to avoid the strike.

It—and thus all of them—had to be made of many smaller, independently mobile globs, a colony creature. Those globs pressed out of the way as the green beam swiped through, creating a hole through the panopticon's body that moved at the same speed as the beam, so that the beam passed through without touching flesh. The eyes around the moving hole grew brighter and bigger, their inner light shifting to the same green hue.

Asad couldn't tell if the panopticon somehow reflected the pirates' own attack back at them, or spontaneously synthesized identical weaponized energy. The results made the question moot: the cluster of huge green eyes fired a volley of the same green blasts into the pirate vessel and cut it to pieces.

As the pieces fell, more eyes down the panopticon's length transformed and repurposed, pupils bulging open, sprouting teeth, snapping forward like heads of snakes to capture and devour every bit of the destroyed ship and the remains of its crew. Within seconds, the vessel had vanished.

Dishita stepped in where Asad had gone tongue-tied. "If you don't let us get the instruments, that will happen to all of us."

The eyes of the panopticon closest to the *Argonautilus* began to glow brighter.

The King lowered its gun so the barrel pointed at Dishita's face. The iris of its speech orifice rapidly expanded and contracted. "You will show us where the timefire hybrid parcels have been hidden. Do this and I permit you to defend us."

"Timefire—" Asad exclaimed, or started to. They had nothing so dangerous on board, not on a mission like this. But Dishita put a hand over his mouth. "I'll show you," she told the King. "I need Epperly and Nguyen with us." She pointed, indicating which crew members she meant. "You too, Asad." The King didn't budge. "Come with us and monitor us if you must."

The King inclined its head. Dishita took that as permission to proceed. With a release of breath, Asad followed. The King trailed right behind him, its footsteps a disconcerting arrhythmic clacking, multiplied as other pirates joined them.

Asad feared to whisper because he didn't know the acuity of the King's hearing. As they took the stairs belowdeck, the King still topside, he risked it. "Who told you we have timefire?"

"Not now," Dishita said. He heard her clearly, though she didn't turn her head.

The unfortunate Dr. Jensen had given himself old fashioned captain's quarters in the bow of the *Argonautilus*. Dishita led the entourage of armed pirates and prisoners all the way to Jensen's door. "It's in there. Asad, can you get it open?"

"Yes," Asad said, angry she had just revealed him as keeper of the codes.

"There's an object in there that looks like a vintage iron safe, but that's not what it is at all. It stores the timefire. Show them where it is." She turned to the King. "We can't afford delay. You have to let us get the instruments right now. Send guards with us if you don't trust us."

The glowing line of the King's eye oscillated as it made an assessment. "I will go with you." One of the pirate crew, its physiology similar to the King's, but with a pink glow to its eye and only three legs, shifted closer, jabbed its gun in Asad's back.

"Down to the cargo hold," Dishita said, and the rest of the party withdrew, leaving Asad alone with Pinkeye (in Asad's mind the obvious nickname).

Instead of one large iris for vocalizing, Pinkeye had three small ones, and when it spoke it sounded like a chorus of serpents. "Youss hasss sssixty ssseconds to ssshow me thessse parssselzzz."

"I'm trying, I'm trying, I have to remember how he hid—" Asad seized the nose of a fancy carving of the face of Frankenstein's monster, as described in the ancient book, not as seen in any vids, and twisted the mask aside to expose, "—the keypad." His fingers flew and the door opened into a museum quality 19th century Terran-style captain's quarters, excepting that everything was made to look like gold instead of wood. Such a strange choice. Maybe Jensen had been out of his mind, not just disconcertingly eccentric. Ironically, the portraits on the wall behind Jensen's desk provided the most anachronistic detail, depicted the team of four scientists who first visited this deadly sea, each face rendered in neon colors.

The safe squatted beside Jensen's berth. "Open it," Pinkeye said.

Asad's heart leaped into his throat. "You can't just open a containment vessel full of timefire! I'll die, you'll die, and even if your King survives the blast and the aftershock, there will be nothing of the parcels left to claim, if the King, if anyone, escapes this sea alive." In truth, Asad understood so little about timefire he had no idea if his words were accurate, but he had not been entrusted with the code to this safe, had not been told of its existence, and if he led with that he didn't think Pinkeye would believe him.

"Carriessss it," Pinkeye said, as if they weren't all about to be eaten by a horde of monsters the size of a metropolis. "Bringsss to my King."

As Asad expected, the safe was too heavy for him to lift. He squinched his eyes shut, sure that Pinkeye would first kill the prisoner before taking on the task of picking up the safe. Instead it said, "Walkksss in frontsss of ussss. Keeepsss fingerzzz toward ssseiling." Asad obeyed. He heard the scrape as Pinkeye pulled the safe forward and lifted it with the arms not holding the gun. He declined to imitate Lot's wife.

They reached the stairs to the deck at the same moment as Dishita and the King and the rest of that motley group. Asad noted Epperly was no longer with them and assumed the worst. Dishita and Nguyen both had tears streaking their cheeks, though Dishita kept her voice all business. "Asad, did you have any instrument training?"

"Kirigami module G," he said, and swallowed. "Minimal."

"That will have to do," Dishita said. "Nguyen can play module J. I'll have to handle both P and R."

No point in asking her if she was capable. She would absolutely fare better at that impossible multitask than Asad would at playing the G module.

They reemerged into an alarming escalation. The *Argonautilus* was trapped at the bottom of a well of blue flesh and blinding iridescent light. The panopticons had surrounded them on all sides, pressed against one another, walling in the ship. If they squeezed in closer they would crush the *Argonautilus*. Hundreds of eyes tracked every flicker of motion on the deck, putting every pirate and expedition member at the center of multiple mobile spotlights.

"We need to assemble the instruments," Dishita called, but the King and his minions weren't even paying attention; they had surrounded the safe. Grateful to see them distracted, Asad pitched in with the assembly.

A scream from Parrish interrupted their work. Heart spiked by fear, Asad glanced up to see the lanky biologist lifted from the crow's nest by a long, bright blue tongue, which slurped back with amphibian speed into a maw filled with deep red light.

They couldn't stop working. Asad prayed to whatever cruel powers that be for the panopticons to take a pirate next. Within a minute, his prayer was answered. One of the more humanoid raiders twirled toward the sky, the poor blighter caught by two tongues, body split like a wishbone when the tongues retracted.

"Positions," Dishita said. The instruments were ready. Asad put the mouthpiece of the G module to his lips.

Whoever had designed the four instruments that together formed a one-of-a-kind defense had a curious sense of humor. The inventions combined woodwind, percussion, strings and electronics. From the pores in their large ocarina-like sound chambers, membranes expanded that together formed distinct shapes as they modulated notes, tones, types of noise. An observer unaware of the particulars might have thought that Asad, Dishita and Nguyen were inflating improbable balloons that swelled to resemble dark-haired, pale-skinned men wearing outlandish paramilitary clothes. One had spectacles and a mustache, one had sideburns and a soul patch. The one that emerged from the G module had a full beard. Jensen had explained it as a tribute to the team of adventurers from centuries before, who had encountered the monsters in their original incarnations and discovered how to ward them off.

Mercifully the musical pattern Dishita picked was simple, perhaps deceptively so given the richness of its overall affect, but easier for Asad to harmonize with than some of the other possible options. The membranous doppelganger of that long ago bearded explorer opened its mouth to sing the notes Asad's playing provided, or maybe it was the other way around, because the tune pulled itself through Asad's throat, lips, and fingers with an effortlessness he had never achieved in rehearsal.

Above the melody, a howling, the cacophony of a hurricane heard through the walls of a concrete bunker. "They're trying to disrupt us," Dishita said. "Don't let them, keep playing." The fact that her words had cut through all the noise even though she was blowing into the mouthpieces of modules R and P might have distracted Asad worse than the protests of the panopticons, had he not been submerged in sheer survival instinct.

Asad snapped his head back and gasped, as if the mouthpiece had released him, not the other way around. Nguyen lay on the deck beside him, exhausted, sweat-sheened.

The forest of monsters was in retreat, the few that remained above the surface curling away, their bodies bowing like the necks of sea monsters to escape underwater, their once blue skins coated with thousands of small rose red growths that tangled in rouge lattices over their eyes. Waves rocked the *Argonautilus* as the panopticons dove en masse.

Asad's gasps changed to incredulous laughter. "We did *that*?"

The Pirate King occluded his view. "Open this container."

The business end of the King's gun hung mere centimeters from Asad's nose. With a giggle that bubbled from a place where absurdity trumped fear, Asad kissed the barrel.

The King must have pulled the triggers, but what emerged was a red flowery mass like the ones that had overwhelmed the panopticons. Asad cackled as the King lifted up its weapon to stare in elongated extraterrestrial consternation.

The wavering caricatures of the four explorers from long ago still stood at full height, though no one was playing the instruments. One made a child's version of a gun with forefinger and thumb and took aim. A bizarre happy warmth enveloped Asad as the King shuddered, and more flower-like growths burst forth from the slit of its eye and the iris of its mouth.

Still laughing, Asad seized the moment to wrest the gun away. This victory probably came too little too late, as the gun was most likely neutralized. The King hardly resisted, either paralyzed or dying.

Pinkeye lurched toward Asad, brandishing a similarly clogged weapon.

Asad hummed the song Dishita was singing in his mind and clamped down on the bulky weapon's triggers. Pinkeye bloomed like a flower garden in timelapse. Asad charged, continuing to hum and even scat Dishita's tune as he dealt similar fates to all the remaining pirates, even the ones that tried to surrender.

When he returned, he trained the gun on Dishita, who was spinning the dial on the safe. The outlandishly-clad explorers had retracted back into the instruments.

Seven of the expedition's crew remained, including himself and Dishita, who clearly had never been who she seemed. "Who are you?" Asad asked. "What are you?" And, as the safe clunked open, "Will that kill us?"

"I am a spy," she said simply. "The timefire parcels belonged to my people. Jensen stole them long ago. He brought them to this sea for purposes of experimentation. I intended to stop him but not like this. The pirates intercepted my message home. I am sorry."

A sadness tried to flood Asad, at the awful stupidity and the needless death wrought by inexplicable motivations, but the odd joy that enveloped him hung on. "Where is home?"

"Nowhere," Dishita said. Whatever she held, Asad didn't get a good look at it before she shrank into it and vanished, leaving nothing behind.

The remaining crew members decided not to waste the journey, and shifted the *Argonautilus* into a form that would allow them to explore under the water. But first they made one more use of the instruments, to put on a concert commemorating the dead.

THE IVY-SMOTHERED PALISADE

Dearest Eyan,

    If luck is on my side, I'll have returned before you ever find this.

If not, if Bryn is reading this to you, please know first and foremost that I love you and never wanted to leave your side. Nor did I leave out of fear. I've learned who slaughtered our peoples in the other three encampments. And I intend to stop it before it happens again. Before we're all exterminated.

If you read this and I have not returned, I beg you not to follow me. Leave your men behind, leave Calcharra, cross the mountains and never return.

I know you better than that. You won't. But you must at least find new hiding spaces. And never stop moving, though even that might not save you. If I've failed, if I don't come back, you're not safe. The muershadows will hunt down all who fight for Lady Garthand.

They are nothing the tales say they are, not a cult of assassins or berserkers driven by sorcery or vengeful demons. You can watch for them all night with blades drawn. You'll see nothing till their hands close around your throat and stifle the screams of your men.

I must tell you how I learned who they are, and why I have to leave.

As I write this, I'm sitting in the water room during the small hours. The sun will rise and set, and at dusk I will go to Manse Lohmar. I'm sure you know its grounds—that huge swath of land carved out of the middle of Rosepike Quarter, so overgrown with thornflower bushes that their branches snag the sleeves of passersby in places where the streets abut its boundaries. And I'm sure, like every living soul in all the seven quarters of Calcharra, you've grown up believing no one lives there.

That's a lie.

I've told you my mother and father joined in the Cabal of Grace that bribed one hundred thieves to break all the locks of Auguste Urnath's debtors' prison, and that they were betrayed and murdered in the first of Lord Urnath's Purges, and that I fled and fell in with the urchins hiding beneath the streets of Rosepike Quarter. Only the first part is true. I didn't escape, but the arms-men who forced my parents to drink the poison broth lacked the stomach to murder a child. So they bound me and dragged me to the Rosepike orphanage.

My first month there I cried and asked for my mother and father every night, and the nurses beat me for it and encouraged the other girls to mock me.

I didn't understand at the time what had happened to my parents or why I'd been taken. Over the years the nurses gave me so many contradictory answers that I learned not to trust anything they said. I wasn't the oldest of the girls in my wing, but I grew into the tallest and strongest, and the other orphans learned that snickering behind my back or stealing my reward-sweets brought dire consequences.

The three wings of the orphanage curl around a bleak stone courtyard, sealed on the fourth side by a black iron fence crowned with needle teeth. On warm days, when the Orphanmaster felt un-usually generous, we'd be allowed to run in that space, though I an-gered the Keepers so often that I spent most such days locked in one of the oven-hot fourth floor cells. Yet I had the same view through the window grilles that the other children did through the fence.

The back of the orphanage faced a flat stretch of thornflowers run riot, tall as a man, a half-mile deep and extending north and south as far as we could see from our vantage. Their blood-violet blooms with their reek crossing anise with onion taunted us as much as their spines and their burrs. Beyond that moat of brambles stood a palisade taller than the orphanage, taller than any buildings we could see, its immense stones so dense with vines you might at first glance mistake it for a forest. I wonder now, Eyan, if our vantage might not have been the only place in Rosepike Quarter where one can clearly view the palisade.

We didn't know the name of the place, only that it had to be centuries old. From my fourth floor cell, my face pressed to the bars, I made out the tops of trees beyond that wall, and past them towers, equally choked with ivy that didn't quite bind shut the mouths of empty windows. The nurses told us many stories about that place, some that gave me nightmares when I was younger, but by my tenth year in the orphanage I no longer believed any of them.

The day I escaped, I stole a knife and wore an extra tunic. In the courtyard, washing linens with the older girls, I simply set my work down, took my tub and washboard to the fence, placed the board on the tub propped against the fence posts, and stood first on one, then wobbly on the other, gripping the posts in my fists. Then I pulled my legs up, clenched the center post between my knees, and started to climb.

The other girls didn't follow me, but they didn't make noise, either. They wanted to see if I'd make it over, or die.

My arms trembled as I gripped the horizontal bar at the top. I swung my legs, hooked one bare foot into the space between two of the spikes, and pulled myself over with a yell. A spike tore my shin and I dropped headfirst into the thornflowers.

I didn't break a bone or lose an eye, but I hurt in so many places I could have just lain there until the Keepers snagged me with their mancatchers, but I made myself crawl. The girls starting shrieking, "Daeliya's escaped," and I heard the thumps of the armsmen's boots. I stayed on my hands and knees, used the knife to slash through the knotted stalks.

I'd forced my way through several yards of spiky tangle when I heard the Orphanmaster call. "I've told the armsmen not to waste their bolts. They'll be ready whenever you lift your head out."

That made my options clear as water. None of them would ever hear me beg for my life.

Perhaps the Orphanmaster hoped I'd bleed to death in that field. But I kept my head and chose my path carefully. When I reached the palisade the sun had set. Small slashes covered me, and bruises on bruises.

From the courtyard, climbing the bluff of ivy had seemed dog-simple. As I stared up at the weave of vines that at that moment looked taller than the thornflower moat was wide, I wondered if a crossbow bolt could be a mercy after all.

But I refused that fate. I found a sturdy stalk, with handholds and footholds, and started to haul myself up. The ivy proved to be layers deep, with some of the crisscrossing vines thick as tree trunks. Raw skin and bone-deep aches strove to bind my limbs, but I forged on.

It seemed like I climbed for hours in the starlight. In the dark, the thornflowers seemed as far away as the stars. Yet I kept ascending, until my arms and legs felt rubbery as gum.

When I reached the top I hoped the width of the blocks would allow me to lie down, but the vegetation mounded at the wall's crest made the surface treacherous. Nor did prospects improve on the other side. I'd thought that because I could see the tops of trees there might be a terraced garden and a short climb down awaiting me on the other side, but the trees loomed immense and ancient, and the grounds they shaded far below were lost in darkness.

I heard something moving on the wall, an animal rustling, and when I turned, the mat of wood and leaves I stood on cracked and tilted. Before I even understood what had happened I was falling, the twisted trunks blurring past as I scrabbled at nothing.

Perhaps it's a blessing that I don't remember the landing.

It should have been the end of me, Eyan, but it wasn't.

I lived in a dream state, awareness surfacing between waves of pain. Most of the time I floated in complete darkness. Sometimes I perceived a wavering light, its edges always shifting. At times I knew I was dreaming. Once I stood before a doorway, the room beyond so bright I couldn't make out its contents. People milled, the intense light reducing them to shadow. A gaunt woman stood in the entrance, blocking my view. A translucent veil covered her head-to-ankle, exposing only her feet, which were gray and wrinkled with age to an astonishing degree. Under the veil she raised her hand to her mouth, commanding silence, and a voice whispered in my ear, "At last. I won't let him know you're here."

I awoke. I lay in a large bed within a chamber that stretched off into cavernous dark, save for a lamp burning on a table. A slender boy sat in its glow, a huge book open before him. He let a page slide from fingers delicate as any girl's.

He could have stepped from one of the orphanage nurses' creepy tales of changelings. Hair like thistledown, arching brows, ears curled almost to a point. Then he noticed my stare and shocked me with his whispery voice. "You're awake. You must be thirsty."

I must have slipped from consciousness, because when I opened my eyes again his cold palm lifted my head. He pressed a flagon against my lips full of a drink like melon juice. Warmth spread through me and the pain receded.

I woke again alone in the black. Dank odors fouled the air, mildew and worse. Somewhere beyond the bed I heard someone bumping around. I called out and the sounds stopped, but no one answered. I lay hardly daring to breathe, yet either I was hallucinating or merely asleep again, for I had a vision of a spiraling stair of gold, more ornate and bejeweled than anything I'd ever imagined from the tales the nurses told. At its top stood the woman in the veil. She didn't speak, but I felt her gaze upon me.

At some point I opened my eyes. The boy with the lamp had returned. He offered food, though at first I was reluctant to try it. Fruits heaped the platter by my pillow, none like I'd ever seen before, as well as mushrooms, lichens, and stranger things. None tasted unpleasant, though they were bitter or salty or sour in unexpected ways.

I could move only my left arm to snatch morsels from the tray. Beneath the covers I'd been mummified in bandages, braced with wooden splints. I discovered this with furtive glances stolen as the boy absorbed himself in another book.

I jolted as he spoke. "I'm re-reading the Cantos of Olderra the Witch." The phrase meant nothing to me. He held up the tome so I could see its pages. "In these stanzas she twines her life with that of her mortal enemy, the warlock Elalef. So long as he's alive, she can't die, and if she dies, he will die too. I've hunted through many translations for hints to how she did it." The rows of symbols looked ominous to me. He recognized my bewilderment. "You don't know the story? This is one of the oldest versions, you can tell from the ridiculous number of repetitions of the 'H' rune." Then his eyes widened. "You don't know your letters."

A spike of anger jabbed through the warmth of the elixir he'd given me. "What's it to you if I don't?" That spike grew hotter. "Who are you anyway? Where am I?"

"I'm Leonind," he said. "You fell into our grove, but you didn't die, and I didn't let my stepbrothers kill you."

"Brothers?" I asked. "What brothers?"

But he ignored me. "Was I wrong to help you?"

I had no answer for that. Instead I asked, "You bandaged me?"

Impossibly, he grew paler, and I couldn't help but laugh a little, which appeared to humiliate him more. "I gave my stepsisters instructions and they did the work," he said. "I've done nothing improper."

Eyan, you know me best of all, so you know his embarrassment just made me laugh louder. Though I learned then that in my condition laughing led to agony. My broken bones singing, I reached out for the flagon, and despite my mockery he brought it, his mouth pressed in a dour line.

I dozed and dreamt of a voice haranguing me with questions: my name, where I came from, why I'd climbed the wall. I told the voice to leap off a tower and drown in a well, but it never stopped badgering.

The veiled woman stood at the end of a long balcony, arched doors regimented along the wall on one side and on the other a filigreed rail with an abyss beyond. She walked toward me on those grotesque feet, her steps silent. "Not so loud," she whispered. "Not so loud." I woke as a heavy object shifted in the dark. I lay there and listened with a panicked heart, but the sound never resumed.

My days and nights unspooled as one. I could only be certain I was conscious whenever Leonind appeared.

Once I shouted at him to leave me alone and struck at him. My fist never reached him. An arm lashed out from the shadows and a stone-gray hand clenched my wrist, strong and immobile as an iron ring. And as cold. I stared at its flesh, withered as salted meat, and saw it belonged to a person, or a semblance thereof, that had arms and legs and a head, but I made out no face or features. The shape defied my eyes, wouldn't condense into focus.

"Are you done?" Leonind asked.

Heart in mouth, I couldn't answer.

"Let her go," he said. Within a second the creature faded into the dark.

I understood at that moment that he and I were never alone and knew what I heard moving whenever he extinguished the lamp.

For a time after that, I was much less inclined to taunt him, though he never did anything to threaten me.

Long months seemed to pass in the dark. Slowly, under his unasked-for care, I healed.

He made it his business to attempt to teach me written words. He said he wanted to share the wonders locked within those leathery books. At first I scoffed and laughed, and savored the sour expression this induced. After my scare, I cooperated.

And I took to it like fire to paper sheaves. Eyan, I don't have time to account for everything to you, not now. We began with simple tales, the ones I knew from the nurses, but he required me to read them aloud from scribbles and if I tried to simply make them up—and several times I did—he immediately knew and his lips curled in a way that combined impatience, contempt, and an odd enjoyment, as if my rebellion entertained him.

We moved on to poetry etched in centuries-old runes. Once I could flex my right arm he allowed me a tablet and a stylus. On occasion I contemplated stabbing him with it but then recalled all the amazing tales he had spun through my mind, the stories of Olderra the Witch, the sagas of the Ice Prince, the ballads of the Nine Child Serpents, adventures I'd snatched for myself from the very page. Forgive my confession, Eyan, but the thought of ending it saddened and shamed me.

I trained another way, too, that galvanized my blood with fear the first time I tried it and every time after. When I was alone in the dark, when I heard nothing else moving in the chamber, I began to restore my mobility. I made myself crawl. I made myself walk. I couldn't tell you how long it took, but those opportunities didn't arise often. Sometimes, confronted with silence, I waited too long, too scared to move, and the lamp would light and Leonind would appear, my chance gone.

A long time passed, I don't know how long, the orphanage rendered a phantom of memory, before I could stand without collapsing. I started to range out into the room, which was vast and filled with detritus—rotted, splintered chairs, tables, shelves.

After the first painful bruise, which forced me to invent a lie for Leonind, I learned to navigate at a snail's pace on my hands and knees, one arm extended in front of me. That's how I at last found the door. I listened at its crack and thought I heard voices outside, though I couldn't be sure. I didn't dare call out, and I shook too hard with fear to press further, anxious that at any moment freezing hands would seize me in the dark.

The lessons continued, and if Leonind knew of my excursions he never let on. Reflecting back, I'm sure he didn't. I think he was so confident I couldn't escape that he never bothered to have me watched.

He said he'd share an odd story with me when I could write out the tale of Olderra and the Antlered Man from memory, without mistakes. At last I presented it to him, and I confess I took delight in his delight.

He claimed this story would scare me. I dared him to try—he had before, without success. What tale from the imagination could weigh upon me in that ghoulish place?

He told me that in the Goldbrook Quarter of Calcharra there once lived a man who by day was a powerful merchant in the quartz-mining trade and by night a lord of thieves, so brazen he'd wear stolen necklaces of platinum and bracelets of diamond when he called on other merchants. No treasuries were raided or ransoms demanded without his blessing. Those who defied his law suffered worse than those he targeted for plunder.

He believed that one estate here in Rosepike Quarter held riches that dwarfed his ill-gotten hoard. Its grounds could have engulfed an entire town, and the walls enclosing it stood taller than any tower. Tales painted this place of fearsome spires as home to a dynasty of necromancers, but the robber-merchant dabbled in the dark arts himself and sneered at the notion that any such person could pose a threat.

At this point in the telling I realized Leonind spoke of the manse itself, and I paused in my next writing exercise and listened in full.

The inhabitants of the manse ignored his offers of parlay. A pair of cutpurses sent to scout the grounds never returned. The robber-merchant stormed through the halls of his own manor, terrorizing his much younger wife and the tiny son who had filled him with such pride not long before.

A man like him had a web of favors to gather, and he reeled in the thickest of all. One of the nine Lords of Night had enlisted his assistance in eliminating a rival prior to ascending to that dark assassins' council. The robber-merchant approached this fell wizard and requested an alliance against the sorceress rumored to rule the manse.

No sooner had that pact been signed in blood than a caller came to the robber-merchant's manor. A wan, willowy girl with snow-white hair, she presented herself as the lady of Manse Lohmar. It's a wonder the thief king didn't snap her neck right then, but they consulted alone, and afterward he announced to his stunned and cowed household that the lady would become his second wife and the manse would become their new home.

His first wife refused with increasing hysterics to set foot in the place. Within that week, she vanished. Leonind's voice tightened like an oud string as he told me this.

The wedding took place in the grand ballroom the day the robber-merchant's servants brought his son to the manse. The priestess who presided over the wedding was like no other, a woman shrouded in red gauze whose voice cracked like brittle bones. The son never saw the girl with snow-white hair again. He heard his father's howls of terror all through the wedding night.

This story didn't scare me, but it certainly scared Leonind. His huge eyes focused somewhere other than the table and its tomes. An intuition told me he described the screams from memory, that he'd meant to tell this tale as if it had happened to someone else but lacked the composure for the task.

The robber-merchant's servants tended to the son, though fear bent their spines and whited their eyes. Even by day they lived by candlelight. His father turned quiet and pale as ash, and at night his screams echoed through the manse's maze of halls.

Then came the day his father regained color, the flush of fury, and ranted without pause. "The old witch tricked me, but I've taken care of that now, oh, yes . . . I'm so sorry, my boy, my boy. We can never leave this dark place, these cursed grounds, never. But we are free of her, and that knowledge will be our sun."

Yet that night his screams began anew, louder than ever before, and in between he yammered and wept, "No! No, no . . . ."

Leonind sat there beside the bed, mouth moving without uttering, until I demanded, "Well?"

And he snapped "Insolent!" and blew out the lamp.

But I refused sleep. I waited long, breathless minutes. Then, braved the dark.

I prowled to the entrance, pressed my ear against the door. And again heard distant voices.

My fingers found the latch, and slowly, so slowly I turned it, pushed the door open. Outside, the gloom only lightened by a shade.

I stayed in the opening a long time, barely breathing, until the dark haze coalesced into outlines and I realized I'd seen this setting before, in dreams. The doorway let out onto a long balcony, with an abyss yawning beyond the filigreed rail. I walked toward the rail in a crouch, and when I reached it I had to stifle a gasp. Above the cavernous pit hung a chandelier larger than a merchant ship, an intricate mass of webs and dust that hadn't shone with light in uncounted years, and yet it sparked in its depths with the dimmest of reflections from a light source deep below. The balcony I stood on was part of a mezzanine that completely encircled the entire vast ballroom. On the farther side I witnessed ghostly stairs.

I didn't dare to breathe as I peered over the railing.

The illumination came from a pair of torches, each held by a wide-eyed armsman. Two more gripped a shivering figure between them, a child, a slender youth or even a woman, I couldn't tell. The figure occasionally struggled, which revealed feet bound at the ankles.

In front of them, a tall, round man in robes bent on one knee in submission before a towering basalt throne. Whatever sat there glistened in the torchlight. It said, "You have prepared to pay the price?"

And when it spoke, I wanted to shield my ears and cover my nose. It sounded like screams bubbling from quicksand. Its mere words poisoned the air with a stench like corpses piled at the bottom of a well, so powerful it even reached me on my perch eight floors above.

The kneeling man swayed and stuttered. "My Lord Audrind, I would have the House of Ayfel trouble me no more." And then stammered, "Is it truly necessary to . . . ."

"You are welcome to change your mind," the thing said. "But you will never leave."

The supplicant sobbed, "Yes, Lord," and the captive whimpered.

"Let it be known then, Earl of Syburgh," said Lord Audrind, "on your behalf I will send my children out into the world where I cannot go, and each night they will seek anew, and never tire of the search, until every sire and babe and servant and soldier of House Ayfel breathes no more."

His voice so sickened me as I cringed behind the rail that I hardly understood his words. I heard the Earl say, "Yes, Lord."

Audrind's chuckle made his voice seem mild. "Now then," he said, "the overture."

A hiss, a scrape, and the Earl cried out. I had seen no one approach him, but he clutched a spurting stump where his left hand had been. One of the armsmen passed his torch to the other and rushed to his employer's side, applied a tourniquet. The Earl's mutilation had been expected and planned for.

"You will leave me to enjoy the aria alone," the thing on the throne said.

The captive must have had a gag in all along, because it slipped loose. "No, father, no, no!"

But the armsmen and the light retreated, leaving the captive to plead in darkness. And then, the shrieks . . . . I am no stranger to death, Eyan, but at no time in my life have I heard such terror and pain expressed in a single sound. And they went on, and on, and on.

Oh, Eyan, so often I've reflected on this moment and been so ashamed, that instead of trying to do something, anything, to help, I cowered and crawled away, groping blindly in the dark for the room Leonind kept me in, which in that moment of dumb-struck terror actually seemed a place of safety.

I found the door, slightly ajar, and fled inside with an awkward thump. I didn't recognize until I'd scurried well into the room what a terrible mistake I'd made.

A flare of illumination washed the chamber in flickering shadow and gleam. I'd gone through another door, into a different room, longer and wider than the one I knew. Runes were scratched on every visible inch of walls, ceiling and floor, some of which I could read. Repeated phrases: Death feeds life. Life breeds death. Death breathes.

Tall and heavy armoires slithering with gold filigree lined both sides of this horrid space, most with their doors open, spilling out once-beautiful gowns now molded and rotting. Other rags, hung within their cobwebbed interiors, reminded me of molted skins.

The glow came from behind the drawn curtains of a canopy bed larger than a house in the Rosepike slums. As I started to backpedal, the curtain parted. The woman in the veil stood there, silhouetted by wavering light, its source hidden behind her.

She wasn't as I'd seen her in dreams. Her filthy veil hung in shreds. Her feet, her legs, weren't of veined gray flesh but spun of bone and shadow and wet gristle. I saw hair through the veil, white as milk. Her eyes—I couldn't look at them.

The same voice that had spoken to me in sleep rasped in my ear. "You arrive too soon," it said. "Hide, or you will stay forever."

Behind me the door from the mezzanine creaked. I threw myself into the nearest open armoire as Lord Audrind slouched into the room. Eyan, I'll never know how he didn't spot me or hear me. Pressed against the back of the wardrobe amongst those chill leathery hangings, I couldn't see all of him, couldn't bear to look at what I did see. Only a massive, man-shaped thing, wet with decay, that paused, chest heaving, his stench threatening to turn my stomach inside-out. The monster started to thrash as if it fought an unseen force, and the light in the room thickened and contracted and pulled as if it were the lure and net and Audrind the fish. The air clotted and I struggled not to gag.

"Your petty games of torture and murder make you no braver, husband," the witch said. "Oh, my lovely children, afore your father turns you out for the hunt, *bring him hither.*"

And the skins fluttered around me in a bat-wing storm and flowed into the room, gaining mass as they did so, faceless gray shapes that swarmed Audrind as he flailed against them.

Fear blazed through me in a white fire. I gave up on hiding, sprinted for the exit.

Arms wrapped around me the moment I sprang into the hall.

To my credit, I didn't scream but fought for all I was worth, and though my attacker was strong he was also small. I punched him several times before I recognized the voice hissing at me. Leonind. "What are you doing? Stop. Stop. He'll hear you."

I fell still and he let me go.

"We have to get you back," he said. And I knew he meant back into the dark.

I backed away from him until I pressed against the rail.

"Please," he said, and for the first time I heard genuine sorrow in his voice. "If my father finds out you're here he'll tell my stepbrothers and stepsisters to kill you, and then they won't listen to me anymore."

And at that moment, Eyan, I began to connect all the strangeness together—the shapes in the dark that were his siblings, the story of the treacherous witch wedding and a father's evil ambitions, the woman in the veil and the monster that feared her. A husband and wife who walked though their flesh rotted, whose unnatural children lurked in darkness.

I finally voiced what I'd wanted to say for so long. "I want to leave."

He clenched his fists, closed his eyes. Grimaced. Opened them again. Of what he muttered in response, I heard only, " . . . someone to talk to . . . ."

I thought of all the brave heroes in the stories he'd forced me to decipher. My sorrow alarmed me, stoked my anger even hotter. "In another place, Leonind. Not here."

He moaned. "I can't. He told me I can't leave. He says the witch's spell binds my flesh as fast as it binds his."

I guessed at a piece of this puzzle he had not shared with me. "Will the curse end if you kill him?" And when he didn't answer I spat. "Coward! One way or the other I'll leave this place."

He stepped closer. "You'll never find the way out. My brothers and sisters will bring you back."

I climbed onto the rail, one leg dangling over eternity. "I will not live here." I couldn't stop my voice from trembling.

"No," he said, with no hint as to in what sense he meant it.

I'd called him a coward, but perhaps I was no better. I knew there'd be no nursing back to health after this fall to hard marble. So I said the thing that either might be the greatest mistake I've ever made or else the thing that might save us all. I told him, "Let me go, Leonind, and I'll come back for you."

I can't swear I meant it as a lie. Eyan, please don't hate me. It was long ago.

From behind the witch's chamber door, a deafening scream muffled Leonind's reply. He repeated it softly. "You swear on your poisoned parents' graves."

As I said "Yes," a gust disturbed the air.

We returned to the room where I'd lain so long in the dark. He asked me to drink the elixir one more time and told me his brothers would bear me out. I closed my eyes, certain they'd never open again, but they did when sunlight seared them. I lay in horse-barn straw in the Steermast Quarter, as far from the Manse Lohmar as Calcharra's battlements allow. Leonind had kept his promise.

But I didn't keep mine.

Many things happened, Eyan, between then and the first time I met you. Most of them you know.

I already despised Lord Urnath for the same reasons you do. Yet Lady Garthand won my heart long before Urnath drove her into exile, when she exposed the Earl of Syburgh's depravities without a single sword drawn, and even Urnath couldn't spare him from the guillotine. That was the day I learned that the cruel cannot always trump the fair, and you, Eyan, couldn't know till now how my heart sang.

As you hear this account you may have recognized the House Ayfel, once enemies of Syburgh, snuffed out overnight after the Earl's son vanished. Everyone believed the one was retaliation for the other. I know differently. The son was the price.

And I'm sure you've heard the word "muershadows" whispered when talk turns to the end of House Ayfel. Or to other horrors. The slaughter of the Candlemakers' Guild. The sudden deaths of the entire Oceanside Prelate.

I lived with the knowledge of who the muershadows really are, and tried to forget that I knew it, that I had ever learned it.

I believe Ariste's son Worulz has become so frightened of Lady Garthand and her forces underground that he's made this dark bargain. I wonder which heir has gone missing. Or perhaps even more than one?

Eyan, it's only because we're so scattered and so well hidden that we're not all dead already.

I can hear you now: "What makes you so sure?"

Last night as the camp slept, as I slept, a hand cold and unyielding as a gravestone clamped over my mouth.

I opened my eyes in complete darkness and for a second believed I'd undergone the worst wakening of all, that I was still in the manse, lying in that pitch-black room.

But my vision adjusted until I could see the crumbling plaster frescoes of this buried cathedral, the old tapestries hanging from ropes that partition our pallets from the rest of the revolutionaries. The thing gripping my mouth crouched beside me, not moving, not breathing, no pulse in its fingers. I knew instantly what manner of being it must be.

An edge pressed against my throat. I flinched, but the object flexed and failed to cut. Then the hand was gone, and the creature with it. A folded letter lay across my throat. I recognized the script, though I didn't need to guess who had written it.

I've enclosed the letter, though Bryn will not be able to decipher its runes. It reads, "You are in grave danger if you stay. You must leave that cell of thieves and never return. You know why. And you know the only place where safety lies."

You told me, Eyan, you thought sorcery must have had a role in the butchery at the camp within the Pauper Catacombs. But I tell you sorcery has been behind every attack on Garthand's fighters, at Toothgate, at Speaking Cavern, even in the massacre of our people as they prepared to storm the Urnath vault.

Every sire. Every child. Every servant. Every soldier. Lady Garthand herself when she returns. Audrind's brood will come for all of us. There will be no warning, no time even for screams. And if you go to the Manse Lohmar yourself to bring the battle to them, you'll meet the same end.

Only I can go, because Leonind has allowed, and because his father still knows nothing of me.

I don't want to go back. And yet, Eyan, the dream that troubled me before that hand touched my face—it could not have been coincidence.

In it, I was climbing down the outside of the ivy-smothered palisade. I looked up to see Leonind following, anxiously seeking purchase. He looked no older than he did when he cared for me in the Manse all that time ago, and I imagine for an enchanted creature such as him this could be so.

Hurry, I said, though I heard no rustle of pursuit.

He descended gingerly, and I knew the heavy sack tied at his hip held something terrible inside. *Hurry*, I hissed again, and kept urging him on until I let go and dropped into the thornflowers.

A wind sighed as he struggled the last few yards. Thin as he was, his clothes billowed on his frame. He either chose to leap or lost his grip, I'm not sure which.

When he landed his legs snapped beneath him. He collapsed as if kneeling.

His elfin face withered tight to his skull and blackened as if licked by fire. His eyes rolled and bulged between shriveling eyelids. His mouth stretched open as his teeth dropped out. He touched my arm with fingers like old twigs, papery and long-dried.

I can't tell you if revulsion, rage, or pity drove me to strike. I kicked him.

He burst in a gout of dust.

Then I knelt and sifted through that dust, searching for the bag and what it contained—his father Audrind's head. Yet I found nothing.

The wind rose again, shrill cackles carried on its breath. I looked up and saw the witch standing with me in the brambles, her veil stretching around her skeletal form like demon wings. She rose into the sky until my gaze could no longer track her.

And then I awoke, that cold hand over my mouth.

So, Eyan, if I've been granted a vision of what's to come, of what will save us, it can only happen if I do as Leonind demands.

May the goddess who guides our Lady bless my steps and grant me luck, that your ears are never cursed to hear this story.

The dusk is thickening. I go.

WITH SHINING GIFTS THAT TOOK ALL EYES

Candace feels no breeze, though the silhouette of the house-plant shimmies behind the window curtain, the long fronds of its leaves wriggling like legs. That curtain should flutter with equal agitation, but it hangs motionless. Candace shudders, goose pimples stippling her arms.

"Donny?" she calls. "Could you shut the window?"

She could swear she heard him moving around in his home office, saw a brief dimming cross the wall as he eclipsed a lamp while fussing with his chair. Candace holds herself still, even holds her breath. All is still with the office save the movement of the leaves. No lethargic mutter of acknowledgement answers her, no floorboards creaking as a body's weight shifts. Only minutes ago, it seems, the time between spliced away by sleep, his hands had pushed back her thighs, and a wild notion takes her that his warm touch had been deception, a ruse carried out by a ghost.

Her wet hair wrapped by a towel, she cinches her robe tighter and steps out of the steam cloud emerging through the bathroom door. Immediately she regrets it. The cold deepens, the goose pimples spreading up her arms to her neck. The plant sways as if it were a palm tree in a storm.

The chill is inexplicable as the animated plant. There's no sensation of air brushing her shower-damp skin. Not a peep from Donny when she calls his name again. He's sitting just out of view—how hard can it be for him to get up and close the window, it's right there behind him, not three feet from his chair.

The weight of his shoulders against her hips perhaps had masked a deception of a different sort. He's back to his usual self, easily distracted, prone to ignoring her. She takes a deep breath to repel the chill and her mounting impatience and walks into his office, which stands empty. Yet Donny was in here, somehow, and heard her, somehow, because the plant is gone from the window. She pulls the white gauze of the curtain aside, unveiling fog thick as cotton batting, the afternoon light diffused to gray.

A screen saver jitters on Donny's outdated monitor, a chubby eight-legged monster chewing away at a pastoral rendition of rolling hills. For a fleeting instant she conflates the monster's teeth with Donny's, the nips at her neck before he descended lower.

She used to find the animation funny, then tiresome—eight years and he's never switched it out. Now the cartoonish grossness grates on her.

At the other end of the house, a floorboard creaks. She slips right to the edge of calling Donny's name again, but stops herself, instinct counseling silence. She retreats in a slow creep, peers down the hall, across the darkened dining room, through an archway, into the room where she and Donny often settle on a hand-me-down couch to watch the few shows they both enjoy on a flatscreen television that might well be the most expensive thing they own. Beyond the TV, behind drawn curtains, the silhouette of a houseplant waggles in the window.

An all-too-familiar pain taps behind her right eye, then presses, exerting a malevolent pressure. *Not now*, she implores. *Not now.*

Donny isn't in the living room. She can't fathom how he moved the plant.

This time, at least, air currents cause the curtain to ripple. Outside, children shriek. The dilemma clenches in her chest. She doesn't want the neighbor kids to see her wearing nothing but a robe, but if anything the house is colder yet and this window is definitely open. She hurries to it, discovers a two-foot gap between sash and sill, struggles with the reluctant latch as one of the shrill voices from across the street calls her name. In the fog, she can't tell which child spotted her. How inconveniently sharp his vision has to be.

As she tugs the latch abruptly loosens and the window slams shut so hard she fears broken glass. She cringes as if Donny slapped his hands together beside her ear, a stunt he loved to pull when they were younger, he loved making her shriek.

A sludge of pain flows down her spine into her belly. Confirmation a migraine is boiling up.

The same kid shrieks her name again. She flinches backward, something snags her bad ankle and her ungainly topple spills her onto the couch. She gasps at the twinge in her back, the cushions so worn that the front frame digs into her shoulders. Donny had pinned her that way once, in this same place, gripping her wrists, her back arched uncomfortably as he leaned to thrust his hips in her face. She had done what she had to do to get it over with, trying to concentrate on how his chest and belly tensed with each movement of her mouth, a sight she had enjoyed in other circumstances.

Why is she thinking of that now? Because the pain echoes through the years? Gaze level with the sill, she registers that the plant isn't in the window, wasn't there when she pulled it shut. Donny is messing with her somehow and not in a nice way. It must be that he's pissed at her still, because they need to go visit her sister in the rehab center and he doesn't want to. She doesn't want to either, but there's no hope for Chrystal at all if no one offers her a lifeline. He's told her that he understood this. He swore to her that he grokked that poor Chrystal was the only family she had left.

But Donny hasn't been able to move that quickly since he hurt his back and he's not skinny anymore. If he was taking out his aggression on her by moving that plant around, she for sure would have seen him do it.

A chair in the dining room slides across the hardwood floor. Her heart backflips. A tiny thunder rumbles in the empty room, like panicked cats scrambling. For an instant she really does believe she hears clumsy cat steps—but that can't be. Those cats she's remembering, two chunky monkeys from the same litter, one of them died months ago, the other one years ago. Candace does believe in ghosts, or at least the metaphor of regret they represent, but not in ones that vibrate floorboards with tangible weight and mass.

Debunking that notion sends the previous one floundering away. She and Donny weren't going to see her sister today, rehab ended five months ago and after Chrystal's release she'd gone right back to her drug-dealing, gun-fetishizing boyfriend. Donny had admirably refrained from saying *I told you so.*

Her memory, what had warped it so? Had the exertions of the morning given her a small stroke? The throbbing in her skull denies access to the answer.

Candace works third shift at a factory that assembles different sizes of syringes. She was showering in the afternoon because she slept in after her shift, she's sure of that. She can't remember if Donny was awake when she got home. Too tired to care, she'd crawled in bed next to him after stuffing in ear plugs to ward off his snoring, the sound exactly like the grunts of pigs rutting.

A morning that began just like hundreds of others, and what happened next intruded in her memory like it came from a different universe. His hand on her belly, under her shirt. His lips pecking at her cheek like a child's kisses, engaging fully when she brought her mouth to meet his. The nips at her neck, the tongue at her nipples, tickling her navel, her knees pushed up to her breasts, his shoulders pressed against the backs of her thighs as he slid down further, started to suck on her, his fingernails stabbing her a little as he worked his way in, up to the knuckles of his index and middle finger. Eventually he would stop, climb back up her and push his way inside, except this time he didn't, he stayed down there, sucking, matching the staccato of her gasping breath. He had not gone at her that way in months, maybe in years. His hydrangea-blue eyes stayed focused on her face, his gaze meeting hers whenever she briefly opened her eyes and bent her neck to watch what he was doing.

She lost herself so she doesn't remember when he stopped, or how. Nor will her memory confirm whether he was out of bed when she woke up, whether she actually saw him in his office when she got up to shower, or heard the clicks of keyboard and mouse.

Another chair shifts, and not only does she hear it, she sees it jerk away from the table. Several of the kids outside scream at once, the sounds coinciding with her own short shriek.

Her mind and heart race together. An animal found its way inside, a squirrel most likely. That's happened before, one crawled through a cracked window into the basement, a frightened and frightening homunculus in a dim, cramped space. Donny put sheets of cardboard over all the other basement windows and the creature followed the light out.

Again, she almost yells for Donny, but stops herself. He can't be in the house, by now he'd have shouted from wherever he was to ask what was going on. Maybe genuinely concerned, more likely cross at having his computer game interrupted, but at least he'd have made some sort of fuss.

Ergo, it was up to her to cope with the squirrel, possum, bird or—she shudders at the thought—rat. She does what she should have done in the first place: finds and flicks a light switch. The sun might be out, but you wouldn't know it from the gloom boxed in the house with her.

Nothing under the table but dust bunnies, and a hint of rosewood and lavender spoiled with the sourness of fermentation that she matches after a puzzled moment to the scent of the plant now missing from two windows.

She regrets more than ever that her botanical and horticultural courses in college are more than a decade past, and that she's been too preoccupied to dig through her books for the plant's identity. (Why has she been so distracted? She can't put her finger on the why. In her mid-forties her powers of recollection have gone blurry in a manner not unlike her mother's did in her final years, though with that awful woman it was hard to tell where the onset of dementia ended and maliciously selective re-editing of personal history began.)

The most curious thing about the plant—which sported unremarkable white blossoms, the tiny needle-like petals evoking miniature dandelion blooms—was that Donny had insisted on bringing it home when they happened across it during an exercise hike, one where he had been unusually considerate of her weak ankles, maintaining a pace she could match without growing winded and sweat-soaked, her hips and knees burning.

Usually, she would stop the hikes to investigate a bush, flower or fungus beside the trail, and he huffed and practically stamped his feet a like toddler until they started moving again. When he hiked, much like when he fucked, he tended to care only about the act itself. On a stroll outdoors, he focused on the forward motion through uneven but beautiful terrain, which he made little to no effort to take in as he traversed it. Finishing the trail for the sake of finishing took precedence. The discovery of this plant caused one of the most dramatic role reversals in their sixteen years of marriage.

That Saturday afternoon on Poor Mountain, she had walked ahead almost twenty yards before she noticed that he was no longer at her shoulder, that only one set of footsteps disturbed the fallen leaves.

Donny had stalled at a bend, his gray-flecked beard emphasizing the direction of his gaze as he focused on something spied between two enormous rocks that in truth were one rock split asunder by some prehistoric upheaval. Once he had caught her eye, he pointed at the slope between trail and cleft. *Any poison ivy?* He trusted her to spot it—no matter how many times she showed him what it looked like, he always forgot.

Candace doubled back, picking her way carefully as he tapped his hiking-booted toe in mounting impatience.

Within the dagger-shaped split in the rock grew the ugliest tree Candace had ever seen, its branches curled in unnatural fashions, curving upward until they looped back in toward the gnarled trunk, reminding her of sea anemones or the spirals formed by nesting centipedes. Reinforcing that grotesque impression, the long fronds of its leaves also curled strangely, down instead of up, paired evenly like arthropod legs along the lengths of the branches. She could easily picture those branches as worm-like bodies that could straighten and crawl away at any moment.

They had walked this path dozens upon dozens of times, but she had never noticed this rock or this tree, as if an egg of massive dimensions had surfaced from the substance of the mountain and hatched a frilly sea worm of leviathan scale. Imagining this, Candace forgot Donny's question until he prodded her. *Well?*

She gave him the all clear. He trotted straight at the creepy tree and dropped to one knee in front of it as if swearing fealty. Hurrying to catch up, a root snagged her ankle and sent her, too, to one knee. Only a miracle kept her from slamming face-first into the rock.

Donny didn't turn his head at her shouted curse. He had unslung his backpack from his shoulders. *Can I have your spade?* he asked as if she hadn't just come within an inch of having her head cracked open.

Nor was he paying attention to the tree. All his focus was devoted to a small plant sprouted between two knobby roots. The

sight of the flower up close prevented her from snapping at him.
(And frankly, she'd been more than happy to spare herself his in-
evitable defensive retort and the plaintive whine that would taint
his raised voice as he made some balderdash excuse.) Unassuming
though the plant was, she didn't recognize it as any species she'd
ever studied. Her own curiosity welled up, though the odd flower
accounted for only part of it.

Your spade? he asked again. She wanted to say, *You should let
me do that*, but a part of her wanted to see whether the many times
he'd observed her collecting samples had somehow rubbed off.
The only collectibles he ordinarily got this excited over were bonus
treasures in computer games.

She complied, and he dug out the plant with a care that made
her proud. It proved to have more roots than she expected for
something so small, the thickest of which he severed with the
spade's serrated edge.

A flash of color from above snapped her head up as if pulled
by a string. This close, the branches reminded her even more of
curled centipedes, but she spied nothing to explain the splotch in
her peripheral vision, dismissed it as a random sunspot floating
behind her eyelids.

Meanwhile, Donny was gingerly stowing his new find into his
backpack. As sometimes happened, her mouth bypassed her res-
ervations. *I've never seen you this interested in a plant.* The subtext
of his resentment of her interests sharpened her words. *What's got
you so fascinated?*

He shrugged. *I've never seen one single plant have so many dif-
ferent-colored flowers.*

He was making fun of her. *You don't have to be that way, I just
asked you a question.*

I answered. He stood up, and for a moment his hydrangea-
blue eyes met hers, gorgeous as jewels but fixated somewhere other
than on her.

I've never seen a tree like that, she said, and pointed, but he was
already walking back to the trail.

You got a pot to fit it in? he called back. Immediately she'd
known who would really be taking care of this plant. He was back
to his subtly infuriating usual, walking a little too fast for her to
easily catch up.

As Candace reached the trail a burst of wind nearly yanked her over, whipping her hair to one side and tugging at her backpack—it really felt like someone had grabbed hold and pulled. This same wind affected that strange tree in the most unsettling way—it appeared to shrink backward into the rock cleft, like the sea worm she had imagined, withdrawing tentacles into its burrow under the sand.

Donny never said another word about the plant, even after she potted it and set the pot in the sill of his home office. As she packed its pudgy roots in the pot, she turned it this way and that, scanning for any sign of iridescence that explained his odd remark about color. The flowers, already wilting, remained resolutely white.

If she gave away that she was allotting any additional thought to his deadpan sarcasm, he'd take the opportunity to snicker at her, so she declined to let him have that opportunity. If he so much as curled his lips in a patronizing smile, she'd long to claw his face off, then lie awake later wracked with guilt that the urge had even crossed her mind.

A splotch of color where none should be yanks her attention back to the present.

Gaze aimed under the dining table, she catches of sight it again: one room over, in the darkened kitchen, a scintillating cluster of green quivers in the gap between cupboard and heating vent. Faintly glowing, the hue blurs into pink before her eyes. Then come blooms of deeper purple, then gold, the various shades swirling like the surface of a soap bubble.

Staring directly at the spot establishes unequivocally that there's nothing there.

She leans into the kitchen entrance, groping for the light switch by the refrigerator, half expecting something to grab her wrist. The other half of her mind berates her superstitious anxiety, using Donny's voice, *Why would you even think that?* delivered with a mocking curl of the lips.

The fluorescent bulb buzzes to life, illuminating a worn, banal, unoccupied kitchen, the linoleum curled up at the corners, exposing dirt underneath.

Another thunder. Not a pitter-patter this time but a heavy thump.

"Donny?"

He responds this time, an indistinct exclamation from the direction of the bedroom.

So he *had* been in bed with her when she'd woken up. She can't believe his presence didn't register, but in the state she's in, tired and disoriented and distracted and maybe even hallucinating, missing something so obvious is distressingly plausible. She's ruefully reflected more than once how the same conditions cause adoring parents to absentmindedly leave their babies inside oven-hot cars to die.

The neighbor kids are still screeching outside, but the sun must have gone down or the clouds thickened to brick wall opacity, as moonless-night dark smothers the windows.

Donny rarely stayed in bed this late. On the days he worked from home, and on the days he was off work, she'd invariably find him at the computer, and if she was quiet enough, she'd sometimes catch him watching porn—he always reacted like she was the one wronging him, snarling at her in that defensive nasal whine to stop looking at things over his shoulder.

Something tickles at the back of her mind, something that contrasts sharp as glass with the amorous adventure of the morning. *He's been sick.* Her struggle to connect with this thought disturbs her deeply, like a chasm encountered on a nighttime walk, only the sudden giving way of dirt altering her to its edge. She recalls pasty, sweaty skin, a fever that blazed, heat that radiated from him as he watched her from between her legs, his lips and tongue squeezing, pressing.

Maybe she's been sick too. Maybe the plant was never in either window. Maybe she'd thrown it away. She has a vague recollection of a withered thing in a reeking pot, that sweet odor gone completely to sour, the dead plant not looking much like a plant at all.

When she turns on the overhead light in the bedroom, Donny cries out like he did the time he tried to move his desk on his own and tore a muscle loose in the small of his back. "Turn it off," he moans, shuddering under the covers.

"Sorry!" As soon as she complies, something punches her bad ankle and she drops like a sandbag.

The pain's as intense as it was when those tendons first snapped, all those years ago when she was small and that van backed out of its driveway and the bumper knocked her over and the rear driver's side tire ran over her foot. Chrystal had seen it coming quick enough to jump out of the way and reacted first with a laugh when she noticed Candace sprawled on the ground.

When Candace's head slams against the bedroom floor, iridescent blotches flower in the void behind her eyes, where that bulging migraine pain unfolds and opens to absorb any and all light and convert it to fire, sun-poisoning her skull from the inside.

The pounding in her ears isn't figurative. The pitter-patter of panicking cats drums toward her, as if they've returned from the grave to clamber over her prone body the way they did in life.

She manages to make noise. Donny's right there, he's right there lying on the bed but he doesn't shout her name, doesn't cry out *Are you okay?*

A prism shimmer casts its glow across the feet of the nightstand, illuminates the underside of the bed.

The little plant's blooms are as colorful as Donny said they were. His voice says *I told you so* but the words come from somewhere other than the shuddering mound on the bed.

Why did he bring the plant into the bedroom? He must have spilled it from its pot—through the migraine haze she perceives the dark stains dribbled down the sheets and box-spring cover. The mud stinks of warm copper and feces. Maybe it's not dirt from the pot at all, maybe Donny had some disgusting bathroom accident right there under the comforter. An urge to laugh gurgles from the depths. He'll expect her to clamber upright and deal with it, won't he? But first he has to help *her*, genuinely get off his ass and help her. "Donny! Donny, help me up, I'm hurt!"

The plant has two new stalks with buds bulging at their tips. When they open Donny stares at her with those hydrangea-blue eyes, but Donny is still twitching on the reeking mattress. His breathtaking irises glisten in the spectral light, focused on her as intensely as they were this morning, as intensely as they've ever been.

Meeting her gaze, Donny's stolen eyes blink. The plant totters and sways at her, its thick, undulating roots rat-tat-tatting on the hardwood. The long fronds of its leaves uncurl to caress her face, their touch across her brow and cheek like the skittering legs of centipedes.

FOLLOW THE
WOUNDED ONE

The beast wore a man's face.

It moved on all fours, the size of a city bus, its vast blue eyes fixed on me above a crooked nose, a grim mouth, a long matted beard. One of its ponderous antlers was broken, terminating in a splintered point. Great bird talons made no noise as they settled in the earth. All its fluid motion, its feathered and scaled detail, registered with crystal clarity in the corner of my eye: the muscles bulging in its legs, the sunlight reflected in the scales of its spiny tail, tall wings that lowered ever so slightly, and raised ever so slightly, like the beating of a slow, silent heart. I didn't dare turn my head to meet the creature's gaze.

I stood in a grove of pine trees which had lost all their needles, their sticky black trunks afflicted with rot, rings of bare branches ascending each trunk like stacks of upturned spiders' legs. A path wide and straight as a church aisle sloped upward through the grove, and as I began my ascent, the beast paced me along a ridge about a stone's throw to my right, never inching closer, never looking away.

A recent rain had soaked the ground; mud and softened pine needles squelched with each step I took. The incline grew steeper, and the black-blighted trees grew taller, older, as if they were columns holding up the arched ceiling of some primeval Gothic cathedral, a ceiling formed by the crisscrossing canopy far overhead. I marched up this astonishingly elongated nave toward some unseen altar.

Though the beast never quickened its pace, it was gaining ground, getting ahead of me, its blue-scaled flank glittering in and out of view in my peripheral vision as it wormed through the black, blighted pines. How did I know this creature was an eater of men? Why did it keep its distance?

Above me a new path defined itself, perpendicular to mine, bordered by agonized, lightning-split trees that had survived to renew their growth in tortured curves, branches groping around each other in a struggle for sunlight. The beast would reach that path before I crossed it, and when it did, it would turn to block my way, the stare of its headlamp-sized eyes piercing me head on, lips parting in its tangled nest of beard to reveal a mouthful of boars' tusks.

Beyond the crossing path, the pine grove opened, revealing a distant cluster of dogwood and elm, a white steeple rising incongruously from their midst like a signal flare.

Wood popped like gunfire as the beast smashed through a ruined tree and forced its way onto the intersecting trail, its spiny tail hissing through the air as it whipped back and forth. I raised my hands instinctively, defensively, expecting to see great cat claws shimmering in blue outline, electric and dangerous, but instead I saw mere hands, my own feeble flesh.

I stared between my useless fingers as the horned head rose above me, eyes large and crazy as broken china plates.

M y hand shook so hard that my pen slipped out, clattered from the table to the bench to the floor.

The words scribbled in the tiny journal lying open beside my silverware weren't a summation of a dream. They described a memory, but one I couldn't fit into any sensible space or time that matched the rest of my life's recent ebb and flow. I had hoped that writing it down would jar it into place. The image of the beast had plagued me for days, irritating as an inaccessible sliver of popcorn wedged between the teeth.

At odd moments, I would glimpse flickers of motion, ripples of brute muscle beneath shimmering blue hide; or the jagged silhouette of a broken horn, swaying as a windblown branch where no branch could be; the illusion evaporating whenever I looked straight at it. Twice on the bus to Wilkes-Barre the corners of my vision had snagged on such phantoms; first stirring a few seats in front of me as I gazed sleepily out the window at rumpled nighttime forest; the next one in the mirror as I navigated the cramped toilet at the back of the bus. And again, after I settled into my dusty motel room with its television bolted to the top of the scarred wooden dresser.

"Settling in" consisted of plopping my shapeless backpack onto the floor, flopping backward on the creaky bed and taking a moment to note the decades of water stains that etched concentric and overlapping circles on the ceiling, a fossil record of neglect.

Soon I could think of nothing other than the itchy residue from the bus ride that was making my skin so unpleasant to inhabit. I stripped and went to test the shower, and gave thanks to providence that it delivered both heat and pressure.

Afterward, I swiped a sloppy zigzag of condensation from the mirror with my bare palm, met a stare from a pair of bright green eyes overhung by bushy black brows. Like it or not, I could not deny I was my grandmother's child before all else, her eyes the same unnerving green as mine.

My long black hair kinked like crumpled wire; my face darkened to hickory where the sun kissed it; at my neckline it glistened Mediterranean olive. My face jackal-lean from living nowhere, subsisting on little.

My hair I could do little about, but I could at least dispose of a couple day's worth of black stubble. Towel held around my waist, I stepped out to dig a razor from my pack.

I'd left the curtain open. A blue blur brushed the window glass with the lightness of a feather.

Blue irises big as dinner plates stared at me.

The beast's head and shoulders filled the view through the window, eyes unblinking, beard divided by a mouth flat as the horizon. Lips parted as if to speak, revealing tusks curled like crooked fingers. I screamed at the window and hurled my towel; I could not have deliberately invented a more fruitless defense.

The towel impotently smacked the glass, while the view now showed me nothing more than an empty parking lot and weeds beyond.

Once my composure returned, I dressed in denim cutoffs, a tie-dye shirt and flipflops, all in consideration of the afternoon heat. The motel had a diner attached to it, a place of gray wood paneling and square aluminum tables that wobbled when you sat at them. I elected not to go there; after my little towel-hurling humiliation, I deserved to splurge on a meal better than the usual fare. Perhaps it would help me get a handle on my hallucinations, if that was in fact what they were.

Lately I'd been having considerable difficulty finding the seam where reality separated itself from the otherworldly and illusory.

When I first came awake to the world of ghosts and spirits, I had believed flesh and phantom were as easy to tell apart as salt and sour. But it's not true. The more aware I became, the more I discovered that the two intermix in unexpected places with alarming frequency.

The restaurant I ended up strolling into, a blue-collar-priced affair around the corner from the motel, did little to help my disorientation. Its marquee proclaimed MACPHAIR'S FUNNIE FACES in red and blue carnival script. Inside, at the vacant hostess podium, a neon pink poster board told me PLEASE WAIT FOR SMILING FACES TO TAKE YOU TO YOUR PLACES. Colorful pastel caricatures portraying dozens of profiles of not-so-memorable customers hung on both sides of the entrance hall. I waited a minute for a host or hostess who didn't show, then decided hell with manners, I wanted to sit down. It was 3 o'clock on a Tuesday afternoon, not like the place was packed.

I slipped into the smoking section and took a booth at the far end, putting my back to the wall. The decor in the dining area continued the face motif—a long frieze of photographic portraits lined the brick wall above the booths, photos of people making goofy faces or wearing troweled-on clown makeup or some combination of the two. Directly above me a woman with a fantastically elongated nose crossed her already close-set eyes and made a comical O with cherry-red lips. Next to her a man in classic clown getup grinned despite the huge blue frown that covered the lower half of his face. Disconcerting, that. I wondered if the portraits were done in-house, with waiters accosting particularly odd-looking tourists (or whatever sort of folk stopped over in an aging coal mining-opolis like Wilkes-Barre) and luring them into a studio and darkroom tucked somewhere behind the ovens, ambushing them with pancake makeup.

I fished out my pocket notebook to see if I could sort out where my beastly visions came from, only to discover I remembered an event that couldn't possibly have happened. I had never been anyplace like that pine stand with its white steeple like an admonishing finger in the distance. After taking deep breaths to recover from that whacked-out revelation, I groped awkwardly under the table for my escaped pen.

"Has anyone helped you?" my waitress asked, nearly causing me to crack my skull. She must have walked up just as I ducked under the table. I registered white hose stretched over gracefully curved calves extending from buckle shoes to a smart black skirt starting just above the knees.

I straightened myself, saw her face and almost screamed. I exclaimed instead, "Jesus, what *happened* to you?"

Black bruises ringed both her eyes, fanned out from each socket as if the blood from each blow had splattered underneath her skin. A pair of Black Dahlia slits at the corners of her tiny lips stretched to her cheekbones, as if you could stick a finger in her little purple mouth and unfold her face. More bruising made a mottled ring around her neck. Hair black as mine matted in a bloodied tangle. Sky blue eyes stared at me out of the ruin, dumbfounded.

I experienced a lurch of displacement, and a familiar electric tingle raised the hairs on the back of my neck. Something had changed; the marks on her face didn't look as vivid as they had the instant before. I had just misinterpreted a particularly creative clown face. "I'm sorry," I said, trying to cover, "the makeup you have on looks so real."

That only seemed to compound her confusion. Her eyes widened and she took a step back, her knuckles white around her pen and pad of tickets.

Two kinds of vision came into focus, and I saw two faces in the same place: one, the visage that first confronted me, that I had misinterpreted as a horror show mask of bruises; the second, a pale, pretty girl with high cheekbones and a pointed chin, whose hair was in fact a striking highlighted blond, though thin brown eyebrows perhaps gave her real color away. The second girl's hair was wavy and tied back in a pony tail, not stained dark red. She bore no signs of injury. The wide blue eyes were the same in both faces.

What did *she* see, as she stared at me?

I willed my vision to root itself in this world, and the pale blonde wearing perhaps a bit too much blush grew solid. I wondered, how on Earth could I defuse this situation?

I raised my hands in what I hoped was a humble gesture. "I'm so sorry. Please forget I said anything. I just got off the bus a couple hours ago, and those fumes, you know, they can get to you. I have a hell of a headache."

She smiled wanly. "Oh-kay." But in the pause before she asked what I wanted to drink, she looked me over once more, curious, serious, calculating. Her eyes lit on the notebook. She had seen something unusual herself, I was sure. And I believed she knew what I had I seen.

I pulled out my wallet, thumbed through the bills wadded in there, last remnants of an unspent student loan, decided it was time for a moderately reckless splurge. I ordered a Murphy's. She blinked—she'd never heard of it. Perhaps she hadn't been at the job long. Now she looked little different from any other slender waitress not far removed from her teens. I noticed a food-stain fleck below the starched collar of her white blouse. I had her at a slight disadvantage, I realized, because the poor woman had to wear a name tag: HI, MY NAME IS KORI.

She asked what Murphy's tasted like, but I lack the vocabulary necessary to explain how you distinguish the flavors of beer. She stopped me as I fumbled through a series of "as sour as but more bitter than" comparisons to tell me she'd see if they had in stock. Turned out, a little to her surprise, they did. I wanted to ask her when she began working there but she dropped a menu in front of me and hurried off.

Agitated, needing a timekiller, I returned to my notebook and started a poem, somewhat rashly sparked by my new acquaintance:

What gold cried from your eyes tinted mine?
What ghosts breathed from your lips chill my skin?
What gods frolic in my blood and yours?

"What's that mean?" Kori asked—she'd sidled up to me quietly as I wrote.

I gave her a sidelong, coy glance. "You might know."

A crease appeared between her brows. "Why would I?"

"Just a guess." I grinned aw-shucks-like. "You seem like someone who'd get poetry." I think it flattered her, though she didn't lose her wariness.

Dinner ended my conversational tactics for a while: a honey-glazed chicken with seasoned mashed potatoes and breaded okra. I'd run so long without a good meal . . .

"What, were you on a hunger strike?" said Kori when she next checked on me.

"I might as well have been," I told her. I asked her to pick my next beer and wound up with a Corona.

By that time, the dining area had gained a bit more population. Two booths down from me, a black family, mom and dad, two small daughters in pigtails, a baby in a high chair. A gray-haired white couple sat at a booth across from me, solemnly poring over their menus through bifocals. They required Kori's attention, which irritated me, because I really wanted to talk to her. I suspected I'd found, so to speak, a kindred spirit.

Next chance that came, I told her I wanted the check. As I did, I focused: did I still see that first face, so black and stark around the eyes? A flicker, a shadow: yes, they were there, the strange marks of the spirit world.

I weighed my options as I counted out cash for the meal. Though I truly couldn't afford it, I fished out an extra $10, pulled a sheet of paper out of my notebook, wrote the motel name and my room number and "I want to talk to you more." Then I stuck the bill and note together and united them with dog ears. This became her tip. She collected all the money without comment, a crease between her brows, attention somewhere other than MacPhair's.

After a minute she returned, the $10 clutched in her fist. "Did you really think that would get you something?" She flashed teeth in what look like a smile, but from the tone of her voice I guessed it wasn't.

I'm not too fleet on my verbal feet in an emergency. The best I could manage was what I hoped would come across as a disarming shrug. She let the bill drop to the table with a flick of contempt, put her fake smile on wider and walked over to the black family's table. I thought about insisting she take the tip, but concluded I'd already pushed my luck too far. As I picked up the bill, I discovered she's kept the paper with my room number. I tried to catch her eye but she wouldn't look my way.

Enough, I told myself, and left.

"Have a nice evening," she chirruped behind me. But I had no idea whether I really would.

As I walked back to the motel, I wondered what the hell I'd been thinking. Just because I'd stumbled on someone else who seemed to share my dual-world nature, I couldn't assume this meant she would instantly feel some bond with me, or have some profound insight to share about my condition. It had only been a month, less than, since I came to accept my own ability to see and feel and interact with things on the other side, and understand that though my nature in the spirit world is different, it's something that's been with me from birth, a head-spinning inheritance. Why would Kori know how it worked any more than I do? Perhaps she knew nothing. And who was I to judge? I couldn't even decipher what manner of being she was. The previous ones I'd encountered, good and bad, had presented their traits in significantly different manners.

Back in my motel room, I contemplated whether to stay put or explore the city. I wouldn't be any safer either way, I suspected. I chose to nap.

I looked up from my notebook as the waitress set the plate in front of me. When I saw what I'd been served, I dropped my pen. A severed wing lay across the abstract china pattern, its brown feathers speckled sandy, its tip darkening to black. My startled breath stirred the edges of its feathers. In response, it twitched.

I sprang out of the booth, my right knee jarred painfully as it banged under the table.

I was alone in McPhair's Funnie Faces. The dining area smelled of upturned clay, the odor growing stronger as a fog rolled in that cast a gray filter over the chipper furnishings.

The frieze of photos that ran above the booths all displayed the same image: a bearded face with piercing blue eyes, antlers rising from its temples, one broken.

I looked for the way out, but the room stretched on and on. The fog thinned; I could detect a pattern within it, columnar, like the trunks of pine trees.

A motion pulled my attention back to the photos. The face had grown closer while I looked elsewhere. Now each photo displayed only one huge, crazily blue eye.

In unison, all the eyes blinked.

I started awake in the motel bed, heart pounding thunderous tomtoms. The sun had almost set, tinging the drawn curtains a bruised purple. An inexplicable anxiety, maybe a remnant of my dream, charged the air, and I stared about frantically, thinking a blue scaly shape was about to emerge from the closet or slide in ghost-like fashion out of the wall.

I noticed a white slip of paper that someone had slipped under the door.

It was the note I gave Kori. On one side, my writing. On the other side, block letters in ballpoint pen read MEMORYTOWN TAVERN 9:00.

T he Tavern turned out to be about twelve blocks away, well within my idea of walking distance. Unfortunately this didn't prove to be a beautiful stretch of Wilkes-Barre to stroll through: a gaudy procession of strip malls, loudly lit signs and cars jockeying pointlessly for position across six lanes of traffic. Hotels I couldn't afford towered to either side, bleak sentinels of commerce. I knew that if I ever ventured into this coal city's downtown, I'd find picturesque buildings with flourishes of brick architecture standing empty and crumbling from disuse, though still in better shape than the neighborhoods of decrepit old houses circling the city's core like a moat of poverty. I'd seen the same thing in Tennessee, in Virginia, in West Virginia, all up and down these mountains.

Given its enticing moniker and the company I anticipated, the Tavern proved disappointing. Even as I approached the building, I caught the unmistakable twang of electric guitar country. Bluegrass or Old Time music I can handle. Though even at that young age I much preferred Duke Ellington to Doc Watson, I'd take either in a heartbeat over Garth Brooks. I could already tell this wasn't going to be a comfortable fit.

Inside, the guitars grated, yet failed to drown out the clumsy twang of a particularly untalented live singer. With my wire-thin frame, dark skin and curly black hair, I stood out like a sore thumb among the clientele, none of whom were likely to appreciate any of the nuances of Melungeon heritage: men in sleeveless motorcycle shirts and denim jackets that strained to hold in their guts; women with their button-down shirts tied across their breasts, revealing no-so-supple bellies that spilled over the tops of their jeans, hair 1980s-big and dyed blond. More than a few of the men sported mullets, the most frightening of which, combining punk spikes with waist-length hair, adorned the awful singer's head. The flannel-shirted man serving as host gave me a once over before mercifully leading me to a table far away from the dais where the band played . . . though nowhere was far enough.

Two mugs of Sam Adams later, Kori was still a no show. I didn't feel brave enough to snoop up and down the rows of booths looking for her. The attention I drew would most certainly be the unwelcome kind.

A sinking feeling yawned into a cavern, a canyon, a sullen acceptance that I'd been had. That Kori directed me to this place, honestly, didn't speak so well of her. I felt betrayed but chided myself for overreacting. Why should I have believed that she would even want to meet with me after our strange first encounter?

Finally, I could stand the wait no longer, and truth be told, neither could my bladder.

A constant electric crackle made the cramped, spotlight-bright restroom even more eerie and constricting. Dark puddles clustered around the drain in the center of the cracked cement floor. I resolved, Kori or no, as soon as I was done I would get out of this place. I pulled the stall door closed, fumbled with the loose lock, then sat.

But where to go from here? I'd come to Pennsylvania with an incoherent notion to reunite with a couple I'd palled around with at UNC in the months before I dropped out. They were seniors, I was a lowly sophomore, both hailed from Wilkes-Barre and both had landed jobs in nearby Strousburg. During one evening involving heavy petting, cannabis consumption and giggles over passages from Lord Byron's "Manfred" read with theatrical exaggeration, Bill and Melissa had invited me to drop in on them in their post-collegiate lives any time I wished.

Ever since I aborted my ill-thought-out attempt to hike the Appalachian Trail—a dubious adventure thoroughly sabotaged by a spirit world intrusion—I had been drifting toward them, because even though when I called the number they'd given me the phone just rang and rang and rang, it still put distance between me and the family I didn't want to go back to. I'm not quite sure what I thought would happen when I found them; there'd been some awkwardness between myself and Melissa that never got resolved, and despite the open relationship, Bill would let flashes of irritation show. Maybe, even if I didn't hook up with them, I could pick up a job here somewhere, build up my cash reserves.

A footstep splashed softly in the puddle on the floor, snapping me out of reverie.

The space below the stall door framed a pair of weathered leather work boots. Based on their size, the man standing outside the stall was enormous. I could just see the dome of his brow above the door, high forehead, white hair in a buzz cut. "Just a minute," I told him. He said nothing and didn't move away from the door.

A chill grew in my belly. Outside that awful music still drenched the place. The oppressive light offered no escape, and that electric hum surged louder, along with the ringing in my ears. My new friend shifted slightly, and I released he was leaning against the door, which would pop open with a gentle push. I scrambled to get my shorts back in order. "Excuse me, can I help you?" I hoped I sounded more annoyed than afraid.

The man exhaled in a drawn-out sigh of satisfaction. I looked up, saw a sliver of his face as he stared through the crack in the door at me; saw a cross section of a tangled beard, a piercing blue eye. I knew that eye. "Shit," I said, struggling to get my fly buttoned and zipped.

All my hair stood on end as a glowing blue speck appeared in the center of the stall door. The speck began to stretch into a vertical line, a knife slice in reality.

I'd seen this done before. He was ripping an opening to the spirit world, right in front of me. I had nowhere to go. "Wait, wait, wait," I said.

He didn't wait.

Something like a knife poked through the opening; as it crooked down into the stall I realized it was the tip of a talon as large as my leg. Then the entire hand appeared, three upward talons and one downward, all together as tall as me, shimmering with blue phosphorescence. My heart battered against my rib cage like the tongue of an alarm bell. I couldn't scream. I couldn't breathe.

The beast from my vision flexed its claws ever so slightly, amusing itself with idle threat. Behind it, on the other side of the door, that mad eye burned.

In the spirit realm, I am a great cat. I knew this, but only from what witnesses have told me, half-remembered mirages, and the evidence left behind whenever I have fought. I had never consciously summoned that form. When I'd been attacked, it responded with claws and teeth and muscle, some ingrained instinct.

This time, nothing happened. I remained as I was, a skinny young man terrified out of his wits. After too many seconds of blank panic, the thought arrived, *Climb out! Climb out!*

I stood straight, reached up. The claws closed, sawing into my neck and chest and shoulders, up between my legs, through my groin. It was like being carved by lightning. The pain stabbed deep, fiery, excruciating. The scream lodged in my throat came loose, and I let the world know how much it hurt.

When my eyes refocused a bearded man was staring down at me. After a terrible second I pieced together that I wasn't regarding the face of my attacker. This fellow's dark beard outlined jowls that cushioned a kind face with the yellowed complexion of a smoker, brown eyes nestled in premature wrinkles. He wore a blue workshirt with his name stitched on it: Albert.

"Buddy, I think you had a few too many," Albert said.

After rolling my wits up—I lay on the floor, wedged uncomfortably between toilet and wall—I said, "Yeah. You're right. Can you please help me up?"

With Albert's help I escaped the restroom, but the darkness and noise inside Memorytown assumed an entirely different timbre, one pregnant with menace. The beast was still in there somewhere, maybe watching me from one of the booths. The searing pain had subsided, but the hairs on my aching chest and legs prickled. I'd taken a hell of a bruising in my fall. As I walked toward the exit, every step hurt.

No sooner had that front door shut behind me than a tiny gray Hyundai flipped on its headlights and pulled out from the parking spot where it had been idling. The car pulled up alongside me with the growl of someone stomping on the gas. Through the driver's side window peered an astonishing face, with haunting eyes ringed by deep black.

"Get in!" Kori said.

I stepped back.

"He's coming," she hissed. "Get in, now!"

We rolled along in silence through the decaying downtown of Wilkes-Barre, not at all unlike what I'd imagined, with beautiful buildings from the 1920s sporting ornate cornices, fleur-de-lis, even a gargoyle or two, all crumbling in great gaping wounds of exposed brick. Kori's Hyundai smelled heavily of some vaguely fruity incense.

Finally I shifted in the passenger seat to look at the double image of her face. "How can I trust you?"

She smirked. Her eyes never left the road. "A little late for that, don't you think?"

"Maybe you should be asking *me* that."

The smirk again. "You're a pussycat. I've got nothing to worry about from you. And you've got much worse things to worry about than me."

"Why aren't *you* worried?"

She glanced at me sidelong with those bright and haunting eyes. "He sees you. You're too big to hide. But he's never noticed me."

I understood immediately who she was talking about. "Who is he? What is he? Do you know him?"

She pressed her lips in a grim line as she waited for a stoplight to change. Her left turn signal clicked, making her face strobe green. "I don't know him. I don't know anything about him. But what he's trying to do to you, I've seen him do it before, when I've been in the sky so high he doesn't see me." She fidgeted as the light stubbornly stayed red. *"Come on!"*

We passed under a bright street lamp and for a moment I saw both her selves clearly illuminated. The pretty bottle blond in a black spaghetti strap top, skin pale and smooth, and the wild creature with black bands around the neck and eyes.

"Is it out of bounds for me to ask what those bands are?"

"It's not."

"Then what are they?"

"Protective coloration," she said.

"Protective from what?"

"Hunters. Enemies."

"What hunters? The same psycho fucker that's after me?"

"Not your business."

"Well then why are you helping me?"

"You're the first one I *could* help."

"The first?"

She finally took her eyes from the road, to glare at me. We'd made several turns. I had no hope of keeping track of where we were.

"Curiosity *did* kill the cat," she said.

"I'm sorry, I do *not* agree," I snapped back. "Answers keep this cat alive."

We weren't downtown anymore, but crossing a long, well-lighted four lane bridge, with American flags hung from every pole. "I suppose I should be afraid of you." She rubbed her forehead with a sweaty palm. "But I'm not in the least bit. I can tell you're a good kitty."

"Not sure there's much to be afraid of. When he came after me—" Under his stare, I had stayed human, even when he attacked. "Right now I'm a cat without claws. How did he do that to me? Stop me from . . . whatever it is we do?"

"You're not declawed."

"How do you know?"

"It's plain when I look at you."

Her statement stopped me cold. It had not occurred to me that there might be a pattern in my face visible to her the way her inner self showed itself to me. What did it look like and who else could see it?

She turned onto a side street that converted to gravel as it curled underneath the bridge. "We're here," she said. She guided the Hyundai over an uneven lot of dirt and pebbles that made the car shake horribly before she ground to a stop. Her headlights illuminated one of the great H-shaped cement pylons that supported the bridge. She flipped on her brights, bringing the image tagged on the pylon into sharper relief.

"Damn," said I.

A huge, crude painting of an all-too-familiar monster flowed across the curved cement. One difference: the deer antlers were whole.

We sat silent in the car a moment. "Do you have any idea what that is?"

"I found the same image once, in a book on creatures from Indian myth. It's called a pie-ya-saw."

"A what?"

"P-I-A-S-A," she spelled.

"What kind of Indian?"

She smirked. "Native American."

I nodded. "So tell me about Mr. Piasa."

"A book I found said the word means 'devouring bird.' It ate young warriors whole."

I felt an electric prickle at the back of my neck, but I was sure it was nothing more than fear.

"The chief of the tribe went to the cliff were it lived and lay at the bottom, pretending to be wounded. But all the men from the tribe were hidden nearby, waiting. It came out hungry and they filled it full of arrows. It took every single one of them to kill it, once it was so heavy with arrows it couldn't fly."

"So it was killed?"

"That's what the book said. But I read somewhere else that a white man made it all up."

"Huh. Leave your lights on." I opened the passenger door. "I want to look closer."

She watched a moment, then followed me.

The painting commanded the eye, a thing of fierce power tall as me and long as a BMW. Though heavily stylized, all its pieces were familiar: the feathered wings, the rows of blue scales, powerful haunches, the deadly talons, the long spined tail that curled above its back, the wild beard, the tusks jutting from a snarling mouth, the unblinking stare, the antlers. It shimmered with the false glow of the airbrush, luminous as the aggressively cheerful art you see tagged on the sides of freight cars.

I touched its gritty surface. "How long has this been here?"

"Since I was a kid."

"So not that long?"

She cut her eyes at me. The headlight glare bleached her skin to a harsh white. At last I could see the jeans she wore, how they hugged the contours of her thighs and calves, the grace added to her height by plain black boots. Her outfit was a small gift to me, and I wished the circumstances would have let me appreciate it more.

I ran a thumb along the black lines delineating feathers in a wing, as sharp as if carved, my own shifting shadow swimming atop the intense colors imbued in every line, shape and spatter. "Someone refreshes this. Touches it up."

"Huh?"

"If it's been here since you were a little girl it ought to be faded. It's not. Somebody takes care of it."

"It's been here as long as I can remember." She wasn't refer-ring to the painting. "I saw it in the sky when I was little. Him. He never saw me." She pressed a knuckle against her lip. "When I was eleven, I had a cousin who was sixteen, he brought me down here. Wanted me to smoke weed with him. I think he wanted to get me stoned and feel me up." She pointed at the painting. "I saw that and started screaming my head off."

I put a hand over the piasa's snarling face, and felt a twinge of anger at this cousin, imagined the frightened little girl beneath the bridge. "I'm sorry," I said. Under my fingers, the creature's eyes blazed. "How is it possible that you've kept away from him all that time?"

"I'm not what he's looking for. I don't take up much space in the spirit world. And I can fly much higher than he flies."

"I spotted you quickly enough."

She nodded. "You're made to see in the dark."

"There's something else I see, too." I bent my fingers into claws over the beast's face. "This is a man, not a creature from legend."

A line of puzzlement creased her forehead.

"I've seen this before. Some folks can make their own shape in the spirit world. They're not born with a shape, like you or me. But they build a shape. That's why he can be something that's a hoax, just because he wants to. He chooses it. But the ones like you and me, we have no choice."

"What makes you think I was born like this?"

I shrugged. "Am I wrong?"

Her lips pressed into a line. "No."

I leaned against the wall, the painting. It felt like defiance. "I know where I get it from. It comes from my grandmother, from her people in the hollers of Tennessee. You have family in Tennessee?"

She tensed. "I'm the only one like me in my family."

"That's not how it works." I went to her, put a hand on her bare shoulder. Her skin was smooth and cool, and I caught a scent from her hair, a sweet vanilla. She looked at the wall but didn't shy away from my touch. "You're not the only one," I said. "There's someone in your family who isn't talking."

She kept staring at the painting. I moved into her field of vi-sion. "But the guy who hurt me, he isn't made like us. He made himself. I don't know how these fuckers get that way, but I've seen it before." An all-too-recent memory bubbled up, a man in a white mask lying in leaves, bleeding from the claw marks I'd torn in him. "And the man who I saw before, that guy was sick, a sick bastard."

"So's this one," she said. "He's come after people before. People like you. I've seen it, from up high, when I'm flying." She shuddered, almost too subtly to see, but I felt it in her shoulder.

I tried to imagine her flying, but couldn't comprehend the mechanics involved. "How does that work, exactly? Is it like an out of body thing?"

"Don't make fun."

"I'm not."

"Yes you are. Stop or I'll stop helping you."

Okay, this was a sensitive subject. So was my life. "Fine. Do you know why he's after me?"

She still wouldn't meet my eyes. Her face with its bands turned away from the headlights, disappeared in layers of shadow. "I told you the old story. The piasa hunted warriors in its territory, carried them off and ate them. I've seen . . . I've seen this one do that. With . . . I don't know who they were, I've seen their form *there*. I never met them *here*." Now she looked at me, eyes red and moist, but her voice was steady. "Sometimes you see something on the news, a body found in a strange place. Once maybe it was under here." She swallowed, looking up at the bridge. "The cops rule out foul play. But I've seen . . . When he comes for them, they can't fight back . . . "

I had to break her silence. "Is he guarding something? Searching for something?"

"In the story, there's no reason. It's just evil and hungry." She pulled away. "I have to help you get out of here. But I don't know if it will let you."

"You said he doesn't see you."

"I've told you, I'm too small. When I fly I'm just a dark speck in the sky, like a gnat to him, nothing he cares about. You, you take up a lot of space. You can't be missed."

I'd been born with a gift of moving in silence. So much for natural talent helping me here. "Do you know a good place to hide?"

"You have to hide yourself *there*, not here."

"Well." I took a deep breath. "I don't guess I ever planned to stay long." I started toward the Hyundai. "I need to get my things.

If you can take me as far out of here as you can take me, I'll owe you. Everything."

She didn't move. "He might be looking for you at your motel."

My gut twisted. That huge face staring in the window. "Yeah, he might be."

"Then we can't go there."

"Listen. From what you've told me, it sounds like he'll find me wherever I am. I need my things. Let's just do it quick."

She put her hands over her face. "Oh, God."

"Look, your battery's probably dying." I tried to laugh, to make it sound like I wasn't scared shitless. "Let's just move, okay?"

On the ride back to collect my things, I coaxed Kori into talking more about herself.

She grew up in Scranton, daughter to a hairdresser and a father who worked on steam engines for Norfolk and Western until asbestos poisoning put him on disability, then killed him over ten slow years. Once their lawyer excised his portion of the settlement, her mother blew it all in a candle-at-both-ends spree. Her mother's main acquisition had been a sleek black Thunderbird that she totaled a mere month later.

Kori's family was large, but not close. Her mother had been the youngest of a family of ten. Her grandparents on that side died before she turned nine. Her grandparents on her father's side hadn't grown closer after her father's death.

She lived at home, paying her mother rent. She'd tackled a few community college courses but hadn't followed through—the classes ate her money and worse, bored her. She didn't know what she wanted—she had at various times imagined being an art teacher, a paralegal, a lab assistant at a hospital—but she knew that for now she'd had enough of school.

Her dream, I learned, was to fly without ever having to land.

"No husband, no children, no split-level?" I teased as we pulled into the motel parking lot. She cut her eyes at me again, then made an exaggerated show of shivering.

"Oh, c'mon, it can't be that bad."

One eyebrow raised. "So says Tigger Tumbleweed."

I climbed out of the car. "You're weird."

"Don't push it." She got out after me.

"You could wait out here," I said, fumbling in my pocket for the room key.

"If you need help, I want to help."

"Okay," I said, jingling the key into the lock. In we went.

The room wasn't as I had left it. I don't mean that maids had cleaned it up. The covers were rumpled in a different configuration, my bag was in a different spot on the rug than where I'd left it. The bathroom door was ajar, exposing darkness.

"Someone's been in here," I said.

Kori stood in the doorway. "How can I help you get out?"

I raised a hand. "I think I'm all right. I don't have much." I grabbed loose clothes from the floor and pulled the zipper of my dufflebag open to stuff them inside. When I moved the bag, I felt a cold electric jolt, as if I'd just shoved my hand through a ghost.

I turned in time to see Kori's eyes widen in terror as a pair of splayed talons as tall as her passed through the wall, one to either side of the door where she stood, huge blue claws curling into the room, grasping for me.

I screamed as much in fear for her as for my own life.

I reached for her, and in that split second of freaked out awareness I actually witnessed the great cougar paw of my spirit form, thin fur over massive blue muscle poised to strike at the threat, drawn up short as the rational piece of me shrieked that I was just as likely to tear open Kori as my enemy.

She made a sharp startled noise as that horrible bearded face appeared in the door, occupying the same space she did. Just as the talons materialized through the wall moments before, the beast's face phased through her body.

Because I could see my great claw, I also saw what happened the instant the piasa's burning gaze locked on me. The muscle and fur shriveled away, dissolved into nothing, immediately reduced to a defenseless human hand.

In the same instant, as Kori slumped to the ground, the creature's eyes widened in surprise. It had been so focused on getting to me that it hadn't realized she was there.

But I had no chance to take advantage of the pause. Before I took another breath the beast struck with both its talons.

The pain was excruciating.

* * *

A delusion of flight assailed me with wind and vertigo.

I dangled in the beast's front claws as it bore me away from the city with ponderous strokes of its enormous wings, carrying me to its den to die.

I didn't understand how we moved. Was I lying on the motel room floor as the piasa carried off my soul, or was this physical? Either way, I'd been bested by the most powerful being I'd ever encountered in my brief time of spiritual self-awareness.

The world glowed dim and silver. We descended into a dark mass that resolved into a green canopy of pine needles. We pierced through the canopy like a nail through skin, and I gasped at the blackness beneath.

Yet I'd seen this place before. Tall slimy pine trunks arranged in cathedral-column rows, their barren branches stabbing out grotesquely like rings of broken spider legs.

We dropped, dropped, dropped, squelched down in the moist layers of brown needles that carpeted the forest floor. The creature settled so its weight pressed me into the mud and pinned me.

That wide bearded face lowered over mine, the breath wafting between its tusks stinking like spoiled meat. The mad eyes were half-lidded, coy, as if it planned to kiss me deeply before goring my neck.

"What," I wheezed, "the fuck . . . have I ever done to you?"

Between the prongs of the beast's antlers, I spied a flicker of movement in the dark canopy overhead—a small bird, silhouetted for the briefest of moments as it descended from a patch of empty sky.

The piasa saw my eyes flicker and punched a talon into my chest to keep me still—I screamed blue murder—then it looked up.

Transmuted by the power of the thing's gaze, the bird's shape exploded in frenzied confusion. Its size kept changing. I saw wings fluttering, arms flailing, heard a cry as a hand caught a branch that broke. I pushed at the talon that had cracked into my ribs with both sweat-slick hands, then screamed again as it pushed in a little deeper.

Kori landed on her back about thirty yards uphill from us. Given the violence of her fall I was certain she'd snapped her spine. She lay so still.

The piasa swung its attention back to me. It again lowered its eyelids in anticipated ecstasy. I noted in a moment of absurd clarity that it had long black eyelashes, elegant as those on any actress.

Kori arched her back and gasped for air, then rolled onto her stomach, using the nearest black trunk for support as she struggled to her feet.

She staggered up the hill, limping, dragging her left leg so stiffly I was amazed she could walk at all. She looked back, directly at me, dark rings around her eyes and neck. The double image of spirit world vision afflicted me even more strangely, because in her place I also saw a bird, wounded, dragging one broken wing as it hopped awkwardly away.

The piasa yanked its talon down my body, ripping my stomach wide open.

I gagged, howled, slumped. I was wide awake, but in too much pain and terror to move.

The beast turned its attention back to Kori.

When its gaze fixed again on her, the bird vanished. I saw only a young, badly injured woman scrambling to escape my fate. She sobbed with every breath. I could hear her as if those breaths were in my ear.

Agony burned deep in my gut. I thought of the eerie eyes of my grandmother, who understood who I was long before I did. *Little panther*, her memory whispered. *You've hurt them enough.*

I had been hurt more than enough. How much of this was real, how much of this was some strange artifice from the spirit realm?

The terrible pain in my chest and abdomen lowered an octave as the piasa plucked out its claw. Above us, Kori stumbled and cried out, clutching at her injured knee.

A slow smile spread across the beast's wide face. It lowered its head, snagged a big branch between the prongs of its undamaged antler, flexed its neck and snapped the branch into three pieces. The noise made Kori jerk up and look back, wide-eyed.

The creature raised itself off me, reached without looking and plucked at the groove it had torn in my stomach. I bucked in agony but did not scream. It moved its claw to the side of my neck and caressed me gently as a lover. The fire of deep pain that only someone who has been impaled or eviscerated could know burned in my chest and intestines.

Kori regained her feet. The double image of woman and bird flickered, both broken. Then the piasa began to pad toward her, keeping its wings tight to its sides as it moved between the rows of trees.

The beast's haunches still loomed above me. It wasn't hurrying. As its long segmented tail drifted over me, I lifted my left hand just an inch above the forest floor, doing my best to maintain absolute silence. I willed myself to see the impossible, imagined that instead of a trembling arm, I would see a gigantic, rippling limb, thick as one of the pine trees, covered in the blue down of my panther self. The very act of raising my arm stirred embers of agony. I bit deep into my lip to stifle a scream.

My hand stayed nothing more than a hand, still trembling.

Kori's ragged breath had grown more distant, but I heard her plainly. Even at a casual saunter, the beast had no trouble gaining on her.

I kept staring at my arm, afraid to even move my eyes for fear the piasa would somehow detect the motion.

I can't say precisely when my perspective changed.

As it moved, the piasa's wings pulsed in a slow rhythm, just as I'd seen in the not-a-dream. It moved in total silence, making the commotion of Kori's limping struggle that much louder.

Ahead of her, the desolate rows of pine trees gave way to a gray glade, and beyond it another line of trees began, innocuous-looking oaks and maples. From their midst rose a pale church steeple, strange as a giant's finger.

Kori reached the glade. The beast would arrive just seconds behind her, freed to spread its full wingspan.

Which is what it did as soon as it left the pines, stretching its wings wide as a small passenger plane's, intending to catch its new prey and win the game. As its front talons came off the ground, my own claws sank deep into the muscles that joined its wings to its shoulders.

It twisted and thrashed its head, stabbing at my face with its antlers. I lashed forward with a paw, unsheathed my already bloodied nails and raked them across the beast's china blue eyes.

Abruptly Kori became both a bird and a woman again, and then purely a bird, whooshing through the air above the glade, a killdeer with red bands around its eyes and black and white rings around its neck, whose wings had not been harmed one whit in the fall, who had risked the beast's horns and claws to draw its magic-killing gaze away from me just long enough.

The piasa tried to fly with its wings wounded and me on its back. I tried to dig my long teeth into either side of its spine before it screamed and rolled, hurling me off.

The fire in my gut still burned, though the burning was muted by rage and adrenaline, transformed into something else, something that fueled me.

From its human mouth the beast shrieked, its paralyzing stare replaced with dark blood.

Now the odds were even.

The nauseating see-saw motion that tilted the room back and forth turned out to be my own aching head jostled as Kori shook my arm, repeating, "Christ, Christ, Christ—"

"Stop it," I moaned. She gasped and jerked away.

I focused on a lamp beside the headboard, took in the water-damaged ceiling of my motel room.

Blood from inside my own sinuses filled my skull with a coppery reek. My dry tongue felt as if it had been baked while packed in cotton. In fact, my entire body was a husk radiating unpleasant heat. I imagined myself as sun-dried clay that would crack if I tried to move.

Despite my instinct, I made my lips and tongue form words. "I could really use some water," I said. "Am I all mud and blood?"

"No." The amazement made her voice sound frantic. "But you have a burn, on your stomach. Where your shirt's torn open. There's blisters."

I guffawed once. "I don't think the ice machine works here." But she had left my side. I heard the sink running, a glass filling. "I don't feel the burn," I told her, then chuckled again. That was accurate. I didn't feel it, yet. "What about you, are you okay?"

"I'm fine."

"Did he touch you?"

"No." She came back to the bed. By then I'd managed the perilous feat of propping myself up on my elbows. She helped me sit up, then handed me the glass and watched me drink. When I finished, she went to fill it up again. Over the running water she spoke. "Did you . . . do you think you killed him?"

I shook my head, which hurt to do. But not as much as it had a minute ago. "I dunno. I don't think so. But I sure hurt him." Something occurred to me and my eyes searched the room. "He's not lying around here somewhere, is he?"

"There's no one here but us." She stared at me, lips parted and eyes huge, an expression both frightened and relieved. She remained a little wide eyed as she brought me the second glassful and knelt beside me on the bed. As I drank I was acutely aware of the pressure of her thigh against my hip. I handed her the glass, and as she put it aside I caressed her cheekbone with the back of my hand.

When she didn't pull away I ran my fingers through her hair, drew her closer. We kissed.

Neither of us broke off until we absolutely had to breathe.

I kissed her neck in quick soft pecks. She sighed and lifted her chin. Every contact with her skin was electrifying, addictive. She affected me like morphine: the pain in my gut and skull didn't recede; I simply didn't care.

Naked, her body bore markings as exotic as the rings around her eyes and mouth and neck. She moved carefully above me, avoiding the blistered burn, as I followed those markings with my palms.

Afterward we lay side by side beneath the sheet, sweat-soaked and uneasy. My own rat-fink flesh began to announce new aches as a result of the exertion. The clay had cracked.

"You can't stay in this town," I told her. "He's seen you now."

She shifted her forearm over her brow, but didn't answer.

"Leave with me," I said.

She replied with a derisive snort.

I turned to her, put a hand on her bare belly. "Don't think twice about it, you have to." I tried to meet her eyes, but she wouldn't play. "Unless, maybe . . . Do you know where that place is, where he took me?"

Her lips pressed in a line. She squeezed her eyes shut. "I followed him in spirit when he took you. I might be able to find it again *there*. Here, I have no idea."

"It has to be close by."

She shook her head, eyes still squeezed closed. "I've never seen anywhere like it around here."

"He's still there, then. He's badly hurt, I bet. But he'll hide out and heal. When he does, if we're still around, we'll be the ones hurt. You've got to come with me."

She threw the sheet aside, climbed out of bed and started gathering her clothes, at the same time stunning in her grace and awkward in her self-consciousness.

"Don't get crazy on me," she said. "I have to be more careful now, but I can't just uproot my life at the drop of a dime."

"You have to!"

Her blue eyes blazed. Incredible, how much of my strange ordeal has been woven around blue-eyed stares. "What makes you think it would do any good? Won't two of us together just be easier to find?"

"Look." I sat up. "It can't be a coincidence we found each other."

"Yes it can." She fastened her bra, agitated.

"No it can't. We're supposed to help each other. I'm sure."

Tears of frustration glittered on her cheeks as she shook her head. "Don't let yourself believe that," she spat. "We're not put on this Earth for any reason." She pulled up her jeans, re-buckled her slim black belt. "We're not put here to help anyone with anything. We just are. If anything, people like us, we're more vulnerable than people whose lives are normal, because people like us get so crazy so easily. We're much more dangerous to each other than we are to any of them." She finished dressing, pulled her hair back into a ponytail. "There's nothing special at all about what we are."

"I never said that."

She was done. "Do you need me to give you a ride anywhere?"

I sighed. "No. I think I've bought time for at least a night's rest."

"Okay, then." She made for the door. I told her I'd come see her tomorrow at the restaurant, but before I finished my sentence, she'd already left.

I lay back in the bed, my mind pulling in a thousand different directions, and didn't sleep a wink.

DRIFT FROM THE
WINDROWS

E den, I'm not a writer. Not like you are. You touch a keyboard, and I swear, five thousand words drop out in thirty seconds. Not for me. I type fast, yes, but I will never have so much to say. Not all at once like that.

Truth is, I'm not much of a talker, either. You know that, right? This, what's happening right now with the words coming from me so easy, that's got to be the state I'm in. My nerves. The chemicals in the air. All those sounds in the other room.

Maybe it's easier that I'm just talking to my laptop. I'm glad I can't see my reflection in the screen. I don't think I could record this if I could see my own face. Even though it's for you.

I need you to understand what all that pain means, what it's for. I hope my words are clear—it's hard to tell, I can barely hear my own voice.

My boss can probably hear me out here. I don't think she cares.

Oh gods, I wish I had known how much you hated San-Morta before we started sleeping together. But when I told you where I worked, you didn't say anything. Why?

Wait, I remember. You told me why you didn't say anything. Because you wanted me that bad. Because you didn't want to scare me off. But you know, I don't think you could have even if you tried. Your purple hair didn't scare me. Your tattoos, the gauges stretching your earlobes, your nipple rings, none of that scared me. Fuck, even the thought of what my dad was going to say didn't scare me. The bastard had a hard enough time accepting me as a scientist. He wanted me married off to a doctor back home. Seven steps of wedding vows around a fire, jewelry through my nose, the whole traditional shebang.

What he said to me when I confessed I loved a woman—I never told you, did I? You asked me, and I told you not to make me speak of it. You were so respectful of my wishes. Is that why you never talked to me about my job? You knew I'd tell you not to write what you planned to write, never ever to do it, and you didn't want to give me a chance to object? Is that it?

You confuse me so much. But I love that about you. Even now I hope that doesn't change. I hope you come out of this with some of that wildness left inside.

Brady here at work told me. He showed me your blog. The entry about what SanMorta does to farmers.

I know all about that, you know. I don't like it either. I don't even care that they can hear me say it right now. I know why people think it's unfair: those farmers don't have much money, and SanMorta has billions. What harm could this company possibly suffer if someone saves a few seeds? But that's not the point you made, is it? In that blog entry.

Brady told me he found what you wrote because that superpopular activist site linked to it. Spread it everywhere. His eyes were so wide, watching me as I read your blog entry on his screen. Because he thought he was looking at a dead woman. That you and I both were as good as dead.

You're not the first to claim my employer deliberately tampers with crops and uses aggressive legal tactics to sweep it under the rug. But what you blogged, about why they do it . . .

You had to know they would come straight to me. That I would have to answer for your words. In all my soul, I can only find the will to forgive you because you couldn't possibly have imagined the consequences.

If I'm to survive—if *we* are to survive—I can never, ever, let them lose their faith in me.

Know I came home to you that day with a heavy heart. Please, know that.

Please.

* * *

S orry, I lost my breath. I think I might have fainted.

It smells like asphalt in here. No, so much worse, like there's a tar pit from prehistoric days in my boss's office, like all the creatures that drowned in it, they're ghosts now and they're haunting this waiting room.

There's a sweet smell inside the tar, like honeysuckle, like you, and it gets stronger every time I hear your voice through that door, but if I try to inhale you, the tar will kill me. One hundred percent tar, just like the old cigarette ads never said. I'll barf my lungs out, and they'll grow legs and crawl away . . .

I'm sorry, Eden. I don't even remember what I just said. I'm fighting to keep these words sane.

But I remember when I got home and confronted you with that printout. And you just said, "Yeah, I tried to get you fired," like it was nothing. It would have taken me a thousand hours of screwing up my courage to admit something like that, but you just blurted it out! My dad beat me for blurting things out. Your dad did too, didn't he? You told me that, and that wasn't even the worst he did. So how did we grow up to be so different?

Concentrate, Amisha. Keep your focus.

Eden, this is so hard. To fight the drugs we're breathing. To finally speak my secret aloud.

It's like I see you in front of me now, me saying, "What were you thinking? I almost lost my job!"

And your blue eyes went steely, and you said, "That would be a good thing. I think they've brainwashed you, Amisha."

And as I sat there in shock, you snuggled against me on the love seat, like you wanted a kiss. And you started talking about the lateral gene transmission, like I didn't know.

I was too stunned by what you had done to say anything else. I just let you go on.

And much of what you said, I've heard before. That, with genetically modified food, the body doesn't recognize when it's ingested something unnatural. That the body gets fooled into replicating unwanted genes. I couldn't help but laugh when your eyes went all wide and serious, and you told me, "They've proven that the mutant cells start clustering in our reproductive organs first. So children are born with that modified DNA already a part of them."

I know I shouldn't have laughed. It wasn't for the reasons you thought. I was laughing because you couldn't possibly have known how close you'd come to describing what's really going on without actually understanding one fucking bit of it.

And then you yelled at me about how SanMorta gets away with it because they have plants—human plants!—in every level and branch of government, and I know I shouldn't have kept laughing.

But then you grabbed me and shook me!

How could you do that?! You know all about what my dad did to me when I was eight. I trusted you with that! Did you do it deliberately? To hurt me the way my dad would hurt me, so I'd heel like a good little dog?

You're the first person I've known who I ever felt I could be intimate with. And I've even told you . . . that you make me feel safe . . .

Sorry, Eden. It doesn't matter now.

I keep forgetting what's important, because of the atmosphere in here. It's so thick with the Mother's musk, it's like my brain isn't even attached to my body anymore.

Is this thing still recording? It is, bless the stars.

I had to show you that you had it all wrong. It's a miracle I was even allowed to come home to you.

And I admit, it broke my heart in a completely irrational way that you agreed so readily to a tour of our lab. I knew then and there that you had to be plotting something that you'd try to hide from me.

But at the same time, you made me so happy. Because I knew then that you had a chance. *We* had a chance.

Oh! Oh no! W-wait, Mother. I'm not finished, don't—Eden, I love y—

She let me go.

Looks like my laptop is still working. She didn't touch it.

I don't think she cares about our lives. I mean, our day-to-day lives. And that's why I have hope. I hope what she took from me will help you . . .

I hope they'll make the things the Mother is doing to you proceed easier.

This stench, it's so thick. It makes my head light. I don't know if I'm talking anymore or dreaming it all.

Funny that I remember this now: I did worry that you'd be disappointed at how mundane this place is. You know, our labs, they don't look much different than what you find in the biology department at Ferris University—sorry, I shouldn't laugh, especially now. I just remembered your shout of "FU" every time I said that name. Fact is, our labs look junkier. Hah. And you know, the "palace of all evil," as you call it, is just a big greenhouse on the roof. Where we keep all the varieties of plants we're studying. To see what gene combinations show promise.

It's really important, what we do. The heirloom seeds you yammer on about—the world is undergoing drastic changes. I have inklings of what's going to happen, and I still struggle to imagine it. The weather turning haywire won't account for even a fraction of how this planet will transform. What humans will endure. But we'll still need to grow food. We have to adapt our crops.

I don't hear those sounds any more. Maybe it's over. Or maybe my senses have stopped working.

But my laptop is here on the desk. I can touch its warm screen. The little line that the recording program displays keeps pulsing as I speak.

Did I say something about how the Mother doesn't care? None of them care. About our daily lives. My co-workers might care, but they're not the ones that matter. These . . . creatures only care about the big picture and where we fit in it.

But Eden, you were all about the big picture, too. Of course, you planned to put everything you found on your blog. I knew you had a camera hidden in that purse; you never carry a purse. Did someone from the activist website give that to you?

Fact is, I could read your thoughts like a picture book. If I lost my job because of your exposé, if you wrecked my career, I'd be free of this place, and you could deprogram me. Lovingly. And I'd see that you did it all for love and love you even more.

What I kept thinking about, though, when I led to you to my boss's office, was how you grabbed me by the neck and shook me. Like my father did because I wouldn't do what he wanted. So many years, I would sit on his lap, and he would sing to me so beautifully in Hindi, and I would wish I knew the words. I had no warning what was waiting inside him.

Or you. But I *do* forgive you.

Some part of me, though, must hate the thought of happiness for us. Because there was a perverse part of my mind that desperately wanted you to catch on. The way all my co-workers treated you better than any real science journalist would ever be treated, all smiles and happy to show you *everything*, even though you're nothing more than an angry woman with your own little angry blog. The way they just smiled and kept chatting about how we use traditional cross-pollinating when you couldn't hide your boredom anymore. The way my boss greeted you like an old friend after the things you wrote.

She looked her dapper best, I tell you that. I can't believe how pretty she can be sometimes. It's all about her mood, I think. How she wants you to feel.

I could tell you were responding to that aspect of her power, too, Eden. But how could you help yourself? No one can, really. Sometimes, I think my boss is just another human, taken deeper into the Mother's mystery than all the rest of us. Sometimes, I think she's a piece of the Mother, an independent aspect.

What I think is irrelevant.

No one can resist her charms. When she selects someone to meet her here for an interview, you can bet they'll show up on time. But it's how they respond to *her* boss that's important. Whether they understand and comply, like I did. Or try to fight back. Or start shrieking.

My boss's boss. The Mother. She was waiting for you in the room beyond the office. They told me I wasn't allowed to say anything about her. That I had to let her introduce herself.

My boss was weaving her spell of words. You didn't notice when the Mother started attaching her limbs to you. I did. I couldn't say anything.

Eden, I'm so sorry.

I was hoping you wouldn't scream.

I grew up reading comic books about the many-armed Hindu gods. Sometimes when the Mother takes me, I close my eyes and imagine it's Parvati embracing me. Preparing me for the times ahead. The Mother lets me think this, I think, even sometimes makes it real for me. She wants me to be willing. I don't know what she does for the others. We don't dare talk about that. I wouldn't even speak it aloud now if anyone else was here.

I guess you could say, the same thing you tried to do to me—set up an ambush to force me off the team—I had to do to you. Otherwise, our lives were forfeit.

When I went to the Mother to answer for what you'd done and she took me in her arms, I showed her how useful you could be, filled my mind with visions of all the things you could do for her once she taught you the right way to think. How your voice on our side would make our cause easier. Thank the gods, I saw that she agreed, that you would be spared.

She showed me what she had in mind for you.

I didn't see any other choice.

The Mother isn't like you—or like dad. She's been honest with all of us here about the harm that lies inside her.

Eden, you were absolutely right about some things. You wrote that the reason SanMorta denies that its GMOs cause genetic drift in humans isn't blind stupidity or bureaucratic incompetence. You said they're doing it deliberately and that they want it to spread.

This is true.

You even almost grasped the reason why. You wrote that it was for population control, that the group you're in touch with believes the intruder genes will make everyone more docile, more vulnerable to disease, more dependent on government.

They'll cause changes all right. I can't think about it because it makes me feel so sick I want to vomit myself inside out.

The Mother is just one of multitudes. She and the ancient things she calls kindred are . . . are kind in their own way. When they make themselves known, they don't want bloodshed. They want to claim this world peacefully.

The things they can do with their minds. The ways their forms can change. We can't hurt them. Their bodies—most of what they are doesn't even exist in this dimension. There is nothing we can do to stop them.

Those of us who are useful, those of us who understand and show that we are with them, we have a chance at lives, at futures. A slim chance but a *chance*.

Those who resist, who don't understand, who are not useful. They will just be crops.

There are some, like your father—like my father—who deserve that and worse. But I want you. I want to spend the rest of my life with you. I want you to be with me when this future comes. It's the only way I can imagine that it will be bearable.

The smells are fading. Those sounds you were making, they've stopped.

The Mother promised me you would still be you when she was done. That you would still look like you. Even, to some degree, still think like you.

Oh, I hope she's kept her promise.

If there's something left in you that questions what I've done, I'll play this because I won't be able to say these things to your face.

But I hope I don't need it. I hope I can just delete it and never worry about us again.

I love you.

AFTERMATH OF AN INDUSTRIAL ACCIDENT

Shadeishi and I pushed the storage room door shut, not knowing whether anyone else had already dashed in to hide, or whether any of the creatures were waiting inside. The screams coming from the students down the hall deafened us to any telltale noise. My own panting breath whooshed in and out—I had a key and had spent precious seconds locking the door, as it couldn't be locked from inside. Shadeishi's face hovered an inch from mine the whole time, her wide, toothy, toothsome mouth silently shaping *Hurry hurry.*

Neither of us were thinking past surviving the next few seconds. Our frantically chosen hiding place offered no other exit, unless we decided to break out a window and drop twelve stories. But that really didn't matter. There was nowhere to escape to. Where the hall outside turned a corner, there were more windows, and as we ran past them I had snatched a glimpse of the company's front lawn, its level green stippled with torn bodies. Outside and inside, we were all prey.

In front of us, the doorknob jiggled violently. Shadeishi and I met one another's wide-eyed stare. A male voice cursed, high-pitched and terrified. Footsteps pounded away, fading into the shrieks of agony from the testing rooms around the corner.

"What is happening?" Shadeishi whispered, as if she hadn't seen. Our offices were right across from that training lab. So much of the whites showed around her fuchsia pupils that I imagined, for a second, they were glowing. And then a rational thought sliced through my own panic—the light that let me see her so clearly: where was it coming from?

This room had once been the main teaching lab, back in the days when RillCorp had need to train hundreds of new labtechs at a time. Now its cavernous length was stuffed with years of biotech-industry flotsam. Rows of shelves storing specimens, show-and-tell props for the company's biochemistry and biology training semi-nars, stood in regiments behind us, blotting out the light source, but it had to be a window with the blinds drawn up. Which meant those creatures could see inside. The glass and metal wouldn't keep them out, if they spied prey in here.

These weren't fancy remote-operated panels; these were ac-tual ratty bargain-basement blinds—typical of RillCorp with its high-tech miracles, showing off in front of clients and engaging in dangerous penny-pinching everywhere else. Maybe I could lower the blinds. If that didn't get us killed instantly as one of the things soared over to investigate the quick downward motion, it could buy us more time. To the degree I was thinking at all, that was the goal in my head as I sidled toward the wall. Shadeishi stayed put and watched me, maybe waiting to see if my choice of action got me eaten.

I stepped softly even though the tortured cries outside masked the sounds I made.

I could see a sink at the far end of the wall aisle, and I offered a cynical prayer to one of Shadeishi's native gods that it still drew water. To cross to it I would have to walk in front of ten tall win-dows, covered with nothing-fancy low-tech-as-you-can get beige blinds. The blinds over the closest windows were turned to let more light in. The blinds over the fourth window from my position were drawn all the way up. They should have all been closed, but we sel-dom visited this room now, and clearly whoever had come in here in the last few months—or was it years?—didn't give a damn about protocols.

My breath loud as a tube train in my ears, I took the lever in my fingers and turned the nearest blinds closed. Nothing smashed through the window to tear me open and drain my body cavities dry.

I glanced back at Shadeishi, who crouched against the door, svelte knees drawn up to her chin, her fists crammed into the sides of her huge Choom mouth. I raised a hand, *it's going to be okay,* the biggest lie I had ever told her, and tiptoed toward the fully-raised blinds.

Would that I could have stopped myself from looking outside.

Our hideaway was twelve stories up. A deep red smear of human blood stained the outside of the window. Beyond the bloodstain, the illusory green sky provided the light that threatened to expose us. Beneath it, on a normal day, an immaculate field of manicured grass dotted with wildflowers would stretch as far as the eye could see.

If the clear sky didn't give the trick away, well, you'd have to be lobotomized to believe the fields were real. A multipurpose quarantine shield sealed away the RillCorp tower from hundreds of square kilometers of industrial Paxton wasteland. RillCorp had taken the extra, exorbitant step of incorporating holographics into the force field that could generate their own light. Visitors flown in through the ceiling port or, if rumors were true, admitted through an extradimensional gate in the executive suites, could treat themselves to a view that erased the slums of Punktown completely. Conversely, the rare passerby on the outside would see a tall wall around an empty lot.

It made my heart swell whenever I thought about my status as one of the very few employees entrusted with the shield's emergency codes. Even then, mortified by the carnage, my heart swelled.

Never before had it been so easy to tell where the genetically engineered and extravagantly irrigated lawn around the tower ended and the quarantine shield began. Shredded bodies buried the grass, piled higher near the faintly outlined egress gate. So many colors of blood pooled against the shield's inner boundaries, demarcating its exact dimensions in massacre hues.

A white coat flapped. Someone was making a stumbling dash across the gore-slathered lawn toward the gate. From where I stood, the slats partially obstructed my view of my fellow employee's progress.

The coat continued to flap in the corner of my eye, but now it moved in the wrong direction, up rather than forward, as if its wearer were levitating. Through the slats I caught the barest glimpse of the gray mass hoisting the poor soul into the air. Thankfully I succeeded in levering the blinds shut and didn't have to witness the end of it.

I dreamed for a moment that it was my backstabbing rival Gio being drained of blood and ripped to pieces outside. The fantasy gave me enough strength to scuttle to the next set of open blinds. The shelves I passed held archival vial cases dulled with age, specimen jars showcasing multicolored tissue lumps, cryocylinders the size of coffee carafes and the olfactory ghosts of a thousand chemicals.

I cursed whatever joker had raised the next set of blinds to the ceiling. Once I got them down, nothing outside could look in, unless they could see through walls, in which case we were fucked anyway. Then maybe Shadeishi and I could eat each other out until the monsters came for us.

I glanced back but couldn't see her. I imagined her, back to the door, gripping the ornate tattoos on her forearms and praying. She prayed to calm herself, not because she believed, or so she told me. If her people's gods were real, she had said more than once, they'd have prevented the humans from finding this planet. Amen to that.

I found the cord that lowered the blinds and contemplated the consequences of a too-quick motion. Behind me, droplets of something pittered onto the floor.

A door clicked open, then slammed shut. Not the one Shadeishi and I had come through. A different entrance. I had forgotten there was more than one way in here. I yelped at the noise, yanked the cord and brought those blinds down with a clatter louder than rifle fire.

A woman shrieked. Not Shadeishi. A man's gruff voice shushed her. Nothing smashed the window to grab me as everything but my panicked heart froze in place.

In the ensuing silence, a faint drip-drip made itself known, accompanied by a soft, wet crackle, like a dull knife sawing at meat.

RillCorp developed weapons, among many other things, but forbade its employees from keeping any on their person, not even stun plasma. I kept a plasma thrower in my nightstand. I'd even practiced shooting it. How I longed for it then.

Through the shelves, I spotted movement. A small Tikkihotto woman in a lab coat, pressed against the opposite wall, the tendrils of her eyes bunching together to focus on me. I knew her: Takhoun. The perverse relief that flooded me, seeing her alive, faded quickly to a pang of wrath, because if she was here, likely Gio was too. Was he doing something to create that noise?

I slunk to a nearby cross-aisle and crept toward her. She started to tremble, violently. No, that wasn't it. She was shaking her head, her eye-tendrils stabbing to my right, where liquid splattered.

I turned.

I recognized the blue-skinned intern suspended in mid-air about six meters away. A soft-spoken Sinanese named Ched. Even in the dimness, his black eyes glistened as his head lolled in my direction.

Suspended in mid-air didn't quite describe it. He jutted out from a high shelf, his hips and back and neck straight, his wagging head almost brushing the shelving opposite. A thick strand of red drool stretched a meter and a half from his lips to the floor. A black smoke-like substance rose from his pulsing chest.

The red strand extended from his mouth twitched and curled upward. Another emerged from his ear. Even more oozed out from the suppurating mound of his chest.

The creature these tentacles belonged to squeezed out from the space where Ched's lower legs were concealed, expanding like a massive snail exiting a tiny shell. Once free of its hiding spot, it slowly rose toward the ceiling, unfettered by gravity.

I've seen specimens in recreational aquariums that simulate Earth's oceans before they were poisoned. The creature's body resembled that of a skate, diamond-shaped with wide side fins and a thick tail-like appendage. Above the fins, scallop eyebeads punctuated the creature's entire circumference. A cone comprised of dozens of red tentacles hung from its belly, the upper lengths cross-connected so their structure resembled the skeleton of an antique hoop skirt. The lower lengths were squirming inside Ched's corpse.

Just minutes ago, Shadeishi and I had been alone in her office, with all its doors locked, and I had parted just enough of her layers of clothing to savor a slow lap at her left nipple. And she had let a long sigh of pleasure slide out of that spectacular mouth with all its rows of pearly molars.

Across the hall the training lab had erupted with shrieks and howls.

Shadeishi and I had scrambled to restore our clothes to order as the volume and number of the screams had redoubled. I'd thrown open her office door.

The training lab allows instructors to peer in from a safe distance through a bay window. On the other side of that window, creatures just like the one looming above me in the storeroom aisle were tearing the lab interns, and the instructors who were inside with them, to ragged, blood-and-ichor-spraying shreds. Smells of feces and burnt flesh had slammed over us.

A high-pitched gargle from down the hall, and a splatter of steaming blood had hit the wall just a meter from where we were gawping. Our fellow instructor Gorrister hung in the red-tendriled net of one of those creatures, his head still connected by a strip of flesh to his shoulders, the tentacles excavating and absorbing organs and tissue from every cavity. The creature's gray diamond of a body had billowed against the ceiling, its eyespots staring in all directions.

Behind us, Shadeishi's office windows had smashed inward as something burst through from the outside, and we ran, to hide in this storage room, which was no hiding place at all.

Poor Ched fell to pieces in a rain of raw meat. The parts of him that remained in the creature's grip shriveled into the surfaces of its tendrils and vanished in a second flat. Completely exposed, I could do nothing to prevent what was about to happen to me. My bladder and bowels both loosened, and the only other sensation that registered was the pounding of my heart.

A shout, then a blast of green flame sprayed from the darkness beyond the creature's gray mass, etching the entire room in a hellish web of shadows.

My feet came unstuck and I backpedaled as fucking fast as I could. The green flames enveloped and clung for a moment to the creature's body, but had no effect on its flesh. It darted toward the source of the flame with the same blur of speed I'd observed of its kind in the training lab, and plunged right into a second, brighter and wider jet of green fire.

The monster plummeted straight down. When it landed it burst in a fountain of glowing red spray.

My brain finally connected fully to my body. I turned tail and ran. At the door where I came in, I found Takhoun and Shadeishi curled together in a frightened ball, something I'd have given my right eye to see under any other circumstances. I had the presence of mind to take off my coat and huddle with them. Because I'm a tall, broad-shouldered and thick-chested guy, the coat covered most of the three of us, at least saving our heads from the sticky film that started settling over everything, its red glow fading to clot brown. The good news, I guess, was that it didn't matter that I was pressed against my current and former lovers with soiled pants, because the reek of the disintegrated creature's flesh bathed us in a stench somewhere between an open sewer and a chemical fire.

A feathery brush against my cheek. Takhoun was using her eye tendrils to inspect me. I smiled for her sake. My panicked panting mixed with theirs.

Of all the things to remember at that moment. When Takhoun and I were constantly fighting, but still fucking. She hadn't yet stabbed me to my face by shacking up with Gio, who she knew I hated. But I had already started spending nights with Shadeishi, not staying in my quarters like I told Takhoun. Shadeishi had just joined the biochemisty department and came personally recommended by Dr. Drachan, my direct supervisor's boss's boss. There was a morning when I had shown up unannounced at Takhoun's and cajoled and browbeat her into giving me head, my hands on her temples, her eyestalks gripping my wrists like she knew I liked. What she didn't know is that half an hour earlier I'd received the same from Shadeishi, disappearing completely into that glorious mouth. I did all of that just to see if I could.

The shiver, the hot pit boring in my stomach, could have been that memory, or a side effect of the aggressive itching where that brown film congealed on exposed skin.

Something poked me through the coat, between the shoulder blades. So glad I didn't jump or scream, because immediately after I heard Gio say, "I've got clean masks; you all need to put them on."

"Ladies first," I said, which produced a gale of nervous laughter from Shadeishi.

I hated that it was Gio rescuing us. This bastard once said right to my face, "You're pretty and you can lick ass like a pro and that's the only reason anyone's let you get this far," as if a doctorate in biochemistry from U. of P. and a decade of superlative evaluations from Drachan meant nothing.

Takhoun drew away first. When Shadeishi's turn came, she gave my arm a quick squeeze of reassurance. Then a foot tapped my bootsole and I sprang up. My coat was smothered in the filth. I tossed it aside, pulled the proffered stretchy filter mask over my face in haste.

Gio, a head shorter than me, muck-stained black hair jutting out behind his own mask, said, "If we're going to live we have to clean ourselves. Let's hope the plumbing works."

My heart sank, that he had a plan and my own survival depend-
ed on following his lead without argument. Then I noticed who else
was with us. Instead of a humanoid-fitted mask, which it couldn't
have worn, the Anul's entire upper body was covered in a transparent membrane, as if it had been shrink-wrapped. Anuls are hideous
and indistinguishable, with big, eyeless hammerhead skulls on their
hunchback shoulders and wide grins full of bovine teeth. But this
one, I knew, because of the thick scarring partway up his left neck-
stalk, as if he had healed from being half-guillotined.

It made no sense for Nuund to even be on this floor. He worked
in the dull black pyramid that crowned our tower, designed by
RillCorp to house the multidimensional physics division.

Two dots winked to life in my mind, and I connected them.
"Those monsters, where did they come from?" I stared at the
Anul's broad face as I asked, certain he had an answer.

Gio cut me off. "We can ask questions later. We need to get the
residue from that thing off our skins right now."

As if we couldn't walk and talk. He set off toward the other
end of the room, where there were sinks, eyewash stations and one
lone decontamination pod. Who knew if any of it still worked?

Of the five of us, I had the longest strides. I wasn't going to let Gio
lead, so I stayed right beside him. The aisles were just wide enough.
That stinking brown sludge covered everything. I mean everything.

"What was that you used on the creature?" I asked, loud
enough so the women could hear me. "And is there more of it?"

"Keep your voice down," Gio hissed. Then, before I could par-
ry, "A block of frozen n-buli dropped into a canister of tenspun
water just before triggering the deravel."

I couldn't keep my voice down for that revelation. "Higher-
dimensional solvent mixed with a corrosive base?"

"Didn't expect the flames," Gio said. I think the bastard was
smiling. That could have killed all of us. But the creature would
have killed all of us if he hadn't done that. I couldn't berate him for
his carelessness without looking like a moron.

"Thank all the colors you killed it," Takhoun said, a vicious
jab at me in that awkward moment. Because she and Gio worked
together in biochemical weaponry, and I worked in biochemical
domestic solutions, and they thought reminding me made me feel
inferior. They never missed a chance to do it.

We were almost to the sinks. I didn't let my hurt show. "How did you know that would work?"

"Nuund's idea. His area of expertise."

"A very lucky guess," the Anul said with noticeable haste.

"Where did they come from?" Maybe Shadeishi was trying to help me out. "They were everywhere at once."

"Any ideas, Nuund?" I grinned his way.

"I've never seen anything like them." The Anul was eager to deflect the question, that was clear.

"Thank goodness these hazmat suits were sealed." Gio pried up the lid on a compression crate. "Those sinks are coated with that goo. I know this isn't how we trained, but I think maybe we can fit in the pod two or three at a time; just be careful what you touch. I don't like the way this stuff is burning."

I remembered my soiled underclothes. And I wanted Gio out of earshot. Might as well make a high road show out of it. I inclined my head his way. "You two first."

Shadeishi shot me a look. Gio noticed. "I think there's room." He and the women didn't say anything else, just took three uniforms and climbed as quickly as they could into the pod. To get naked together.

I funneled my anger into something productive. See, I had noticed an object on a nearby shelf that I recognized by its shape. I picked it up, ignored the way the itching intensified as I worked my fingers through the nozzle trigger, and brandished the spraywand point blank in Nuund's face. "Know what this is?"

Those bovine teeth parted in alien shock. "No," he said slowly.

"How lucky for me that I do. It's a discontinued pesticide, but with a special history. We discovered a secondary effect that led us to test it on a certain kind of tumor. The kind they call orb weavers—you should know it well; your race imported them here." The orb weavers manifest as ever-growing pink pearls on the outside, as ruthless fibers on the inside that wind throughout the host's nervous system. They started with the Anuls, who harvest them as prize delicacies even when grown on their own kind, or so the rumors went.

"Too toxic for practical use, which is a shame. It turns those hard pearls to jelly in seconds. I think it would have the exact same effect on your skeletal system."

Nuund gulped, both his unscarred and scarred neck flexing, a surprisingly humanoid reflex.

"So quit lying and evading. Where did these things come from? The only way you could have gotten to our floor that fast is if you had advance warning to run."

Now the Anul straightened. "I don't know what they are. But they are from a different dimension. And that residue is all around us. You can't be so stupid that you'd want to introduce another volatile compound into this mix."

"Don't call me stupid. Answer my questions."

Damned if he didn't smile, a reflex many Anul have learned in order to better relate to us humanoids. "I was on your floor for a personal conference with Gio and his assistant. And if you had been watching the trainees work like you were supposed to, you would have seen exactly what caused this."

My first response, *That makes no fucking sense at all*, was immediately overwhelmed by the second. "You were spying on me? All three of you?"

I meant, I think, to point a finger in his face. But I was holding the spraywand, which pierced the protective membrane he wore as if it wasn't there. Bonus, it went right in his mouth. He grabbed at me to shove me away, and I think that's when I squeezed the triggers.

I could never have anticipated that the compound would react so swiftly with whatever substances make an Anul an Anul. Maybe he was right, and the creature's residue altered the effect. His flesh inside that breathable membrane didn't just liquefy, it boiled. The new substance sprayed out through the hole I'd made, all over me, before the membrane melted and burst.

My agony went beyond the boiling sluice. My hands before my face had activated with horrible life, the brown gunk that covered them alive and crawling, as if hundreds of tiny teeming worms had fused with my flesh. I could feel it on the inside, too, as if my nerves and tendons and blood vessels were squirming with their own will. And it wasn't just my hands. I could feel it in my feet, my thighs, my belly, my face.

I didn't scream. Because it wasn't fair that I should die like this and Gio and Takhoun go on. Shadeishi deserved it too, for abandoning me.

They had no warning, as I yanked the pod hatch open and threw myself on them.

I had the strangest dream.

I had dashed into the bathroom in my quarters. Shadeishi and Takhoun were both out there, waiting for me in the boudoir. Dr. Drachan was there too, ready to observe. He loved to watch just as much as I loved to impress. And Gio was there, too, bound hand and foot to a chair. He was going to have no choice but to watch it all too. Then we were going to kill him, together. I needed to primp every centimeter of my visible self.

But when I faced the mirror, all my urges drained of blood.

I didn't understand how I could see my own reflection. Instead of eyes I had raw sockets. A long yellow bone jutted from the side of my face, its underside studded with a double dozen Choom teeth.

The jaw wagged.

"What's wrong with you?" I said in Shadeishi's voice.

Then I screamed, except it wasn't my mind, my brain, that generated the scream. The sound came from a tumor that yawned open where her/my neck should have been.

I came awake.

My nerves sang with pain, such a ridiculous amount, so far off the scale of the one-to-ten rating the nurses ask for in that archaic ritual that I started to laugh. What good could screaming do against such epic torture?

When I laughed I made no noise. A part of me moved that my brain registered as a mouth, but it was in the completely wrong place inside my body.

Freaked, I tried to stand up. Nervous impulses told me I'd raised to all fours in a crawl, yet I still stared at the pod's translucent ceiling. The foul stench that had contaminated the storage room was a thousandfold stronger in here, and violating my senses in many more places, as if I smelled it through every pore.

Confused and frightened, I scuttled in no direction and all. Though I was up in a crawl, way more of me than there should have been still dragged on the floor, and I could swear some parts were striving to pull in different directions, independent of what I wanted.

Then, as if someone slowly turned a dimmer switch, the painful background static frying my mind gradually shifted into something like evangelical ecstasy. My understanding of my new physical form restrung itself, and I became hyper-aware of which nerve conduits were mine, which belonged to the three people I had partly absorbed, and hell, even which people they were.

I even knew why this was happening: the higher-dimensional creature's equivalent of DNA, acting with an astonishing level of collective intelligence to create a habitable ecosystem for itself. I was its chosen center of higher neural function. Not Shadeishi or Takhoun or Gio. Especially not Gio. Me.

Forewarned by my nightmare, I hoped never to encounter a mirror. But sans my good looks, I had something else to enjoy. I was already physically the largest of the four of us, and growing stronger by the second. I controlled our body. I could make us do things.

I made us crawl out of the pod and toward the storage room exit. There was no reason to fear the creatures anymore. They would sense the kinship and leave us alone. Perhaps they already did. I had become aware of a substance all about that was like a fluid suspension, yet not, and of concentrations of hungry energy that floated within it, and knew these to be my new kindred. This awareness ended at a boundary that conformed to the exact size and shape of the interior of the force shield surrounding RillCorp.

It wasn't fair to all my colleagues, but especially, especially to me, to suffer these horrors and indignities alone while the vile slummy soup of Punktown thrived on, oblivious.

A part of my brain remained aloof from all this, and regretful that neither Shadeishi nor Takhoun fully shared my nervous system. I longed to convey my intentions to them, so that they'd help me rather than resist. Then the three of us could together absorb what was left of Gio and maybe have something like a joyous existence in this new shape.

I did try to speak one last time, and some mobile parts of me flapped, but those were neither jaws nor tongues.

Takhoun started to scream, perhaps because the movement I enforced on our configuration hurt her. The membrane stretched over her mouth muffled the sound, but she must have been drawing air from somewhere, because it bulged, a rudimentary balloon that wouldn't quite inflate. One set of her eyestalks strained beneath the surface of the slimy, scarred mass that had absorbed her head.

The change rewiring us would eventually quiet her. I did not relent.

One of their arms scrabbled against my back. I didn't immediately know who it belonged to. Within this collective body I animated parts that were clearly mine with the eager siphoning rhythm of a pumpjack and drew body fluids from each of them into me, and the tugs of resistance subsided.

New limbs that were wholly my own needle-pricked into life, helpful in maneuvering my cumbersome bulk down the long hallway and into the lift that would take us to the lobby.

One of the gray floaters hovered within the elevator, its net of tentacles drawn up to its underbelly, the remains of its meals all over the walls. It left us alone as we rode. I stared into the beautiful patterns circulating through its cloudy flesh, the meat and blood of my co-workers digested and redistributed to more beautiful use. I was loath to leave that view, but I had a mission to finish.

The marble tiles of the reception lobby grated like sandpaper against my ever-lengthening belly. When I reached for the ornate entrance doors, vesicle-covered tendrils extended from the conical tumor slung beneath my shoulder blades. It felt little different from extending an arm. My limbs simply bent and bent beyond the range I'm used to, pushing the doors open and outward.

As I pulled us all down the grand, gore-smeared stairs leading to the lawn, the artificial sunlight pained my eyespots. I paused to let my eyes adjust. The doors swung shut, some part of me trapped in the doorjamb. I crawled on and that piece ripped away.

Shadeishi shrieked. She still had her voice! Maybe that lost mass was part of her. Further evidence—the remains of her legs, which I still recognized, could never forget, kicked fruitlessly at my flank as I began to cross the meat-splattered lawn, toward the faint outline of the exodus gate, where an employee properly entrusted could enter the codes to bring the shield down.

Above us the green sky was blotted by diamond shapes. The creatures waited in a motionless swarm. Perhaps they understood what I was up to. Bully for them.

I didn't care anymore what had materialized them inside our building. The part of me that remained aloof wondered, when I unleashed them, would this squalid city even notice a new plague in its midst?

Oh, I hoped so. Yes I did.

At the exodus gate I rose, bringing my new limbs to the barely visible bubble that contained the emergency panel. It turned opaque, and was rock-solid to my touch. Of course it didn't recognize me. I'd forgotten that it needed to read the pattern of my original human hands. Where were they?

I flipped completely upside down. I had not planned on doing so. I tried to right myself, and slammed back hard into the exact same position.

I could feel motion that I didn't control. Through the eyespots on my exposed underside I saw hands, not mine, scrabbling at the console, saw the bubble evaporate and let Gio, what was left of Gio, access the input field.

The codes. Gio couldn't know them. He was never a favorite of Dr. Drachan's. I was!

His hands weren't connected to my nerves. I couldn't stop them.

But his eyes. I could tear them out. I could end this rebellion. Any pain I experienced would be worth it.

Twisted in this position, my spine to the ground, I couldn't stretch my tumor-limb far enough to be of use—but my original human hands were free after all. I tore at the layers of skin that blanketed Gio's face.

Agony seared me across both flanks, and through the core of my net of nerves. I screamed and twisted the vestiges of my torso, struggling to understand what had torn me open and gripped my arms.

Takhoun had pried a wet limb free and wrapped it around my left wrist. On my right, Shadeishi had clamped my forearm in her long jaw. She bit down, harder and harder, scissoring quickly through softened flesh to bone that snapped.

But what made me shriek so disgustingly wasn't that, nor was it the eyetendrils sprouting out from Takhoun's side of our body. She shared with me her view of what I looked like now, every awful, viscous color of my melted face, and bombarded me with her utter contempt.

But even that wasn't why I couldn't stop shrieking. Above us the illusory green sky dimmed to the black of self-destruction.

All the rest of Punktown would ever know was that a lot in its industrial wasteland had abruptly transformed into a crater. Those unaware of RillCorp would never learn that we existed and did great things, that I existed and did great things, that our corporate culture was a beacon in their cesspit, and I was one of its brightest lights.

It wasn't fair. Couldn't they see? It wasn't fair.

THE NIGHT WATCHMAN DREAMS HIS ROUNDS AT THE REM SLEEP FACTORY

1.

He saw himself—too slow to react—
enveloped in a death ray, reduced to gray ash,
barely a snack for the dust mop.
As he continues to observe (from some vague space
above the killing ground) his faceless attackers
sweep him onto a blueprint (a scheme of the
sub-sub basement); the particles that were once
his body vanish in the ocean of blue ink;
then They fold his prison shut (darkness/
blink)—He comes to

in the sub-sub basement (still under construction/
constriction) where the naked hoses from
the venom machine undulate leglessly along the walls.
He clutches his brow, remembering the blueprint
(so briefly brushed across) crawls until he finds
the tiny Box, the Key he must turn in the Clock
on his belt to prove he passed by.
A click, a turn,
(a choral aria loosed from its enigmatic works)
another round done.

2.

He saw himself—too slow to escape—
clamber to the top of the scaffolding, force it to topple

to land him on the other side of the Hungering Pool, but the Pool
outmaneuvers him, grows too fast,
pulls its far shore away so he plops in the water, into the path
of the Time Shark's distending jaws, soulless radium numbers
staring from its eyesockets as he slips
beneath its submarine bulk, finds a drain,
learns to breathe water. He emerges

from the mouth of a water fountain, in time to see
an army of Flesh Fish burst from the ventilation ducts, veins
like Man-o-War tentacles dragging beneath their bellies,
a slimy swarm gliding into the employee lounge
to claim the lives of dozens of his faceless co-workers, reduced
to gray meat in milliseconds. He locks the lounge door
(fish on the other side) and finds the tiny Box, the Key.
Faceless Investigators will soon arrive to sort the mess.
He locks the Fear Induction Vault as well, so They
won't find the body inside (he no longer remembers
who that man was, or why he murdered him.)
Another turn of the Key in the Clock
(which bleeds as he forces it in)
Another round done.

3.

He saw himself—too slow to comprehend—
peer out a long window slit to watch child-forms
caper on a beach: tall six-winged penguins with
bulbous eyes, bloated caterpillars with elephant
trunks, horses with corduroy skin—all slash-frozen
as mushroom clouds erupt on the horizon. He slams
the window shut against the blinding blast, too late: Faceless,
he gropes for the Eyewish station, pawing along the cold,
throbbing wall, pushes through a hatch that

drops him on the stony floor, eyes restored (not a moment
too soon)—a boot booms down a paper-width away.
He runs, all eight legs a piston blur, spins to face

his would-be killer, sees his own face snarling down at him.
He charges the kicking legs, whips his tail, stings, stings,
dodges the falling body—clambers onto the empty
husk of head, crawls inside—stands up, dusts off his uniform,
rubs his aching neck, limps off to find the Box and Key.
They're here, in a mirrored hall. A million times
reflected, he slides the Key in the Clock, strokes
(it makes a choking sound) wonders how many
rounds he's done tonight, how many split seconds of REM
recorded, what will he remember, retain,
if anything at all? If the Clock knows
it holds its peace.
Another round done.

4.

He saw himself—too scared to slow down—
running deeper underground, the Manager in hot pursuit—
black-robed, bald, the Manager had merely grinned
despite the blows he took, sawblade blows
to forehead, chest, a pretty "X" carved in the throat. He tried
every trick to bring the Manager down,
but despite even thumb-blinded eyes, still coming, chasing,
the threat of imminent arrival like hot breath on the nape of his
        neck.
In the Meathouse now, playing cat and mouse
among the malformed pig-sized embryos swinging on hooks
above the sloping floor; a voice, the Manager's master, CEO,
commanding from somewhere below.
Living bait, he leads the blinded Manager into the Cosmic Oven,
claws for the On button, learns to breathe fire.
Out the other end, he descends

through one more door, to meet the yellowed gaze
of the CEO, who lies on a pallet, a creature of green bones,
yellow fungus eyes staring from a head like softened fruit.
Surrounded by faceless, white-robed sycophants,
the CEO commands to Stop!

He hears the voice inside his head, knows
not to look in those eyes.
He watches as his shined guardsman's shoes
ignore all desperate orders, step on the pallet,
into the bones, cave in the CEO's head like a puffball.
Confused sycophants follow like ducklings
to the tiny Box and Key, which turns in the Clock,
which (gives birth to birds)
turns the outside world open,
marks the ticker tape, says Goodbye.
Another night gone.

epilogue

He saw himself—as realization slowly dawned—
not shake his baton, blow his whistle, lift a finger,
as the grinning Rat-men climbed
from the submerged turbine shafts to seize the
bewildered sycophants, virgin-white offerings borne
away to the sub-sub basement (some for breeding/
some for feeding). The Clock on his belt
detaches, grins, pats him on the back

Good work, it says, as his back
sprouts unfeathered wings, the teeth
in his mouth lengthen, his skin reddens,
hooked talons grow from his hands, his head.
And he understands the night stretches long ahead,
and who pays his salary
and that he was the Manager
all along.

AFTERWORD AND ACKNOWLEDGMENTS

M y third grade teacher meant well when he read "The Tell-Tale Heart" and "The Raven" to our class as a Halloween treat.

As a grown up, I acquired a beat up old copy of the book he read from, *The Gold Bug and Other Tales of Mystery* by Edgar Allan Poe, part of the "Educator Classic Library." It contains what even now I'd profess to be a harrowing illustration of the old man with the pale blue vulture eye getting smothered with a pillow as he repeats "It's nothing but the wind in the chimney—it is nothing but the wind in the chimney . . . "

My fellow pupils reacted to the reading with appreciative campfire-tale chuckles. For me, the exposure to death, murder and obsessive insanity opened my mind's eye to terrifying vistas. The experience was a watershed moment, at first delivering endless night terrors, some of them described in "Six Waking Nightmares Poe Gave Me in Third Grade."

Eventually, years of grappling with the push-pull of morbid curiosity and fear led me to an embrace of most all things horror. (Any fan of written horror who has read more than one of my stabs at the genre might correctly conclude that the stories of Clive Barker catalyzed that acceptance.)

Along that path, and afterward, I was subject to astonishingly vivid nightmares. Quite a few of those are cataloged in "The Night Watchman Dreams His Rounds at the REM Sleep Factory," providing me with material to mine for story fodder. (In that poem, you'll find quick sketches of dreams that ultimately provided seeds for published stories, including "The Sun Saw" and the title tale.)

In a sign that my immersion therapy worked, I almost never have dreams like that any more. To be honest, I miss them.

Occasionally, a nightmare comes close to the intensity I experienced as a yung'un, sprouting into stories like "A Deaf Policeman Heard the Noise" and "Blue Evolution" in this book, or like "Her Acres of Pastoral Playground" in my previous horror collection, *Unseaming*.

Speaking of *Unseaming*, I want to thank everyone who made that book (on the scale at which I work) a shocking success: the readers who bought it and posted praise, the reviewers who encouraged those readers, the Shirley Jackson Award and This Is Horror Award judges. It got me thinking, early on, what a companion volume might look like.

I hope that if anything signifies "companion volume," it's the participation of amazing artist Danielle Tunstall and her model Alexandra Johnson, who provided the Chesley Award-nominated cover for *Unseaming* and are back for *Aftermath*. I'm so grateful to them for taking part.

Many thanks, too, to my "intern," designer Brett Massé, who provided invaluable help with the visual elements of *Aftermath* and other Mythic Delirium Books projects. Thanks as well to my colleague Patty Templeton, who introduced Brett to me. (If you'd like to consider Brett for a project of your own, by all means visit brettmasseworks.com. Consider this my recommendation.)

There's another way this book connects to *Unseaming*: continuity among stories. I'll spell such things out here, assuming that if you, blessed reader, have gotten *this* far I won't be spoiling anything.

"Follow the Wounded One" is a direct sequel to "The Hiker's Tale" from *Unseaming*, and "The Cruelest Team Will Win" happens in the same setting. (The latter even features a cameo from the main players in "Follow.") "Nolens Volens" ties not only to "The Sun Saw" but to "Gutter" from *Unseaming*. The poem "The Paper Boy" also ties in with that set. For a tale that loops in (loosely in some cases) *all* of these works, and draws in "The Button Bin" and "The Quiltmaker" from *Unseaming* on top of that, seek out my novella "The Comforter" in the anthology *A Sinister Quartet*.

Obviously, "Longsleeves" and "The Ivy-Smothered Palisade" take place during different eras in the centuries-old, unchanging city of Calcharra. A third Calcharra story, "The Butcher, the Baker," can be found in *Beneath Ceaseless Skies*, and more are on the way.

My eternal gratitude to my wife Anita Allen, who took her skills for arranging stories honed by years working on Clockwork

Phoenix anthologies and *Mythic Delirium* issues and applied them to the wildly diverse pieces gathered in this volume. Thanks, too, to dear friends C. S. E. Cooney and Christina Sng for allowing me to include our collaborative poems.

Even more thanks to early readers Nathan Ballingrud, R. S. Belcher, A. C. Wise, Craig Laurance Gidney and (again) Christina Sng, for looking over the rough-hewn manuscript and finding it worthy. Thanks as well to Laird Barron for his generosity and his standing endorsement.

I would be remiss not to thank all the friends, colleagues and editors who gave these stories their original (and sometimes subsequent) homes and otherwise inspired their existence: Elizabeth Campbell; Paul St. John Mackintosh; Stephen H. Segal and Ann VanderMeer; Joseph S. Pulver Sr. and James Lowder; Romie Stott; Nathaniel Lee; Rhonda Parrish; Graeme Dunlop and Jen R. Albert; Marvin Kaye; Jason V. Brock; Sean Moreland; John Benson; S. T. Joshi; C. S. E. Cooney for prompting the "Claire-dare" poems; Scott H. Andrews and the Hexagon retreats; Scott Dwyer; Scott Gable and C. Dombrowski; Allen L. Wold; Carlos Hernandez; Stephanie Berkeley De La Fuente and Martha Simmons De La Fuente; Tina Ayres; Scott Silk; Sonya Taaffe; David C. Kopaska-Merkel and the members of the Science Fiction Poetry Association; Brian M. Sammons; Shalon Hurlbert; Nicole Kornher-Stace; Anya Martin and Scott Nicolay. As the stories in this book span decades, there are many deserving others I have surely left out—to them I apologize!

A double dose of thanks to Scott Nicolay (I seem to have good luck with Scotts) for introducing me to Jeffrey Thomas, who allowed me to play in his delightful Punktown universe and spurred the creation of the story that gives this book its title. Not only that: Jeff applied his keen proofreader's eye to these stories and poems, and wrote a rip-roaring introduction that ties all this chaos together with kind words that I find humbling. Thank you so much, Jeff; my hat's off to you!

Lastly, who could have know this project spanning years and years would come to fruition during a worldwide pandemic? To anyone reading this, thank you, best wishes and stay safe! May these horrors you *can* control grant you some respite from those you can't.

—Mike Allen, Roanoke, Va., April 2020

ABOUT THE AUTHOR

Nebula, Shirley Jackson and two-time World Fantasy award finalist **Mike Allen** wears many hats. As editor and publisher of the Mythic Delirium Books imprint, he helmed *Mythic Delirium* magazine and the five volumes in the *Clockwork Phoenix* anthology series. His own short stories have been gathered in three collections: *Unseaming*, *The Spider Tapestries* and *Aftermath of an Industrial Accident*. He's won the Rhysling Award for poetry three times, and his most recent collection of verse, *Hungry Constellations*, was a Suzette Haden Elgin Award nominee. A dark fantasy novel, *The Black Fire Concerto*, appeared in 2013.

For more than a decade he's worked as the arts and culture columnist for the daily newspaper in Roanoke, Va., where he and his wife Anita live with a cat so full of trouble she's named Pandora. You can follow Mike's exploits as a writer at descentintolight.com, as an editor at mythicdelirium.com, and all at once on Twitter at @mythicdelirium.

COPYRIGHT INFORMATION